FRANCIS DUℕ.

Francis Duncan is the pseudonym for William Underhill, who was born in 1918. He lived virtually all his life in Bristol and was a 'scholarship boy' boarder at Queen Elizabeth's Hospital school. Due to family circumstances he was unable to go to university and started work in the Housing Department of Bristol City Council. Writing was always important to him and very early on he published articles in newspapers and magazines. His first detective story was published in 1936.

In 1938 he married Sylvia Henly. Although a conscientious objector, he served in the Royal Army Medical Corps in World War II, landing in France shortly after D-Day. After the war he trained as a teacher and spent the rest of his life in education, first as a primary school teacher and then as a lecturer in a college of further education. In the 1950s he studied for an external economics degree from London University. No mean feat with a family to support; his daughter, Kathryn, was born in 1943 and his son, Derek, in 1949.

Throughout much of this time he continued to write detective fiction from 'sheer inner necessity', but also to supplement a modest income. He enjoyed foreign travel, particularly to France, and took up golf on retirement. He died of a heart attack shortly after celebrating his fiftieth wedding anniversary in 1988.

VINTAGE MURDER MYSTERIES

With the sign of a human skull upon its back and a melancholy shriek emitted when disturbed, the Death's Head Hawkmoth has for centuries been a bringer of doom and an omen of death – which is why we chose it as the emblem for our Vintage Murder Mysteries.

Some say that its appearance in King George III's bedchamber pushed him into madness. Others believe that should its wings extinguish a candle by night, those nearby will be cursed with blindness. Indeed its very name, *Acherontia atropos*, delves into the most sinister realms of Greek mythology: Acheron, the River of Pain in the underworld, and Atropos, the Fate charged with severing the thread of life.

The perfect companion, then, for our Vintage Murder Mysteries sleuths, for whom sinister occurrences are never far away and murder is always just around the corner . . .

FRANCIS DUNCAN

In at the Death

VINTAGE

1 3 5 7 9 10 8 6 4 2

Vintage
20 Vauxhall Bridge Road,
London SW1V 2SA

Vintage is part of the Penguin Random House group of companies whose
addresses can be found at global.penguinrandomhouse.com

Penguin
Random House
UK

First published in Vintage in 2016

First published in Great Britain by John Long in 1952

penguin.co.uk/vintage

A CIP catalogue record for this book is available from the British Library

ISBN 9781784704834

Typeset in India by Thomson Digital Pvt Ltd, Noida, Delhi

Printed and bound in Great Britain by Clays Ltd, St Ives plc

Penguin Random House is committed to a sustainable future for our
business, our readers and our planet. This book is made from Forest
Stewardship Council® certified paper.

MIX
Paper from
responsible sources
FSC
www.fsc.org   FSC® C018179

This is
a
MORDECAI TREMAINE
Story

CONTENTS

THE CHIEF INSPECTOR
COLLECTS HIS BAG

IT WAS half past ten in the evening. Chief Inspector Jonathan Boyce, of Scotland Yard, was playing chess with Mordecai Tremaine; and a hundred and twenty miles away in the city of Bridgton a fledgling constable was discovering his first body.

The Bridgton authorities were commendably prompt in deciding that it was more than a local affair. It is true that two unsolved murders in the area in less than six months may have developed in the Chief Constable a certain sensitivity to criticism; but whatever the reason the chess game was still in progress when the telephone rang in Mordecai Tremaine's flat.

Chief Inspector Boyce paused in the act of removing a bishop from the impudent threat of one of his companion's foraging pawns.

'I told you,' he said, 'that I had a feeling in my bones.'

Mordecai Tremaine's outstretched hand lifted the receiver to cut short the telephone's insistent clamour. He said into the instrument:

'Yes, he's here. I'll tell him.'

Jonathan Boyce was already on his feet. Mordecai Tremaine waited expectantly. Behind the pince-nez that seemed, as always, to be sliding to disaster, his eyes were bright and yet oddly shadowed with doubt.

After a moment or two the receiver went back. Boyce said:

'All right, Mordecai. This is it.'

Tremaine swallowed hard. He looked like a small boy who had been waiting eagerly in the pavilion for his turn to bat in the school eleven, and who, now that the testing time was upon him, found his stomach beset by butterflies.

'Where?' he said, trying to keep his voice steady.

'Bridgton. We'll get the details at the Yard. They're sending a patrol car to pick us up.'

There was a brusqueness in Boyce's manner that had not been there before the telephone had interrupted what had been a promising game of chess. He was the policeman now, engaged already, as far as his mind was concerned, upon his official duties. But there was, nevertheless, affection in the grey eyes regarding his companion from under the wiry eyebrows.

'You're sure, Mordecai,' he said, 'you're sure you want to go through with it?'

'Yes, Jonathan,' Tremaine said quietly, 'I want to go through with it.'

He knew what had prompted the remark. Boyce understood him. Understood the romantic and sentimental side of his nature that went with his enthusiasm for crime detection. Understood how the fascination of the chase was succeeded by a black despair when the end came.

Maybe that was the way Boyce himself felt, although he was careful to betray no sign of it. For after all you couldn't hunt murderers without paying the penalty in torture of the soul. You couldn't hide from the fact that when you'd unravelled the problem that had been intriguing your mind it was a creature of flesh and blood whom you were delivering to judgment.

In the patrol car that carried him through the dark streets towards Scotland Yard Tremaine leaned back against the leather upholstery and tried to find out whether he *was* certain that he wanted to go through with it. He was still trying to make up his mind when Jonathan Boyce came back under the archway at the Yard entrance with Sergeant Witham at his side carrying the murder bag.

The murder bag! A thrill of excitement competed with his doubts. This was the outward sign, the visible proof that he was engaged upon the hunt.

Somehow the sight of it resolved his fears. It emphasized the fact that he was a privileged spectator; that he was being given the opportunity of seeing what he had long desired—a murder case from the inside.

As Boyce climbed back into the car with his sergeant Tremaine's eyes remained fixed upon that prosaic-looking bag, which was by no means as ordinary as it seemed. There was always a murder bag packed and ready at the Yard available for just such an emergency as this when the next officer for duty on the rota of senior investigators should be called upon, at a moment's notice, wherever he might be, to take up a new trail of murder.

Each bag contained everything likely to be of assistance in the investigation. Tape measure, magnifying glass, dusting powder for finger-prints, scissors, tweezers, rubber gloves—the whole paraphernalia of what might be termed the first-aid equipment of detection made up its contents.

It was the first time Tremaine had seen a murder bag at such close quarters, but it was not because he was a stranger to murder. He had been early upon the scene on more than one occasion when murder had been committed; Jonathan Boyce had, indeed, once described him as a murder-magnet, and the Press had been quick to give him a reputation as a solver of mysteries.

The thought of that reputation sometimes made him quiver, for he knew his limitations, but it undoubtedly had its uses. For instance, it had been the means of persuading the Commissioner when Jonathan Boyce had asked that august gentleman whether Mordecai Tremaine might accompany him on his next case.

It was not the Commissioner's usual practice to allow members of the public to go into partnership with those of his senior officers who were on the murder rota; elderly retired tobacconists, no matter how great their enthusiasm for crime detection, were not as a rule encouraged to go gallivanting into things that didn't concern them.

It had been an achievement, therefore, to have obtained the right to be sitting here in a patrol car bearing one of those senior officers and his sergeant upon the first stage of a murder enquiry.

There was no question, of course, of any publicity; the Commissioner's blessing had not extended to newspaper headlines and a departure with trumpets. Mordecai Tremaine was expected to observe a decent humility, and to do nothing to encourage criticism of Scotland Yard.

But a steady softening-up campaign on the part of Chief Inspector Boyce, during which he had poured praise of Tremaine into the Commissioner's ear; and a dinner for two during which Tremaine had made a satisfying personal contact with the great man himself, had produced results. The Commissioner, agreeably surprised and not a little amused, to find that the amateur detective about whom the usually taciturn Boyce had become almost lyrical, was indeed the benevolent-looking and talkative elderly gentleman the newspaper reports had presented him to be, had agreed that the next time the Chief Inspector was required to make a sudden journey with the murder bag, Tremaine should go unobtrusively with him in the role of unofficial observer. From such a quarter, he had evidently told himself, no harm could come.

Besides, in the communicative mellowness induced by a fine old after-dinner port, the Commissioner had become aware of Mordecai Tremaine's sentimental soul and of his weakness for *Romantic Stories*. It had lured him into confessing that he, too, was a reader of the heart-stirring fiction supplied by that soothingly unsophisticated magazine—at least as often as he could seize upon a copy unobserved.

Tremaine had wondered since—a little uncomfortably—whether the permission he had been granted was a reflection of the uneasiness in the Commissioner's mind when he had awakened in the cold light of the following morning to the realization of just how much he had bared his heart. Had it possessed, he had asked himself, anything of the nature of a bribe?

It was understandable that the Commissioner of Police for the Metropolis should experience a certain reluctance to have

4

his taste for romantic literature revealed to the world; was there an implied bargain, an expectation that consent should beget silence?

Each time the thought had come Tremaine had dismissed it hastily. The bond of sympathy between fellow readers of *Romantic Stories* placed them above such unworthy considerations.

He glanced out of the window of the car and saw that they were swinging left out of the Edgware Road into the darkness of Praed Street. A few more moments and they had halted outside the grey bulk of Paddington Station.

Boyce glanced at his watch.

'We've made it nicely. Come on, Mordecai. They're holding the train for us for a few minutes.'

Hurrying down the platform along the length of the crowded train, doors closed now and evidently on the point of departure, Tremaine felt importance welling up inside him. He was towering above all these quite ordinary midgets who were bestowing curious glances upon the little procession of which he was a part.

But later, as he was half-dozing in one corner of the compartment as the train rattled and tore its way through the night, the illusion fell away from him. Once more he was a very unheroic mortal, tortured by doubts.

Murder. You could read about it and discuss it with a certain sense of exhilaration, savouring the problems it presented, studying and dissecting the characters of murderer and victim; you could find in it an absorbing interest.

It was when you came up against the thing in its actuality that its atmosphere changed; that from being a fascinating problem to intrigue the brain it turned into a dreadful darkness in which your mind was squeezed in a dry, numbing horror.

What were they going to find at Bridgton? What kind of personality, what hopes and fears and desires had lain behind the inanimate assembly of blood and bone, flesh and muscle, that was awaiting them at the end of this swaying, unreal journey through empty countryside and sleeping towns in which only the street lights spoke of humanity?

He had never stayed in the city although he had passed through it several times when he had been travelling to Wales or the north-west. He remembered it as a pleasant enough place, sprawling, after the manner of all industrial areas, but with the goods yards and smoking chimneys relieved by the hills upon which it stood, and by the river that brought the romance of the sea into its heart.

He knew it, too, as the home of the sturdy and independent merchant venturers who had sent their argosies across the world in days when men had believed that unknown terrors lay in the western seas. And he knew it, also, his thoughts ran irrelevantly, as the scene of two unsolved murders that had, not long ago, held the headlines for a day or two and then been forgotten.

Two murders. He struggled to recall what he had read, but his mind would take him no further. He was left only with frustration and depression.

He opened his eyes and peered resentfully at Jonathan Boyce's stocky form, stretched comfortably on the opposite seat; at the winking glow of Sergeant Witham's pipe reflected in the window just beyond that impassive individual's peacefully reclining head. Confound them both! Didn't they have any feelings? Were they so little moved by the gravity of the business upon which they were engaged that they could sit thus calmly, speaking no word?

He knew, even as the thoughts tumbled through his feverish mind, that he was being unfair. Witham might be a stranger to him, but Jonathan Boyce he knew well enough. It was not because he was cold-bloodedly unconcerned that Jonathan was silent. It was not because this was only one of many similar journeys he had made, so that he had come to regard such things as routine.

If Jonathan had said no word of the errand upon which they were bent it was because that was the way he worked. He would discuss nothing until he had arrived upon the scene and could see for himself with all the facts available to his hand. He would take no risk of a chance remark or a theory evolved out of insufficient evidence remaining in his mind to lead him subtly astray when he came to examine his witnesses and begin the inevitable probing.

It was fatal to start an investigation with a preconceived idea; however much one might conscientiously try to push it aside, it would persist insidiously—and sometimes obstinately—in holding the foreground. And all kinds of apparently solid facts would build themselves upon it to point in the wrong direction and perhaps allow the real criminal to escape in the confusion of thought.

Tremaine closed his eyes again and did his best to allow the rhythmic pattern of the train's passing to lull him into sleep. There was nothing to be gained by fretting his nerves to ribbons. He was committed now and he would soon find out what was in store for him.

2

THE BODY IS ON VIEW

BRIDGTON, in the early hours of the morning and with a chill wind searching along the deserted streets and invading the station platform, was uninviting. Tremaine shivered as he followed his companions past the ticket barrier. The romantic exhilaration of Paddington had quite gone. He felt stiff, and begrimed with travel; he knew that he was beginning to show that he needed a shave.

There was a car waiting just beyond the station entrance. A smooth black polish about it would have labelled it as a police car even if the uniformed constable had not been at the wheel to confirm it.

A burly figure detached itself from the car and moved across the pavement.

'Chief Inspector Boyce?' The voice was low, but firm with confidence. At Boyce's affirmative nod: 'Good morning, sir. Glad to see you. My name's Parkin. Local inspector.'

There were quick introductions. Boyce drew Tremaine forward.

'This gentleman is Mr. Tremaine—Mordecai Tremaine.'

Inspector Parkin's eyes had already taken in, not without a flicker of surprise, the third member of the group, so obviously not the Scotland Yard stamp. He said:

'Mr. Tremaine? Not—?'

'Yes,' Boyce said. '*The* Mordecai Tremaine.' Apart from the one slight emphasis his voice was expressionless. 'He'll be working with me—with the Commissioner's approval but unofficially, of course.'

'Quite so, sir,' Inspector Parkin returned briskly. 'Chief Constable sends his compliments,' he added. 'Thought you might like to go straight to the spot. Probably find him still there.'

Boyce's wiry eyebrows went up fractionally. If the Chief Constable was still on the scene of the crime it looked as though he had been making a night of it. Coupled with the speed with which the Yard had been contacted it was significant. Somebody, evidently, had ideas that this wasn't any ordinary affair.

'What's the set-up?' he asked. 'Didn't have time for any details before we came away. Chap named Hardene, isn't it?'

'That's right, sir. *Doctor* Hardene. Doctor Graham Hardene.'

'Big noise locally?'

'Not exactly that. Good practice—among the right people. But nothing sensational.' Inspector Parkin stole a brief glance at his companion. 'Got to be a politician to make the headlines in these days—even in the provinces.'

In the gloom he saw the curving smile that came and went in Jonathan Boyce's face and he settled back with an inward relief. He thought it was going to be all right. This chap was human; they ought to be able to work together without the hullabaloo that sometimes happened when the Yard's temperamental *prima donnas* came down lording it over the local men.

'It's in my area,' he went on. 'The super's away—broke his arm last week when we were out on a job. In the ordinary way I'd have been handling it. Sir Robert—that's the Chief, of course, Sir Robert Dennell—instrcted me to tell you that he was putting me entirely at your disposal. I don't suppose you'll be familiar with the district, so if there's anything local you want followed up—well, you can rely on me, sir.'

Boyce turned, studying him shrewdly for a moment or two. And then he grinned.

'It looks as though I've fallen on my feet,' he said. 'I never did like the idea of a cat-and-dog life, anyway. Fire ahead with your side of it. And don't be too liberal with the sirs,' he added. 'Keep 'em for public occasions.'

Tremaine was silent during the journey. He had indeed no time for speech, for he was busy with the double task of listening intently to all that Inspector Parkin had to say and of studying the route they were taking as well as the darkness would allow him to do so.

At that early hour the streets were almost empty. There was only the occasional patrolling policeman to be seen. They swept along the broad street lined with gloomy-looking whole-sale warehouses and offices that led from the station, over the bridge that gave the city its name, catching a tantalizing glimpse of spidery cranes and the masts and smoke-stacks of shipping at anchor; and then they were leaping at the imposing hill, flanked by luxury shops but devoid now of hurrying life, at the head of which stood the University.

Bridgton was a fascinating mixture of the old and the new, of the romantic and the practical: it possessed the sober dignity and the mellowness that go with historical traditions, and the bustling activity of a thriving industrial town. Narrow cobbled streets, in which houses of the Tudor and the Elizabethan periods still stood and were inhabited, wound deviously at the rear of broad thoroughfares whose shops, splendid with glass and chrominum, were filled with the myriad products of the twentieth century.

Inspector Parkin's level, efficient voice, just sufficiently tinctured with the accents of the West Country to be in character, came to Tremaine's ears with the effect of a synchronized sound track. The streets through which they were passing were streets along which the dead man must also have passed many times; the irregular façades and the angular buildings etched against the still darkened sky must have been familiar to his eyes.

Tremaine stared out at them as the inspector's voice went steadily on.

A constable on patrol in the suburb of Druidleigh, the outskirts of which they had now reached, had made a routine excursion up the drive of one of the houses on his beat which he had known to be empty to make sure that no tramp or other unauthorized person had been taking liberties with the premises. He had found that the front door had been opened and had made a prompt investigation in case whoever had been responsible for such an act of illegality was still in the vicinity.

Entering the hall he had stumbled over the body of a man. By the light of his torch he had discovered it to be Doctor Hardene. He knew the doctor by sight; he had, in fact, passed him outside his surgery earlier in the evening.

Also on the floor of the hall the constable had observed a fragment of stone, about as long as a man's forearm and much thicker at one end than at the other. It had evidently been applied with considerable force to the side of the doctor's head.

'Anybody else about?' Boyce queried.

Not, Inspector Parkin said, as far as the constable had been able to tell. He had listened for any sound from inside the house and had made a quick search with the aid of his torch, without result. He had then contacted the divisional station from the nearest call-box.

'What kind of chap was this Hardene?' Boyce asked. 'Was he the sort likely to have had any enemies?'

Was there the slightest of hesitancies before Parkin replied? Tremaine half-turned his head, trying to discern the expression on the inspector's face, but the interior of the car was too dim.

'At the moment,' Parkin said, slowly and as though he found it necessary to pick his words, 'I wouldn't know.'

They had left the main road and were traversing the streets of the suburb. They were wide streets, some of them quite imposing avenues lined with trees. Here the houses were big detached stone edifices, obviously erected during the spacious days of Victorian commercial prosperity.

In the gloom they possessed an imposing air of solidity, but Tremaine caught an occasional glimpse of crumbling stone pillars and ragged shrubberies. He saw, too, the scattered notice boards, discreet enough but plainly revealing that what had once been a family residence was now reduced to acting as an office block. Druidleigh, it seemed, was no longer the place it had once been.

'This where the money lives?' Boyce enquired, turning his head momentarily to glance from the car.

'Where it used to live,' Parkin told him. 'Most of the old families have been moving out during the last twenty or thirty years. Flats, offices, and nursing homes—that's what most of these places are now, although you'll still find a house here and there that's kept in the old style.'

They were running now along a pleasant road that was flanked on one side by the open spaces of Druidleigh downs. Bridgton was fortunate in the possession of these downs, many acres in extent and well within the city's boundaries. The police car turned between the stone pillars at the entrance to a rather unkempt drive and stopped outside a large house, typical of this particular road and about which there hung the almost perceptible atmosphere of a place which has not been lived in for some time.

It was growing light now. Tremaine climbed from the car and shivered a little in the sharp morning air.

There was a constable on the steps leading to the main door. His hand went up in a salute as he recognized Inspector Parkin.

'Sir Robert's car's still here,' Parkin said, indicating a smart grey saloon drawn up a little way beyond them in the drive. 'So we ought to find him inside.'

The Chief Constable was standing in the hall, a tall, spare and grizzled man who eyed Jonathan Boyce keenly in the moment before he held out his hand.

'Glad to have you with us, Chief Inspector. You haven't lost any time getting down here.'

'Caught the first available train after your message came through, sir,' Boyce said.

He saw the enquiry in Sir Robert Dennell's eyes and included Mordecai Tremaine in a comprehensive introduction that took it for granted that there would be no question raised as to his right to be present.

'Naturally you've heard of Mr. Tremaine, sir,' he added swiftly, as the Chief Constable stirred as though in doubt. 'It was the Commissioner's idea that he should come along on this occasion.'

Tremaine's conscience gave him a sharp reminder of its existence, but it must be confessed that he did nothing to remove the impression created by Boyce's shameless perversion of the truth.

'The Commissioner's?' said the Chief Constable. 'I see. Quite so. Heard of you, of course, Tremaine. Come to see things from the beginning, eh?'

'Subject to your approval, Sir Robert,' Tremaine put in. 'If you feel that I'll be in the way—'

'In the way? Nonsense, nonsense. May be able to teach us regulars a thing or two!'

There was a note of forced joviality in the Chief Constable's voice but it was not, Tremaine divined, because he was trying to make the best of a bad job. It was because his mind was preoccupied, not because he was resentful of the unexpected appearance of an amateur detective.

As the Chief Constable turned away, obviously having dismissed him from his immediate thoughts, Tremaine was conscious of a sense of surprised relief. He was in! The final hurdle had been taken, and from now on he could go his way without the feeling that someone might suddenly awaken to the fact that he had no business to be on the scene at all.

The grey light of morning was creeping into the house, rendering no longer necessary the emergency lamps by the light of which the police had been working. Tremaine glanced about him. Two men in plain clothes were busy with a measuring tape; another was seated on the lowest stair making pencilled notes in a pad on his knees. The whole scene was drably prosaic; the three of them might have been concerned with nothing more abnormal than the fitting of linoleum.

Even while Tremaine was telling himself that he should have known better he could not keep back a sense of disappointment. This unhurried, dispassionate routine was not the atmosphere one expected to find at the end of a night journey into a murder case. Where was the drama? Where the excitement of the chase and the sense of the law's inevitability?

And then he saw the huddled shape lying to one side of the hall and his heart gave an odd and painful jerk. *Here* was reality. This silent thing had once been a living man, breathing, loving—and hating. Whose hand had been raised against him in the darkness, striking him down into an oblivion from which there could be no return?

He glanced at Jonathan Boyce, intent on his task and missing nothing, apparently untroubled by thoughts of the solemnity of the moment, talking now to Inspector Parkin. On the floor, just beyond the dead man, was a black leather bag of the Gladstone type. Boyce said:

'Hardene's?'

Parkin nodded, and as Boyce took a step forward in the direction of the bag, Tremaine instinctively followed him. The bag was open, so that it was possible to see something of its contents. Boyce took a torch from his pocket and shone it into the interior. Tremaine caught a glimpse of a stethoscope, a packet of gauze, and of a black case that looked as though it might contain surgical instruments. And then, as the torchlight probed, he saw something else—the unmistakable outline of an automatic pistol.

'I've often wondered,' Boyce said drily, 'just what a doctor carried in his little black bag. I didn't know it ran to guns.' He looked at Parkin. 'Did Hardene's practice lie in this area?'

'Yes. I imagine he covered a fairly wide district—although we haven't checked up on that so far. As you saw for yourself on the way most of the houses here in Druidleigh are big, detached places standing some distance apart, and a lot of them have been turned over to offices and suchlike, so that his patients must have been pretty scattered. Although his own house and surgery would be about half a mile away I'd say that the houses round here would be well within his hunting ground. Besides, he was fairly well known and had a lot of patients among the people who matter in Bridgton, so that he'd probably travel farther afield than the average doctor.'

'But although he was familiar with the neighbourhood he might not necessarily have been aware that this particular house was empty—or he might not have remembered it. Is that reasonable?'

'I see what you mean, sir,' Parkin said. 'He might have been brought out here by an emergency call without realizing that there was no one living here. And by the time he did realize it he'd run into trouble. Judging by the bag he certainly came out on duty.'

Something made Tremaine look in the Chief Constable's direction. Sir Robert Dennell was regarding Boyce with a peculiar intentness. There was a taut expression on his grizzled countenance. He had the air of a man who had a problem on his mind but who was loath to allow it utterance.

Boyce made a significant gesture towards the bag.

'If he came out as a doctor attending a patient,' he observed, 'he seems to have made an odd choice of instruments.'

'There *may* be a simple explanation for that pistol,' the Chief Constable said, and Tremaine noted the fact that he had been in no doubt as to Boyce's meaning. 'These roads bordering the downs are pretty lonely after dark, especially at this time of the year, and there've been a number of complaints about tramps. It's possible that Hardene may have brought the gun along as a precaution.'

'I see, sir,' Boyce returned. 'Did he ever make any personal complaint of having been molested or approached by tramps?'

Sir Robert Dennell looked at Parkin. The inspector said: 'Not to my knowledge, sir.'

Boyce stooped over the dead man. Gently he drew back the edge of the covering blanket and shone his torch. Although the daylight was much stronger now it was still gloomy at this end of the hall. Tremaine swallowed hard and looked in his turn.

It was not quite as bad as he had expected. The weight of the stone that had been used in such a murderous attack had been sufficient to kill without leaving as much visible evidence as he had thought, and that part of Hardene's skull which had received the fatal blows was turned away from him.

He saw a man of middle age, with hair that was still thick although heavily grey. The lips were drawn back slightly over the teeth, but the grimace did not detract greatly from the undoubted personality of the face with its strong features and firm jaw. There was something a little ruthless to be seen, even in death, but it was clear that Doctor Graham Hardene had been a fine figure of a man who had carried his years well.

Maybe, Tremaine reflected, therein had lain the secret of his successful practice in this once exclusive and still reasonably well-to-do neighbourhood.

The same thought had evidently occurred to Boyce.

'What was his reputation with the ladies?' he asked, as he replaced the blanket.

'He knew how to handle them,' Parkin returned. 'But I've never heard anything against him in that connection. Being a medical man, of course, he had to avoid any scandal.'

'Married?'

'No. At least,' Parkin added, 'not visibly.'

'How long had he been in practice here?'

'About four or five years.'

Tremaine noted that Parkin's replies came without hesitation. It was obvious that as yet he could have had little time in which to check back on Doctor Hardene's antecedents, but he had already made himself acquainted with at least the basic facts. And he was quite prepared to pass on his knowledge to the Scotland Yard man. He did not intend to hold back with the double object of making Boyce's task more difficult and of gaining kudos for himself.

'Any line yet on the time of death?' Boyce asked.

'Not before nine and he was found at ten-thirty. It probably happened not long before the constable discovered him.'

Tremaine said:

'What happened to his car?'

It was the first time he had made a direct comment and it brought the eyes of the Chief Constable and Inspector Parkin upon him. Tremaine felt embarrassment creeping over him. But he knew that this was the testing time; that upon the impression he made now would depend whether or not Sir Robert Dennell would accept him completely. He added:

'I didn't see it in the drive, and I imagine he didn't usually make his rounds on foot.'

'It was parked on the other side of the road,' Parkin said. 'We found it, as a matter of fact, a few yards *off* the road in the shelter of the bushes on the edge of the downs.'

'With its lights on or off?'

'Off.'

The Chief Constable stirred, like a man who wanted to make an important comment before the moment for it had passed.

'It doesn't follow, of course, that it was Hardene himself who parked it there. He may have stopped outside the house in the ordinary way and it may have been the murderer who ran it into the bushes and switched off the lights in order to avoid attracting attention and give himself a chance to get away.'

'Was the car locked?'

'Yes.'

'And the ignition key?'

'In Hardene's pocket,' the Chief Constable said.

He was looking at Tremaine with respect. The indifference with which he had greeted his arrival had given way to a subtle appraisement. Tremaine had the feeling that Sir Robert Dennell was telling himself that here, after all, was someone whom he would have to take into account in his calculations.

But the Chief Constable did not make any further comments on the subject of the car. He said, after a moment or two:

'If there's anything you want to know, Chief Inspector, don't hesitate to contact me. In any case I'll be glad of a word with you this afternoon after you've had a chance to look around. Say three o'clock at my office. Parkin here will show you how to get there. I'd like you to come along as well, Parkin.'

'Very good, sir,' Boyce said.

His voice was quite level, but there was significance in the eyebrow he raised in Mordecai Tremaine's direction.

Tremaine returned a brief but meaning glance. He watched the Chief Constable's stiffly erect figure go out of the hall with a sense of inner excitement that was steadily replacing the chill of this early morning arrival.

A doctor who carried an automatic pistol when he went to meet his patients, and who had made what was apparently an emergency call at a deserted house; a car parked in the bushes with its lights out—and a Chief Constable who quite evidently had something on his mind and who seemed to have spent a great deal of time at the spot marked 'X' despite the inconvenience of the hour. These, he felt, were highly satisfactory ingredients. It was going to prove an interesting murder.

3

THE LADY IS TROUBLED

SERGEANT WITHAM was left behind to watch developments at the scene of the crime. With Inspector Parkin and Jonathan Boyce, Tremaine set off for the house where Doctor Hardene had lived.

A few hundred yards beyond the site of the murder the road bore sharply to the left, away from the downs and towards the more thickly populated part of Druidleigh. As the car took the corner Tremaine caught a glimpse of the bridge spanning the deep, rocky cleft through which the river ran.

The house they were seeking proved to be situated in a quiet avenue leading back from what seemed to be a major road skirting the downs. Hardene had evidently enjoyed the benefits of a secluded residence together with the professional advantage of being near enough to the beaten track to include within his practice the fairly closely packed population of the neighbouring more compact part of Druidleigh.

Sauntering along the pavement was a man who acknowledged Inspector Parkin's appearance with a gesture that would not have been remarked by any casual bystander. The house was, then, already under police supervision.

'Housekeeper's name's Colver,' Parkin said. 'Mrs. Colver —widow, I gather.'

'She knows about Hardene?' queried Boyce, and the other nodded.

'Yes. We got in touch with the house last night—just after he was found. The constable recognized him straight away and in any case there was plenty of evidence on him—wallet, personal card and so on.'

'How did this Mrs. Colver take it?'

'Shocked. Couldn't believe it. Reaction seemed genuine enough. But don't take my word for it. I didn't spend many minutes with her—things were moving too fast—and in any case she was supposed to have been called out of her bed, so that you'd have a job to say whether it was the kind of attitude you might expect or not.'

Parkin's finger was on the bell. In a few moments the door was opened by a middle-aged woman. She recognized the inspector and a kind of taut foreboding settled in her face.

She said no word but stood back to allow them to enter and then led the way to a room which, judging by the number of chairs it contained and the periodicals piled on the centre table, had been the doctor's waiting room. Parkin made the introductions and she nodded. It was a defensive gesture, as though she felt she must avoid actual speech as long as possible.

Boyce said:

'I'm afraid this is very distressing for you, Mrs. Colver, but I'm sure you understand how necessary it is to make thorough investigations.'

Again the nod, tight-lipped. But Tremaine saw the nervous quiver of the fingers resting on the table against which she was standing and knew that she was inwardly fighting to prevent her agitation from revealing itself in her face.

Boyce went on as though he believed her to be at her ease.

'As Doctor Hardene's housekeeper I'm hoping that you'll be able to give us quite a lot of help,' he said conversationally. 'I daresay, for instance, that you're familiar with such things as his surgery times and his methods of working.'

An expression that was both puzzled and wary came into her face.

'I was the doctor's housekeeper,' she said. 'I didn't have anything to do with the surgery. Miss Royman can tell you more about that.'

'Miss Royman?'

'Receptionist,' put in Inspector Parkin. 'She'll be along soon. Due to arrive just before nine.'

'I see,' nodded Boyce. 'It was her job to handle Doctor Hardene's appointments, medical records and so on, whilst you were chiefly concerned with the domestic arrangements?'

The housekeeper was looking more at ease. Something of her tension seemed to have left her.

'Yes,' she told him. 'Not that I didn't help him sometimes when he wanted things after Miss Royman had left.'

'You mean you might make appointments or take telephone calls for him?'

'I didn't make appointments. I'd pass on any messages to the doctor or Miss Royman. Sometimes people would ring up when neither of them were here.'

'Quite so. Did Doctor Hardene have many calls of an urgent nature after his normal hours?'

The housekeeper's rather thin eyebrows drew together as she considered the question.

'I wouldn't say he had many calls,' she said slowly. 'Most of his patients were private. They wouldn't ring him up unless it was really important.'

There was a touch of pride and a certain asperity in her voice. She was basking in the reflected glory of her employer's exclusive practice. She resented any suggestion that Hardene had been a struggling G.P. at the beck and call of his panel.

'But there was,' Boyce said, 'an emergency call last night, was there not?'

'That's right,' she said. 'That's why he had to go out.'

'Did you answer the telephone—or did the doctor?'

'Doctor Hardene did. He came out and told me that he'd been called away to one of his patients. I was in the kitchen—putting things ready for the morning.'

'Did he tell you the patient's name?'

'No. He said that he'd been expecting a call because she'd been worse when he'd paid his routine visit in the morning, and that he couldn't say how long he might be. He said that it would depend upon what her condition was like when he got there.'

'He told you it was a woman then?'

The housekeeper looked uncertain.

'Well, I thought it was a woman,' she said doubtfully. 'From the way he spoke. But he didn't say her name.'

Boyce pencilled a brief note.

'What happened next?'

'He just went out,' the housekeeper said, a little at a loss. 'He was already wearing his hat and coat when he came from the surgery and he was carrying his bag. He went out through the hall and a few minutes later I heard his car drive away.'

'And you didn't see him again?'

'No,' she returned, in a low voice, 'I didn't see him again.'

'Was it usual for you to wait up for him when he was called out on such occasions?'

'He didn't like me to wait up. He told me I couldn't be on duty all the time and that I was to go to bed. I used to leave a tray of something for him in the kitchen so that he could help himself when he came in.'

'And that is what you did last night?'

'Yes. I cut several sandwiches and left them with a glass of cold milk and then I went to bed.'

'What time was that?'

'Just before half past ten. I usually go to bed about then,' she added.

'Did you wonder why Doctor Hardene hadn't come back?'

'Not especially. He'd told me he didn't know how long he would be, as I said. I don't think I paid any attention to it.'

'Do you know what time he left the house?'

'It was some time after nine. But I don't know exactly. It might have been nearer ten. I just can't say.'

'And you can tell us nothing more about the time between Doctor Hardene's leaving the house and your being aroused by the police officers with the news that he'd been murdered?'

'What else is there I can tell you? I went to bed. I didn't know anything about what had happened.' She seemed to sense disbelief in Boyce's attitude. A sharp, defensive note crept into her voice. 'It's true! I didn't know anything about it! How could I have known!'

Boyce held up his hand.

'Please don't distress yourself, Mrs. Colver. It's my job, you know, to ask questions. I don't want you to imagine that I'm doubting your word.'

She realized that she had made an error and was obviously anxious to eradicate the impression she had made.

'I—I understand,' she said. 'I'm sorry. It's been such a terrible shock. I still can't realize it's true. I don't think I know what I'm doing or saying.'

Her voice was not quite level and she had a distraught air that suited her words, but Tremaine thought that underneath he could detect a harder note. Watching her he thought that her eyes were upon Boyce with an intentness that was out of keeping with the rest of her attitude. It was as though she was deliberately adopting a pose and was furtively studying Boyce to see whether he had been taken in by it.

Boyce said:

'Quite so. Your relationship with Doctor Hardene was perfectly amicable? You found him a considerate employer?'

'The best you could wish for,' she said warmly. 'You couldn't work for anyone better. Whoever did such a terrible thing must have been mad. Mad and wicked!'

'You can rest assured, Mrs. Colver, that we shall do all we can to find the murderer. You can help us a great deal in that task by telling us anything you know—*anything*—that might have a bearing on what happened last night.'

'I'll do whatever you want. I'll not be able to rest until you've found the man who did it.'

'We don't know,' Boyce said quietly, 'that it *was* a man.'

Tremaine saw the quick fear that stabbed into her face and knew that Boyce must have seen it, too.

'No,' she said, breathlessly. 'No. Of course not. I meant the man—or—or the woman.'

Boyce went on impassively, as though he had noticed nothing:

'Did Doctor Hardene have many visitors? I mean, of course, outside his patients.'

She shook her head.

'He didn't have much time for entertaining people. He was out a lot, and whenever he was at home he was generally working in his surgery. It wasn't often anyone called to see him, although there were a lot more enquiries of one sort or another after he decided to put up for the council.'

Boyce glanced at Parkin. The inspector gave an affirmative nod.

'He started taking an interest in local politics a few months ago. There was talk about his standing for the council at the next election.'

There was a wariness in Parkin's voice. It reminded Tremaine of his attitude earlier when the police car had brought them from the station. He was like a man carefully speaking only the truth but who knew that there was more that he might say and was scrupulously trying to avoid saying it.

'What about his relatives?' Boyce said, turning back to the housekeeper. 'Did you ever have occasion to speak to any of them, or did the doctor ever mention them to you?'

'I don't think he had any relatives,' she told him, doubtfully. 'At least, I never heard him speak about them.'

'How long have you been working here as a housekeeper?'

'Ever since he first came here. I answered his advertisement for someone to look after him.'

'Thank you,' Boyce said. 'All right, Mrs. Colver. That's all I need to trouble you with for the moment. I'm sure you understand, of course, that I may want to ask you a few more questions later on, and if anything occurs to you that you feel I should know about please get in touch with me or with the inspector here right away.'

He looked at Tremaine enquiringly. Tremaine shook his head.

Although he did not put any questions to her it drew the housekeeper's attention upon him. She gave him a glance in which both suspicion and fear seemed to be contained. She hesitated, as though she would have liked to stay and find out just what part he was playing, but Boyce had made it quite evident that the interview was at an end, and, reluctantly, she went out.

'I wonder,' Boyce said thoughtfully, when the door had closed behind her, 'what she's afraid of?'

'I thought,' Tremaine observed, 'that she was inclined to protest too much. I mean about how well Hardene treated her.'

'Yes, she made it sound too good to be true, didn't she?'

'I'll check on it,' Parkin said.

Boyce was looking about the waiting room, idly turning over the periodicals lying on the table.

'We can take it up with the receptionist,' he remarked. 'Miss Royman. She ought to know what the domestic atmosphere was like.'

Parkin nodded. He glanced at his watch.

'It's twenty to nine. We should be seeing something of her any moment now.'

It was, in fact, some five minutes later when Margaret Royman arrived. The plain-clothes man who had been on duty at the door conducted her to the waiting room. She was disconcerted when she saw the three men facing her.

'I–I'm sorry,' she said, a little haltingly. 'But if you haven't made an appointment with the doctor I'm afraid he won't be able to see you this morning. He's extremely busy.'

'It's all right, miss,' Parkin said, coming forward 'No need for you to worry. You're Miss Royman?'

'Yes.'

'Doctor Hardene's receptionist?'

She nodded.

'Yes, I am. But I don't understand. Why did that man let me into the house just now? Where is Mrs. Colver? Isn't the doctor here?'

Her glance went to each of them in turn. They saw the flicker of uncertainty in her eyes and also the colour recede slowly from her face.

'Nothing–nothing's happened to him?' she asked, in a whisper.

'What makes you think anything might have happened to the doctor, miss?' Boyce said quietly.

'I don't know,' she said quickly. 'There's no reason why anything should have happened to him. But who are you? And where *is* Doctor Hardene?'

'We are police officers,' Boyce said. 'I'm afraid you must prepare yourself for a shock, Miss Royman.'

There was no concealing the look of dread that came into her face then.

'What—what do you mean?'

'Doctor Hardene is dead.'

She stared at him with wide, haunted eyes, one hand at her lips.

'Oh no—*no*! It can't be true.' And then, with an effort, she managed to get herself under control; her voice held a steadier note. 'He—he was perfectly all right when I left him last night. He wasn't complaining of being ill or—or anything.'

'He didn't die naturally,' Boyce said. 'He was murdered.'

He shot the word out deliberately, but in spite of her former agitation it produced surprisingly little reaction. She accepted it with a kind of numb fatalism.

'Who—did it?' she said, and seemed to hold her breath whilst she waited for him to reply.

'That, Miss Royman, is why we are here. To find out who was responsible. It's possible you may be able to help us and we shall be very grateful for any information you may be able to give.'

There was a brief flare of what might have been relief in her eyes, but she was clearly still very unsure of herself and her manner was hesitant.

'I'm afraid I don't understand. I had no idea when I came in just now that anything so dreadful had happened. I don't see how I can possibly be of any assistance.'

'Please allow me to be the judge of that, Miss Royman,' Boyce said, and he allowed a certain harshness to underlie his tone.

She looked at him doubtfully. She straightened one of the periodicals lying on the table with a nervous movement.

Mordecai Tremaine had profited by the opportunity he had been given to study her. Margaret Royman was undoubtedly a very attractive young woman even if she was at this moment betraying a certain tension which had brought taut lines into her face. She was, he judged, about twenty-three or -four, a little taller than the average, but with a figure neither too slim nor too plump and quite obviously possessed of the knowledge of how to dress to advantage on a moderate salary.

When she had entered the room his romantic soul had warmed instinctively towards her. She was endowed with that fresh quality of youth which was irresistible to a constant reader of *Romantic Stories*. It was therefore especially disturbing that her attitude should be giving rise to such doubts in his mind. The news of her employer's death had certainly appeared to produce the distress that might have been expected, but equally certainly that was not the whole story.

He wondered what was on Margaret Royman's mind. And he wondered too what was making her afraid, because afraid she undoubtedly was.

'You say Doctor Hardene was perfectly all right when you left him last night, Miss Royman?' Boyce said.

'Perfectly,' she returned, steadily enough now. 'That's why this seems so—so dreadful.'

'Quite so. Now, miss, you have my word for it that you may be able to be of great help to us. To your knowledge did the doctor have any enemies?'

'Enemies?' she echoed. 'I'm afraid I don't know what you mean.'

'I mean,' Boyce said, 'that working closely with Doctor Hardene you may be able to tell me of any persons with whom his relations were not as good as they might have been.'

The slight movement of her shoulders was clearly intended to be a shrug of helplessness.

'I don't know anybody who doesn't have a brush with other people at some time or other. Doctor Hardene wasn't any exception. But that doesn't mean that he made enemies

–not enemies who would want to kill him.' Her eyes fell away from his glance. 'After all,' she added, 'people don't kill other people simply because they don't happen to like them.'

The note in her voice seemed to be an invitation to him to agree with her.

'People kill other people,' Boyce said, 'for all sorts of reasons that don't seem to make sense to anyone else. It doesn't do to overlook even the smallest possibility in a matter of this kind. Can you call anyone to mind who might have had, say, a misunderstanding with the doctor? A disagreement, perhaps—some argument over what you yourself may have considered to be an unimportant point? Not necessarily a violent quarrel.'

'No,' she said, in a low voice. 'No, I can think of no one.'

She waited for a moment or two, as though expecting further questions, and when they did not come she looked up again at Boyce. Her manner was that of someone who had steeled herself to face an ordeal which was inevitable but from which every nerve in her body was shrinking.

'You haven't told me,' she said, 'how—how it happened. Or—or where.'

'No,' Boyce said, as if he was surprised at his own lapse, 'no, I haven't. Doctor Hardene was apparently called out last night—an emergency call from one of his patients.'

She stared at him in surprise.

'One of his patients? Who was it?'

'That's something we're unable to tell at present. It seems that the doctor answered the telephone himself when Mrs. Colver was busy in the kitchen. You don't happen to know, miss, which of his patients might have been likely to call him out? I understand he was expecting something of the sort to happen.'

'Was he?' she said, and Boyce raised his eyebrows.

'Didn't *you* know, miss? I thought maybe that being in close touch with his work you'd have a pretty shrewd idea how things might be going.'

'Doctor Hardene didn't discuss his patients with me,' she said, a hint of frost in her manner. 'My work for him was almost entirely secretarial.'

'I realize that, miss,' Boyce returned evenly. 'It merely occurred to me that since you'd probably have to deal with the medical record cards and such like during the course of your duties you'd be more or less bound to pick up a certain amount of knowledge about the people Doctor Hardene was attending.'

His tone was devoid of any note of suggestion or of irritation, but it was clear enough that he was giving her an opening.

Margaret Royman's taut form lost something of its rigidity. She said, slowly:

'I see what you mean, Chief Inspector. I'm sorry. I—I'm afraid I haven't quite got over the shock and I'm not being very helpful. Yes, of course, I couldn't help learning something about the doctor's patients although I naturally haven't a great deal of medical knowledge.' She frowned. 'I can't think, though, of anyone who might have called him out—unless it was old Mrs. Carhew. She's had heart trouble for a long time and it's possible she might have had another attack.'

'Can you give me her address, miss?'

'It's in Regency Avenue,' she told him. 'I'm not sure of the name of the house, but it'll be in the records.'

Boyce turned towards Parkin. The local man pursed his lips and shook his head.

'Not much help. Regency Avenue's a good five minutes walk from the downs. No chance of his having mistaken one house for the other.'

'Sure that's the only one, miss?' Boyce said.

'It's the only one I can think of without going over the cards,' she returned slowly. 'I can have a look through the records if you'd like me to, just to make sure I haven't overlooked anyone.'

'It doesn't matter, miss. We'll have to check back ourselves as a matter of routine in any case. Besides, it's not certain yet that the call was from a patient Doctor Hardene had been attending. It's always possible that the housekeeper was mistaken in what the doctor said to her.'

A door-bell rang with a peculiarly shrill note. Margaret Royman made a sudden movement.

'That's the surgery bell. There was a rather full list of appointments this morning.' She added, as though she had suddenly awakened to the wider implications of what had taken place: 'Doctor Hardene was due at the hospital later this morning and he was to have taken the chair at a political meeting this afternoon. I must go through his diary and see that everyone is notified.'

She hesitated then and glanced doubtfully at Boyce.

'Will that be in order, Chief Inspector? I mean to tell people about what has happened?'

'Tell them,' Boyce said, 'that Doctor Hardene won't be keeping any appointments. That will be sufficient for the time being. It'll be in the newspapers later, of course, and then there won't be any need of explanations.'

Tremaine thought he saw her flinch and thought also that there was sudden fear in her eyes. He watched her as she went out of the room, admiring the freshness of her young beauty and the grace of her movements, but wondering besides whether it might not be a good idea to keep a very tight grip on his emotions.

He knew his own weaknesses well enough. Pretty young women appealed to all that was sentimental in him. He wanted to see them pursuing the orthodox path to romance and marriage, and it distressed him to find any kind of cloud on the horizon.

But at least he was aware—even though he disliked admitting it—that a pretty face was no guarantee that all was well within. It helped him to ensure that he did not make a fool of himself.

Boyce looked at Parkin.

'We'll see whether the doctor's papers can give us any help.'

There was an unspoken question in his voice and the inspector knew what he meant.

'I haven't done anything in that line yet, sir. There may be something useful to be picked up.'

Doctor Hardene's professional quarters appeared to have consisted of three rooms—a well-furnished and comfortable waiting room for the benefit of his patients, and, on the opposite side of the entrance hall, two smaller rooms, one in which the receptionist carried out her duties and one he had used as a surgery.

Margaret Royman had already begun to deal with the papers on her desk when they entered. She looked up in a startled fashion.

'It's all right, miss,' Boyce said, lifting his hand in a reassuring gesture. 'No need to disturb you. We shall have to spend some time with the doctor's things but there's no reason why you shouldn't do what you have to do at the same time. In fact, you may be able to help us if we come across anything that looks a bit—well, doubtful.'

She made a slight inclination of her head, apparently relieved. Tremaine gave Boyce a sideways glance.

It wasn't like Jonathan to be careless. He must be well aware that he was giving Margaret Royman the opportunity of destroying anything she might be anxious to prevent inquisitive policemen from finding, which meant that he was doing it deliberately.

It rather looked, Tremaine reflected uncomfortably, as though the attractive Miss Royman was being presented with enough rope to hang herself—if she was unwise enough to make use of it.

4

DEAD MAN'S EFFECTS

THE surgery was a small room but it was neat and orderly so that there seemed to be no lack of space. A roll-top desk, an examination couch, and three chairs made up the main furniture. On the wall, over the built-in gas-fire, were several framed, rather macabre coloured cartoons depicting the fate of an unfortunate compelled to call in his doctor in the eighteenth century. The anguished expressions on the faces of the patients and the surgeon's fearsome array of implements must have evoked mixed feelings in Harden's own patients. Obviously he had possessed a certain sense of humour.

The desk was locked but Parkin produced a bunch of keys.

'These were in his pocket. Daresay one of them will do the trick.'

One of them did. The inspector rolled back the lid. The surface of the desk was not as tidy as the rest of the room had promised. It looked as though Hardene had merely pulled the lid down over the results of his day's work.

Glancing over Boyce's shoulder Tremaine saw that most of the papers scattered over the desk were covered with the inevitable scrawl of the medical man wearied by years of notetaking as a student and resentful of being turned into a clerk; they were routine prescription and other forms. Several textbooks occupied the small shelf at the back—he saw one on skin diseases, one dealing with chest conditions, a work on toxicology and a well-thumbed medical dictionary.

Boyce began at one side and dealt methodically with everything the desk contained. He made no comment until he had finished.

'Nothing there,' he said, with a shrug. 'Not to my eye, anyway. We'll get a medical opinion, of course, just in case.'

At the rear of the desk was a small drawer. It, too, was locked, but the small key that fitted it was on the bunch Parkin held.

Boyce pulled it open and his expression changed.

'This,' he observed, 'looks a little more interesting.'

The drawer contained several used cheque books, a small, blue-covered note-book, and a number of loose papers, including half a dozen newspaper cuttings. Boyce flicked through the pages of the note-book.

'Supposed to be a diary but he seems to have used it as some sort of appointments book,' he remarked, and handed it to Parkin.

Whilst the local man stood glancing at the note-book Boyce turned his attention to the remaining contents of the drawer. The cheque books he placed on one side for examination later and then he picked up the newspaper cuttings.

The door communicating with the room where Margaret Royman was working had been left open, so that Boyce had only to glance to one side in order to see her. It meant, also, that her voice was clearly audible when she used the telephone, and Tremaine heard her make several calls, cancelling appointments of various kinds that Hardene had evidently made for this particular day.

Her voice sounded normal enough, allowing for what was no more than a natural hint of strain, and she parried the questions which it was obvious she was asked with a calm that left no room for suspicion on the part of the people at the other end of the wire. There was nothing in her attitude to which Boyce could take exception or that could arouse doubts in his mind and Tremaine felt a sense of relief.

He realized that Boyce was holding one of the newspaper cuttings out to him and he took it and read it through.

It was a report of the death of a pawnbroker, Charles Henry Wallins, who had been found lying on the floor of his shop with severe head injuries from which he had died without regaining consciousness. From the fact that he had been wearing pyjamas and dressing-gown it appeared that he had been disturbed at some time during the night and had gone down to investigate. He had been an elderly bachelor who had lived alone over his shop premises.

Since Wallins had managed his business on his own it had been difficult to state definitely whether anything had been stolen, but a window at the rear of the building had been forced, so that it had seemed clear that some unauthorized person had made an entry.

The goods in the shop, however, did not appear to have been disturbed nor had there been any signs of a struggle. A small safe in a room behind, containing a few pounds in money, had been intact and unmarked.

The report added that the police theory was that the unfortunate pawnbroker had disturbed an intruder, who had attacked him with a heavy marble statue which had been found near the body—and which had proved to be an unredeemed pledge—and had then made a panic-stricken escape without staying to carry out the robbery for which he had come.

Tremaine realized then that a second clipping was pinned to the report he had been reading, evidently a follow-up account of a later date. It said very little, merely that the police were pursuing several lines of enquiry but that there had been no further developments.

Jonathan Boyce had by now finished the cuttings he had retained and he handed them across with an expressive lift of his wiry eyebrows.

His meaning became clear enough when Tremaine glanced down at the printed reports, for they, too, dealt with death by violence.

This time the victim had been a seaman, believed to be a Patrick Marton, whose dead body had been found by a charlady taking a short cut across Druidleigh downs on her way to her place of employment in one of the large houses on the far side of the downs which had been taken over by a government department.

The dead man had been lying under a clump of bushes just off the path. The sight of a foot sticking out of the leaves had attracted the charlady's attention and had led her to make the discovery that had first paralysed her with fright and then sent her white-faced and palpitating for assistance.

Marton had been shot through the heart at close range. His pockets had been rifled and his empty wallet had been found near the body. Enquiries had shown that he had been paid off some two or three months previously from a ship which had docked at Bridgton from the West Indies. He had joined the crew at Kingston, Jamaica, and had signed on merely for the one voyage.

After his arrival at Bridgton he had apparently done no work, but his landlady had said that all his bills had been paid promptly and he had never seemed to be short of money There was no trace of his having possessed a bank account and nothing valuable had been found in his room.

Investigations, said the reports, were still being made, but little information as to Marton's antecedents had so far been obtained.

There was a frown on Tremaine's face. This was what he had known about Bridgton; this was what had been on his mind in the train coming down.

Both accounts had stirred his memory and he was recalling now references he had seen in the national dailies. No arrest had been made in either case; the usual reports that the police were in possession of certain facts had been published, but the weeks had gone by with no news of any developments and the murders had gradually slipped into the accepted list of unsolved crimes.

Boyce was regarding him significantly.

'Seems to have taken quite an interest in crime,' he remarked. He took the cuttings again and handed them to Parkin. 'Mean anything?' he asked.

The inspector did no more than glance at the cuttings. It was evident that he recognized them.

'They're all from the *Evening Courier*—local paper,' he returned. 'Off-hand I'd say they were about six months old.'

'Anything special about the pawnbroking killing? Or about this fellow Marton?'

Parkin cleared his throat a little more noisily than was really necessary.

'Only,' he said, 'that we haven't pulled in the people who did it.'

Tremaine admired the impassiveness of Jonathan Boyce's face. It was impossible to tell what he was thinking. He merely

34

nodded, as if he considered the matter unimportant, and turned back to the desk.

Despite the surface confusion, Graham Hardene appeared to have been a man of fairly—and conveniently—methodical habits. In addition to the contents of the drawer, the desk contained a number of completed cheque books, neatly held with a rubber band, three account books—two filled and one about half used—several half-yearly bank statements, and a loose leaf folder holding details of various investments.

'That seems to be the lot,' Boyce said, straightening. 'He's made it nice and easy for us. We'll put the rake through this little collection as soon as we've finished looking around.'

He made a neat pile of the items he had considered worthy of further examination and placed them on one side of the desk. Tremaine expected that he would take them with him but a little to his surprise Boyce left them on the desk and then led the way out through the room in which Margaret Royman was working. She was still speaking on the telephone and she did not look up as they passed her.

There was a uniformed constable in the hall. He saluted as Parkin approached.

'Newspaper reporters, sir,' he announced. 'I didn't disturb you since you were with the Chief Inspector.'

'All right, Constable. It's time they were around, anyway. What have you done with them?'

'They're still outside, sir.'

Parkin nodded and opened the front door of the house. Just inside the entrance gate a group of men stood talking to another constable. One of them carried a camera.

The constable at the gate turned at the sound of the opening door and came smartly to attention. Parkin scanned the newcomers, then turned to Boyce.

'*Daily Echo* and *Evening Courier*,' he said in a low voice. 'Both local. Young fellow is Rex Linton—does the crime for the *Courier*. Other chap belongs to the *Echo*. Don't know the chap with the camera but he's probably working with Linton. The

Echo doesn't go in much for the sensational stuff—it's more of the business man's paper.'

'Not much competition between them, I take it?'

'No. They aren't tied up financially, but one being a morning paper and the other an evening they don't get in each other's way and they seem to work together all right.'

The newspaper men at the gate were regarding them with interest. Parkin walked down the path, and one of the group, whom Tremaine judged to be the reporter who had been called Linton, detached himself from his companions.

He was a well-built youngster, clean-shaven, neatly dressed, and with an air of confidence to which Tremaine found himself responding sympathetically.

''Morning, Inspector. Anything for us?'

'Too early yet,' Parkin returned. 'I daresay you've already got the main facts?'

The reporter nodded.

'Somebody knocked Doctor Hardene on the head and left his body in one of the houses facing the downs.'

'Right,' Parkin said. 'It gives you enough for the first editions, anyway. You can always build up with a few personal details—I've never known you fellows not be able to do that!'

Rex Linton grinned a little wryly.

'No crumb of comfort, Inspector? How did Hardene get there, for instance? Was he called out during the night?'

'He had an emergency call,' Parkin admitted. 'But there's nothing yet to say that it was connected with what happened.'

The reporter was looking curiously at the two men who had accompanied the inspector, and Parkin noticed his glance.

'This is Chief Inspector Boyce,' he said drily. 'Of Scotland Yard.'

There was a sudden gleam in the newspaper man's eyes.

'So you've called in the Yard already! I must say, Inspector, you haven't lost any time—on this occasion.'

There was a barb in his words, although there was no pure malice in them. Tremaine saw Parkin frown and saw, in the same instant and not without embarrassment, that the reporter's interest now seemed to be centred upon himself.

'You haven't completed the introductions yet, Inspector,' Linton said meaningly.

'This gentleman is accompanying the Chief Inspector,' Parkin told him, and his voice made it plain that he did not intend to deal with any further questions on that particular subject.

Linton raised his eyebrows and glanced at Tremaine with an even deeper curiosity, but he made no other comment.

Jonathan Boyce had so far taken no part in the conversation. He had patently been leaving it to Parkin, as the local man, to take the lead. But he saw that Linton was about to accept matters philosophically—at least for the time being—and take his departure to hand in his story, and he stepped forward.

'Just a moment, Mr. Linton,' he called, and the reporter turned eagerly. 'I daresay you know most of what goes on in the city—reporters usually do. Perhaps you can help me.'

'I'll do what I can—naturally.'

Boyce was looking unusually mild and benevolent. Tremaine smiled inwardly at the soothing guilelessness of his manner. It was clear that Jonathan had diagnosed a mutually beneficial tolerance between the police and the Press in Bridgton and was intending to turn it to advantage.

'What can you tell me about Doctor Hardene?' Boyce went on, and the reporter stared at him.

'Well, it sounds rather the wrong way round,' he observed, a trifle doubtfully. 'My editor sent me out to conduct the interviews not to be one of the victims!'

Boyce chuckled.

'The point is, Mr. Linton, I'm a stranger here, which means that I'm starting at a disadvantage. What I'm getting at is whether you can tell me anything about Doctor Hardene that may help me to put him in his place in the general scheme of things.'

'As far as medicine goes there isn't much I can tell you about him,' the reporter said. 'His practice must have been a decent one but he wasn't one of the local big names. Just an average G.P. I'd call him with enough of the bedside manner to put him on the right side of the people who live around here. He didn't land himself in the headlines until he thought he'd turn politician.'

'And then,' Boyce said softly, 'he did get the limelight, eh?'

Tremaine glanced at him with suddenly narrowed eyes. So this was what Jonathan was after. He recalled that moment when Inspector Parkin had referred to Hardene and politics and the wariness had come into his manner, as though he knew more than he wanted to say. Trust Jonathan not to have missed it.

'Don't think I'm trying to make out it was all over the town,' Linton was saying. 'It made a bit of a stir, of course, but that sort of thing naturally makes people talk.'

'What sort of thing?'

'Hardene seems to have sold himself the idea of setting up as a crusader. All for the rights of the common man and politics pure and undefiled—you know the kind of thing. That wasn't so bad—in fact it was quite a good line—but then he started making it personal. At one of his meetings he dropped a broad hint that there'd been some funny business over contracts for work done for the council. He didn't actually mention any names but it was pretty clear to everybody what he was getting at.'

'Or *who* he was getting at,' Boyce said.

Linton returned his glance with a grin.

'That's about the size of it. One of our city fathers—a building contractor called Masters—went up in the air over Hardene's accusations and there was quite a scene at one council meeting.'

'Masters, then, is a member of the council?'

'Yes. That's the point. He belongs to the opposite side. Naturally, there were official denials and all that sort of thing, but mud always sticks and there were plenty of people only too willing to hear something of the kind said against Masters. There's no doubt he had his knife into Hardene afterwards.'

'Did Hardene ever withdraw his accusations?'

'If he did I've never heard of it,' Linton returned. 'In fact, I understood that things were growing worse between them. Masters isn't the type to let anybody get away with something that belongs to him—even if it's only his reputation.'

'Was there any truth in what Hardene said?'

The reporter shrugged.

'I wouldn't know. That ground's too slippery for me.'

'All right,' Boyce said, after a fractional pause. 'I appreciate your help anyway—local people know far more about the reasons for things happening than a stranger can hope to learn on his first appearance.'

'Can I take it,' Linton said, 'that you'll be having a few extra details for us later, Chief Inspector?'

'Certainly.' Jonathan Boyce's tone was affable. 'You need to satisfy your editor; I need to satisfy my superiors. There's no reason why we shouldn't get along together. When it's possible to give you information without giving it to the wrong people as well I'll see that you get it.'

He nodded and turned away. For an instant or two the reporter hesitated, as though he would have liked to pursue the matter, but it was clear that as far as Boyce was concerned the interview was over, and Linton strolled slowly back to rejoin his companions.

Tremaine caught Boyce's eye upon him, and grinned in answer to the twinkle he saw there. Parkin said, as the door closed behind them when they reached the hall once more:

'You won't find any difficulties with either the *Echo* or the *Courier*. They're out for all they can get, of course, but we don't go in for the news-at-any-price stuff.'

'I think we'll live and let live,' Boyce returned.

He led the way back to Hardene's surgery. As he entered the inner room Tremaine saw his eyes go at once to the newspaper cuttings and other items he had left upon the desk, and then turn momentarily upon Margaret Royman, still seated at her place in the adjoining receptionist's room.

She was apparently fully occupied and did not glance up, but Tremaine saw the flush of colour rise to her neck and he knew that she was aware of Boyce's scrutiny and was by no means as busily engaged as she was pretending.

He was conscious of an unpleasant feeling of doubt. It was clear that Jonathan Boyce had left the items he had taken from the locked drawer in Hardene's desk in a place where Margaret Royman could easily have reached them if she had possessed any reason for wanting to do so. And it was equally clear that she had in fact been examining them during their absence.

Why? What did she have to conceal, and of what was she afraid?

5

HOME IS THE SAILOR

WHATEVER ideas Boyce might have had concerning Margaret Royman he kept them to himself. His next step was to carry out an inspection of the remainder of the house.

The housekeeper was called upon to lead the way, and although she did not offer any more information than she was required to give her replies were open enough.

There was not a great deal to be seen. Two rooms on the top floor were used merely as lumber-rooms; the rest were adequately although not expensively furnished. It was, in fact, the home of a bachelor who had not been particularly interested in his surroundings other than as somewhere to eat and sleep.

The only exception to the general male austerity was to be found in the housekeeper's own room. This was a large apartment in the front of the house bearing clear evidences of feminine occupancy.

Two framed photographs stood on the dressing-table. One was that of a man in middle age and the other was of a youth seated in a wheeled chair, with a low brick building in the background with wide glass doors standing open to a verandah.

The housekeeper saw Tremaine's glance and with an automatic movement she straightened the first of the photographs, which was a little out of position.

'My husband,' she said briefly. 'He died ten years ago.'

A vase of flowers stood in front of the window and gaily patterned chintz had been used to improve the appearance both of the dressing-table and the rather heavy, old-fashioned bed.

'I see you've done your best to make things attractive, Mrs. Colver,' Tremaine ventured, but the housekeeper's lips came together in a forbidding line and he tried no more efforts at conversation that went outside the needs of the official enquiry.

They went back downstairs and the housekeeper returned to her duties.

'Not,' Boyce observed, 'the chattiest of creatures.'

They were leaving the house when a car driven by a chauffeur in uniform drew up outside. They waited as the door was opened and its occupant, aided by the chauffeur, descended awkwardly to the pavement.

He was an elderly man whose build must once have been imposing but who was now bowed over the sticks he needed to help him make a slow progress towards the entrance gate. They watched him as he shuffled nearer, irascibly throwing off the arm the chauffeur put out to help him.

He stopped as he became aware of their presence and looked at them questioningly. Parkin stepped forward.

'Good morning, sir. Did you wish to see Doctor Hardene?'

The elderly cripple stared at him with sudden antagonism, clearly resenting being interrogated, but the touch of authority in the inspector's voice stayed him from a sharp retort.

'I did,' he returned briefly, and left it to Parkin to make the next move.

'Did you have a definite appointment with him, sir?'

'Of course I had an appointment with him,' the other said irritably. He lifted one of his sticks on inch or two in Parkin's direction. 'What is all this? Isn't Hardene here? He knows perfectly well I arranged to see him this morning.'

'I'm afraid Doctor Hardene *isn't* here, sir,' Parkin said, unruffled. He opened the gate and placed a guiding hand on the other's arm. 'Perhaps you'd be good enough to come into the house. It'll be easier to talk in there.'

The elderly man studied him without speaking for a moment or two, as though uncertain whether he should raise an objection, and then he glanced over his shoulder in the direction of the chauffeur who was standing at the gate.

'Wait for me in the car, Sage.'

He shook off Parkin's hand and began to make his way up the path towards the house. The inspector glanced significantly at Boyce and made no attempt to repeat his gesture of assistance.

It was Margaret Royman who opened the door to their ring. She saw the elderly man leaning on his sticks and came forward to help him over the threshold. This time, Tremaine noted, he did not disdain the aid he was offered; there were, evidently, degrees of objection.

'I'm so sorry, Mr. Slade,' Margaret Royman said. 'I tried to get you at your house but you'd already left.'

'What's it all about, my dear? Has Doctor Hardene been called away?'

Margaret Royman looked towards Parkin for guidance. The inspector said:

'In a manner of speaking, sir—yes, he has been called away. Let me introduce myself. My name is Parkin. I am a police-officer. This gentleman is Chief Inspector Boyce, of Scotland Yard.'

'Scotland Yard?' The other looked startled. 'Has Hardene been up to anything?'

Parkin did not give him a direct reply. He glanced enquiringly at the girl.

'Is this gentleman one of the doctor's patients?'

'Yes,' she returned. 'It's Mr. Martin Slade. Doctor Hardene had an appointment with him for this morning. I tried to get him on the telephone to tell him not to come but I was too late.'

Parkin nodded. He turned back to Slade.

'May I ask, sir, what leads you to suppose that Doctor Hardene may have been—up to something?'

Slade was looking a great deal less antagonistic now; Parkin's attitude was making it plain that something serious was in the wind, and his reaction was no longer so aggressive.

'I suppose it was this political business. Hardene was asking for trouble with the line he was taking a week or two back and I thought maybe he'd gone too far.'

'You were thinking particularly of his crossing swords with Mr. Masters?' Jonathan Boyce interposed, and Martin Slade turned awkwardly to face him.

'Yes. After all, Masters isn't the kind to let things slip.' He hesitated then and peered into the Yard man's face as though a doubt had just occurred to him, and he might find confirmation of it there. 'But I can't imagine him going to Scotland Yard about it—after all, it wasn't all that important. What brings *you* here, Chief Inspector? Where *is* Hardene?'

'Doctor Hardene,' Boyce said unemotionally, 'is dead.'

He left it at that. Slade stared at him.

'Dead? But how? I didn't know he had anything wrong with him.'

'He was murdered. His body was found late last night in an empty house facing the downs.'

For a long time Slade did not make any reply. He stood quite still, leaning heavily on his sticks, staring at Boyce. His face was a mixture of bewilderment and unbelief.

'Murdered!' he breathed at last. 'Murdered! Bless my soul. I never dreamed Masters would go that far.'

'Nobody,' Boyce said, 'has accused Mr. Masters of being responsible. Nor, as yet,' he added, 'has anyone else been accused.'

A slow smile came into Martin Slade's eyes.

43

'Quite, Chief Inspector. I was speaking out of turn. My apologies. It seemed to me that if anybody had killed Hardene it was most likely to have been Masters, but I agree that it won't do to go throwing anyone's name around without proof.'

Boyce gave him a reflective glance, but he made no attempt to pursue that particular matter.

'Did you know Doctor Hardene well, Mr. Slade?'

'I was one of his patients,' the other returned. 'Not that he seemed able to do anything to get rid of these,' he said ruefully, and raised one of his sticks.

'I meant outside your professional relationship,' Boyce said, and the other shook his head.

'I didn't like his politics. We didn't have much to say to each other—except maybe when I was telling him what I thought of him.' A grim humour came into his voice. 'Miss Royman can tell you all about that.' He gave her a sideways glance. 'Eh, my dear?'

Margaret Royman looked embarrassed, and Slade gave a dry, slightly malicious chuckle.

'No need to keep it back on my account. After all, if the police don't hear it from you they're certain to have it from the Colver woman. When Hardene acted like a fool I told him so and I know she didn't miss much.' He turned his regard upon Boyce. 'Doctors like to think they're a race apart, but when you've had to endure as much pain as I've had you get to know their limitations and you can see quickly enough when they're trying to pull the wool over your eyes.'

Boyce nodded. It might have been a nod of sympathy, of understanding, or merely of acknowledgment that he had heard.

'I'm sorry if we've taken up your time, Mr. Slade. But you'll appreciate that in matters of this kind there are certain official enquiries to be made.'

'And you didn't intend to be in a hurry to say who you are, eh? That's all right, Chief Inspector. Well, I daresay you'll want to know when I saw Hardene last. It was two days ago. I'll tell you now because you're certain to find out for yourself.

We had a fine old row. Hardene wanted me to take a new course of treatment and I told him that he couldn't fool me with any of his fairy tales.'

'Were you still on bad terms when you left him?'

'I wouldn't be here now if we had been. He talked me round—as usual. Got me to agree to go into it again after he'd seen some specialist or other. That's what today's appointment was about.'

'I see,' Boyce said. 'And you didn't meet again after your consultation of two days ago?'

'No.'

'Thank you.' Boyce looked like a man completely satisfied. 'That's all, Mr. Slade. If I should need to get in touch with you again on some routine matter no doubt Miss Royman here will be able to give me your address.'

'You'll be able to find out all about me all right,' Slade said. 'And as you can see I'm not likely to run far even if I do begin to think you're after me!'

He indicated his sticks with a grimace, and, turning, began to shuffle down the hall. With the dislike of the physically sound of appearing to stare at the afflicted they tried not to watch his slow and ungainly movements. Parkin opened the door for him but was careful not to offer any further assistance, and Slade descended the two or three steps outside and moved clumsily towards the gate.

The inspector came back into the hall.

'Shouldn't think Hardene found him easy to handle,' he observed.

'Know him?'

'Not off-hand. I'll take it up, of course.'

The elderly cripple had reached the gate by now. The hall door was still open and they saw him fumble with the latch and edge his way out to the pavement. Mordecai Tremaine took a few steps forward into the open air. The action meant that Slade was still within his vision, although the laurels flanking the pavement had concealed him now from Parkin and Boyce, standing just inside the door.

He saw the chauffeur slip from the driving-seat and open the rear door. Slade seemed to be on the point of moving his sticks aside so that he could clamber into the car when suddenly he stopped. It might have been that his infirmity made it difficult for him to mount the step or that he had been the victim of a sudden attack of pain on account of his exertions, but for a moment or two he did not move.

Instinctively Tremaine moved forward with the idea of helping him, but before he could take more than a step along the path Slade had recovered and had climbed into his seat. The door was closed upon him by the chauffeur. The car was driven away and Tremaine turned thoughtfully back towards the house.

'Poor devil,' Boyce remarked, although he could not have seen the incident. He glanced enquiringly at Parkin, obviously with the intention of making the local man feel that they were operating as equals. 'What did you make of him?'

'He didn't make any bones about his disagreement with Hardene,' Parkin said, clearly pleased, 'but maybe he was a bit more worried about it than he made out.'

'You mean he knew we'd find out sooner or later so he thought it was just as well to admit it right away? Could be,' Boyce said. 'That means, though, that he must have been pretty well at daggers drawn with Hardene, otherwise there wouldn't be any need to panic.'

The Yard man was about to close the door of the house so that they could make their already delayed departure when a sound at the entrance gate made them turn. A man had lifted the latch and was on the point of setting foot on the short drive.

He was a burly, thick-set man, bearded, and wearing a seaman's jersey that emphasized his bulk. He looked up suddenly to see them standing on the steps, watching him, and he hesitated, his hand on the gate. And then, abruptly, he turned away again, as though he had changed his mind about coming in.

Jonathan Boyce, however, was too quick for him.

'Just a moment!'

The Yard man took the steps in one stride and his grasp was on the other's shoulder, gentle but insistent, before he could close the gate and retreat to the pavement.

'I'd like a word with you.'

The other looked disconcerted. Although he stood his ground it was with evident reluctance.

'What's this all about?'

It seemed to be developing into a routine question. Boyce opened the gate.

'I'd be glad if you'd come in,' he said, and when the other hesitated a slight edge crept into his tone. 'I am a police officer. There are one or two enquiries I'd like to make.'

'Police?' The expression on the thick-set man's face was one of mingled alarm and watchfulness. He backed away. 'It's nothing to do with me. I don't know anything about it.'

'Nobody,' Boyce remarked, 'has said that you do.'

By now Inspector Parkin had taken a step or two along the path. As though he would have liked to make a break for it but realized that it would be folly to do so, the thick-set man came through the gate.

'What's it all for?' he said sullenly. 'You've got nothing on me.'

'I'm investigating a serious crime,' Boyce went on. 'You aren't compelled to answer any questions, but naturally I shall draw my own conclusions from any refusal you may make.'

The man's eyes narrowed.

'So it's like that, eh? All right. I'm in the clear. What d'you want to know?'

'Are you one of Doctor Graham Hardene's patients?'

'A patient?' The other's lips curled. 'Not me.'

'Then why were you coming to see him?'

'Anything wrong in it?'

There was truculence in his tone and the Yard man's own voice hardened.

'That remains to be seen. Why *did* you come here?'

'They told me about him down at the Mission. I thought I'd try my luck with him.'

'The Mission?'

Boyce glanced at Parkin as he echoed the word and the inspector nodded.

'There's a Seamen's Mission in King Street, just off the docks.'

'That the place you mean?' Boyce said.

'That's right.' The thick-set man was looking more sure of himself. 'They said this Doctor Hardene was the sort who'd give guys like us a hand sometimes.'

'I see. What's your name?'

'Fenn,' the other said, and hesitated. 'George Fenn. I can prove it,' he added.

'Glad to hear it,' Boyce returned drily. 'What's your ship?'

'The *Altiberg*. In from Halifax. I signed off her yesterday.'

'Trouble on board?'

'No. Just had all I want of looking at salt water. I'm after a shore job.'

'Ever been in Bridgton before?'

'No.'

'What made you pick this particular port?'

'I didn't,' Fenn said. 'The ship's owners did. I was in Halifax looking for a ship. The *Altiberg* didn't have a full crew and she was coming the right way. That's all there is to it. Here.' Fenn thrust a hand into his hip pocket and brought out a soiled-looking wallet containing a number of papers. 'Better take a look at these, hadn't you? Maybe you'll believe what I'm saying then.'

Boyce took the wallet without comment and glanced quickly through its contents.

'Seems all right,' he said, as he handed it back. 'So you're fed up with the sea and want a billet on dry land. What about the Employment Exchange?'

'Just come from there,' Fenn said. 'Check on it if you want to. I should worry.'

'Couldn't they fix you up?'

'They'll get in touch with me,' the man returned, a hint of sarcasm in his voice. 'In due course, when they've cut through all the red tape.'

'So in the meantime you thought you'd try Doctor Hardene?'

'That's about it.'

'What made you change your mind just now?'

Fenn looked straight at Boyce for a challenging moment or so and then his glance went beyond the Yard man to rest upon Parkin and Tremaine.

'Maybe I thought there was too much company. It was this guy Doctor Hardene I was aiming to see.'

'I'm afraid,' Boyce said, 'it won't be possible for you to see him.'

'You mean you've already put him inside?' Fenn made an indeterminate sound that might have indicated anything from shocked disapproval to casual interest. 'Why? What's he been up to?'

An odd note of eagerness crept into his voice with the questions. Boyce studied him thoughtfully.

'It won't be possible for you to see the doctor,' he said, his eyes on the other's face, 'because he's been murdered.'

Fenn's jaw tightened. Over Boyce's shoulder the watching Tremaine saw the startled expression in the man's face; it came unwillingly, as though he was struggling against it, and was replaced almost immediately by a blank stare.

'Murdered, eh?' Fenn said at last, with too much disinterest. 'I reckon in that case it's just as well I've only just got here.'

'You might put it like that,' Boyce remarked.

Fenn had the air of a man who desperately wanted to ask questions but was afraid that if he did so he would give himself away. He stared up the short path leading to the house, his eyes probing the front of the building as though he thought he might draw knowledge from the grey stones and the curtained windows.

'I might want to get in touch with you,' Boyce said quietly. 'Just a matter of routine,' he added, as Fenn's head went up at his words and the other's gaze swung back from the house.

The Yard man exchanged the merest of glances with Parkin. Without a comment the inspector turned away and went back up the steps.

Fenn was obviously disconcerted.

'What's it got to do with me?' he queried resentfully. 'I've never even seen this guy Hardene.'

'I said it was routine,' Boyce told him, mildly. 'If you've never set eyes on him you haven't anything to worry about. I suppose,' he added, 'you've no objection to telling me where you were last night?'

'Why should I have? I was down at the Mission—playing billiards.'

'Where did you sleep?'

'At the hostel. It's right next to the Mission.' Fenn's eyes narrowed. 'Was it last night he was killed?'

'I didn't say so,' Boyce returned levelly.

He asked several more questions but they seemed to be without special significance. They were merely enquiries about the dates and times of the *Altiberg*'s sailing from Halifax and her arrival at Bridgton. Fenn's answers, although grudging, appeared frank enough, and Boyce did not attempt to press him.

Inspector Parkin came out of the house once more. Boyce glanced back at him and then nodded to Fenn in dismissal.

'All right, that'll be all for now.'

Despite his initial show of resentment at being detained and questioned, the thick-set seaman seemed oddly reluctant to go.

'Bit high-handed, aren't you?' he said complainingly. 'You've been asking me plenty but you've been doing mighty little towards telling me what it's all about.'

'It'll be in the local papers,' Boyce said, and gestured significantly towards the gate.

Fenn hesitated a moment or two longer, then, realizing that it would be useless to delay any longer, turned on his heel. They watched him go out to the pavement, closing the gate hard behind him without a backward glance.

Parkin came along the path.

'Lucky,' he said. 'One of our patrol cars was only a few streets away with a plain-clothes man in it. They'll tail him all right. I thought he might have caught sight of our chaps here and might have got wise to it if we'd put one of them on to him.'

'Good man,' Boyce said. 'That fellow's no fool.' He turned to Tremaine. 'What did you make of him?'

'I'm wondering,' Tremaine said slowly, 'just how fortunate he is.'

Jonathan Boyce's bushy eyebrows went up.

'Fortunate?'

'I'm thinking,' Tremaine said, 'of the newspaper cuttings we found in Hardene's desk. Especially of the cuttings about the seaman whose body was found on the downs. I'm wondering whether *he* came to see Doctor Hardene, too.' He saw the expressions on the faces of his companions and coughed apologetically. 'I know it's rather a leap in the dark,' he added, 'but it might be useful to read up all the reports on the case. His name was Marton, wasn't it?'

'That's right,' Parkin said. He was frowning, as though he was struggling to recall some elusive fact from his memory. 'I've a feeling,' he went on slowly, 'that there *was* some mention of Hardene at the time. I'll get the file looked up.'

Boyce stroked his chin thoughtfully.

'I'm willing to lay good money that Fenn knows a lot more about Hardene than he admitted. The question is, did the people at the Seamen's Mission give him Hardene's name as that of someone in the city who took an interest in seamen with hard-luck stories to tell, or did Fenn mention Hardene's name first in order to find out his address?'

'I daresay,' Tremaine observed, 'that either Miss Royman or Mrs. Colver will be able to tell us whether Hardene was in the habit of helping lame dogs and whether he had a particular interest in seamen.'

'You're biting at something,' Boyce said. 'Just what's on your mind?'

'Doctor Hardene was obviously interested in some way in the seaman called Patrick Marton,' Tremaine said diffidently, 'otherwise he wouldn't have taken the trouble to keep all those cuttings. Marton was shot. And when Doctor Hardene went out to keep his mysterious appointment last night he carried a revolver in his little black bag. I'm wondering whether the bullet that killed Marton could have fitted that particular gun.'

'If it could,' Parkin said, 'it couldn't have fitted any other gun. Unless the ballistics people have been wrong for years.'

Jonathan Boyce thrust his thick hands deep into his pockets.

'Yes,' he said slowly. 'Yes. I see what you mean.'

6

THE ALIBI SEEMS COMPLETE

JEROME MASTERS was quite evidently a prosperous man. The original nineteenth-century Druidleigh had been extended in more recent days to take in the shoulder of land on the far side of the downs that lay in seclusion against the river gorge and from which there was a magnificent view of the sea some five or six miles distant. To live in this airy and tree-spaced retreat was to display the hallmark of success in Bridgton, and the house Masters had employed his own men to build for him was one of the most imposing residences in the area.

'If there's money in muck,' Boyce observed, as he clambered from the police car and stood staring up at the big house rising above them beyond the well-kept, sloping lawns, 'there certainly seems to be plenty in bricks and mortar.'

'The city's been expanding for years,' Parkin explained, following him to the entrance gate, 'and Masters has been expanding with it. At one time it was pretty much a one-man show, but a couple of years or so ago he turned his business into a limited company and since then he's been giving a lot of his time to politics.'

'Popular type?'

'So so.' Parkin shrugged. 'He's self-made and a bit—rugged.'

'I see,' Boyce said, and grinned. 'Some like what they call a blunt independence and others think he's too much of a good thing and needs taking down a peg or two.'

Parkin made no reply but his silence was eloquent enough.

Standing in the drive was a new car of expensive make.

'Very nice,' the Yard man observed. 'What a fool I was to want to be a policeman!'

Masters was at home and expecting them—a telephone call had seen to that. Tremaine saw a heavily built man, thick in the neck and beginning to display what threatened to be an unhealthy corpulence. There was a certain coarse arrogance about him. Not, he decided instinctively, a particularly nice individual, although he apparently possessed the qualities that bring success.

The room into which they had been shown overlooked the lawns. It was furnished austerely as a study, but the desk was bare of papers and the books on the shelves along the wall behind it did not look as though anyone moved them except to dust them.

Masters rose from the padded swivel chair in which he had been sitting with a newspaper in his hand and glanced questioningly at Parkin.

'Well, Inspector? Your call came at a damned inconvenient time. I'm a busy man.'

His tone made it clear that he regarded himself as a man who did not receive orders but gave them to other people. If Parkin noticed the hint of threat that was also there he did not show it either in his face or in his manner.

'I assure you, sir, I wouldn't have troubled you if the matter hadn't been important.'

'All right,' Masters said, with grumbling resignation. 'Let's have it then. Beats me why you couldn't have dealt with the business when you rang up instead of making a personal visit out of it.'

He looked at Parkin's companions and waited—significantly.

'This gentleman is Mr. Tremaine,' Parkin said. 'And this is Chief Inspector Boyce, of Scotland Yard.'

'Scotland Yard?'

Masters lost some of his overbearing manner, and Boyce smiled secretly. It was odd how mention of the Yard could take the bluster out of even the most truculent of people. He had observed the phenomenon before.

Maybe, though, it wasn't so odd. Not when you came to think of some of the cases the Yard had broken.

'Sorry to be a nuisance to you, sir,' he put in. 'But the Chief Constable called us in and I was sent down to work with your local men. You'll appreciate, I'm sure, that it means I have to make certain enquiries.'

'Enquiries? What enquiries?'

Masters spoke sharply, but it was not with the sharpness of his former careless arrogance. He was not quite so sure of himself. In fact, Tremaine concluded, watching him curiously, he was distinctly rattled.

Jonathan Boyce saw it, too.

'Before I deal with that, sir, might I ask whether you are in a position to tell me what your movements were last night?'

Masters glared, opened his mouth, seemed about to say something, and then closed it again, with a subtle change in his expression.

'I realize that this may seem a little unusual, sir,' Boyce said gently, 'and of course I have no authority to compel you to answer any questions. I'm assuming that a gentleman of your—prominence—would naturally have no objection to giving the police all possible help.'

'I don't know what the devil this is all about,' Masters burst out angrily, 'but it seems damned irregular to me. If

54

you're accusing me of something, why don't you come right out and say so?'

'Come, sir,' Boyce said, 'you know better than that. If I'd made up my mind that you were responsible for any criminal act it would be my duty to give you the official caution before asking you any questions. No, this is just a routine call to help me get one or two things straightened out in my mind. I'm not saying I won't be compelled to take notice of what I might describe as any—unwillingness to help matters on, but at the moment I haven't any fixed opinions.'

'You'd better sit down,' Masters said.

He seemed to have recovered a little. He seemed, too, to be realizing that so far he had not shown himself in a very favourable light, and was anxious to re-establish himself.

'Now,' he said, with an attempt at bluffness, when they had taken chairs, 'let's get to the point, Chief Inspector. What is it you want to see me about? Somebody been laying complaints about me? Plenty of people ready to tell tales about a man in my position. You know how it is.'

'Yes, I know how it is,' Boyce agreed. 'About last night, sir?' he added, with a slight but significant raising of his voice.

A shadow of irritation crossed the other's face but he managed to suppress it quickly.

'Oh yes, of course. I dined at my club. Had some business to attend to in the city and didn't come home as a matter of fact. After dinner I just stayed around for a while and then drove back here.'

'I see, sir.' Boyce made a brief note. 'About what time would that have been?'

'Time? Well, I couldn't say exactly. Didn't expect to be cross-examined about it. Round about eleven, I suppose.'

'D'you mind giving me the name of your club, sir?'

'Not much use to mind, is it? You'll find out soon enough.'

'Quite so, sir, but it makes matters that much easier and there's no sense in asking for unnecessary work.'

'It's the Venturers'. In Exchange Street. That's down in the city. Parkin will confirm it for you.'

'The Venturers' Club,' Boyce said, imperturbably, adding another note. 'Thank you, sir. No doubt you go there pretty often?'

'Most of the people who count in the city are members. It's a good place to get hold of anybody you want to see or to find out what's going on.'

Masters shrugged heavy shoulders, as though relieved at having got rid of a burden.

'Well, there you are. I think I've been frank with you, Chief Inspector. Now suppose you're frank with me and say why you want to know all this.'

'I'll do that right enough, sir. It was never my intention to go away without speaking of it. I've reason to believe that you're acquainted with a Doctor Graham Hardene. Is that correct, sir?'

The other's eyes narrowed. Involuntarily his hands clenched.

'That infernal busybody! Yes, I know him all right, and *he's* going to know *me* a good deal better before he's much older.'

'I doubt it, sir,' Boyce returned coolly. 'You see, that's why I'm here. He's dead.'

'Dead?' Masters looked taken aback. 'But . . . I thought—' He broke off. His glance rested in sudden dismay upon the Yard man's impassive face. 'What has Hardene's death to do with *your* being here?'

'Everything, in a manner of speaking, sir. Doctor Hardene was murdered.'

'Murdered!' The word came out in a gasp. Masters sank back in his chair. His big but flabby body seemed suddenly to have been deflated. 'I—I didn't know,' he managed to get out. 'There wasn't anything about it in the papers.'

'There wouldn't be—yet. It happened late last night. It seems that the doctor may have been tricked into leaving his house by a telephone call purporting to come from a patient who needed him in a hurry. He was found by a constable on patrol lying in the hall of an empty house facing the downs. His head had been beaten in. I'm afraid it's rather an ugly business.'

Boyce's grey eyes were fixed upon the other's broad features, not accusingly but in a shrewd watchfulness that missed no change of expression.

'Why call on me?' Masters began, and then he heaved himself up in his chair. 'Look here, *I* didn't do it! I know there was a lot of talk about Hardene and me, but I didn't have anything to do with killing him! You can't fix the thing on me!'

His glance went to Inspector Parkin and a vicious look came into his face.

'This is *your* doing, Parkin. Just because everybody in Bridgton knows that Hardene was making a dead set at me over his damned pretence at being so righteous you're looking for a nice, easy way out. Well, it won't work. Wait till I get hold of the Chief Constable. I'll have a word or two to say to him about this!'

'No call to take it that way, sir,' Boyce interposed. 'In any case, this is *my* investigation. No one's making any accusations—it's a good deal too early—but you must realize that it's my duty to follow up every possible line of enquiry, and in view of the fact that your quarrel with Doctor Hardene was common knowledge and that both of you said some hard things I had no alternative but to talk to you about the matter.'

His voice was quiet but there was an implacable note in it that steadied Masters. Boyce waited a moment or two longer and when the other made no further comment he rose to his feet.

'I'm obliged to you for your help, sir. It may be that I shall need to call on you again and I may have to ask you for a statement, but subject to my confirming what you've told me about your movements last night there's no need for you to feel that you're under any kind of suspicion.'

Masters raised his head. His lips were working. Tremaine waited for him to speak, but before the words could come there was a knock on the door and an instant later it was opened.

'Oh, I'm sorry, Jerome, I didn't realize you were busy.'

It was a woman's voice. Tremaine saw her standing in the doorway, a rather frail, grey-haired woman who was leaning heavily upon a stick. She was not very tall and her form was slight, but there was character in her eyes and in the set of her determined chin.

Masters made a great effort.

'It's—all right, my dear. We were just finishing. This is my wife,' he went on, reluctantly, but seeing no way of escape. 'My dear, this is Chief Inspector Boyce, of Scotland Yard. I think you know Inspector Parkin. This is Mr.—er—Mr.—'

'Tremaine,' interposed that gentleman.

Mrs. Masters gave Parkin a brief nod and turned her regard upon Jonathan Boyce. Her eyes, Tremaine noted, were very bright; there was not, he thought, much that she would miss.

'Scotland Yard?' she observed. 'Isn't that rather unusual, Jerome?'

'I'm afraid he's brought bad news, my dear,' her husband said. He was speaking very carefully, as though he was talking to an invalid. 'It's about Doctor Hardene. He's been murdered.'

'Murdered?' She leaned more heavily on her stick, and her lip curled. 'I would hardly have described that as bad news. Not from your point of view, Jerome.'

'But, my dear . . .' Masters threw a glance at Boyce and swallowed hard. 'Murder is such a terrible thing. Surely at a time like this we should let bygones be bygones.'

'Nonsense. The man was doing his best to ruin you and it's just as well that he's dead. Who knows what more trouble he might have stirred up?'

There was appeal in the look Masters gave his visitors but he did not make any attempt to contradict his wife openly.

'I see you're what I might call a practical woman, Mrs. Masters,' Boyce said. 'You don't believe that being dead does anything to change the colour of what a man did in his lifetime.'

'I don't believe in hypocrisy,' she told him bluntly. 'Doctor Hardene levelled a number of unpleasant charges against my husband, and as far as I'm concerned the fact that he's dead means that there will be an end to the trouble. Whether he was murdered or not doesn't come into it.'

She waited, as though she expected Boyce to take her up, but the Yard man refused to be drawn.

'I've asked all the questions I need to ask for the time being, ma'am, and I don't want to take up any more of your husband's time. I know that he's a very busy man.'

She stood aside to allow them to pass, a faint smile on her face.

'And you're a very clever one, Chief Inspector,' she remarked. 'You know that it's useless to argue with a woman!'

Boyce and his two companions were shown out of the house and they walked back down the drive towards their car.

'A woman of character,' Tremaine observed, and Parkin gave a dry chuckle.

'You aren't the first to find that out. There isn't much of her but she's the sort who knows what she wants—and gets it. Outside his house Masters is the strong man, the fellow who gets things done and expects everybody else to jump around when he says so or else. But inside it's a different story. She's got him under her thumb all right. You saw the way he curled up when she came in?'

Boyce nodded.

'Odd how so many of these blustering types turn out to have their heel of Achilles. Still, that part of it's no concern of ours—as far as we know. What we came to find out was whether friend Masters could have been responsible for landing that piece of rock against Hardene's skull. At the moment it doesn't look much like it. How long would it have taken him to drive home from his club?'

'Say fifteen minutes,' Parkin returned. 'Probably not quite as long. The city's pretty dead after about ten o'clock and there wouldn't have been much traffic about. It was a dry night as well, so there wouldn't have been anything to hold him up.'

'So if he didn't get home until eleven, he needn't have left his club until a quarter to. The body was found at half past ten, which means that if Masters did it there needs to be a sizable hole in his story. Even if we fix the time of death as late as five minutes or so before the constable found Hardene it's clear that Masters couldn't have done the job and made himself scarce unless he left his club just after ten at the latest. I can't imagine him being stupid enough to pitch up an alibi with nearly three-quarters of an hour unaccounted for.'

'That's true, sir,' Parkin said. 'Masters is sharp enough. It doesn't seem to make sense that he'd say he left his club at a quarter to eleven knowing that there'd be plenty of witnesses to say that he left a good deal earlier.'

'And yet,' Tremaine observed, 'he was shaken about something.'

They had reached the car by now. As they climbed in and drove off along the road he looked speculatively at Parkin.

'It was Masters who was on your mind when we met you this morning, wasn't it, Inspector?'

Parkin returned his glance wryly, and with something of respect.

'Did I make it so obvious?'

'Obvious enough,' Tremaine said. 'You were certainly keeping something back. You had Masters pretty well lined up as the man we're after, didn't you?'

Parkin nodded.

'Yes,' he admitted soberly. 'You see, coming on top of that open row between them it looked like the kind of thing Masters might have done. You've seen him for yourself now; he can make a bad enemy. As a rule politics don't get down to personalities here, but now and again you do get a flare-up and Masters and Hardene were both the type to take it seriously. Both of them were trying to get themselves in the headlines—Masters hasn't been on the council long and he's been trying hard to get himself noticed—and it was developing into a race to see who could finish off the other first. When I heard about Hardene the first thought that came into my head was that Masters was our man, but the Chief Constable had decided to call you in and I didn't want to speak too soon in case I gave you any prejudices that might have got in your way. I knew that I might be wrong. In fact, it's looking as though I was.'

Tremaine made no further comment. He leaned back against the upholstery, staring out of the windows of the car at the pleasant downland which was Bridgton's pride, and it was Boyce who took up the conversation.

'Well, we're certainly moving,' he remarked, 'but it looks as though the next step's going to call for the routine grind. There's all the stuff in Hardene's surgery to be checked over, a list of his patients to be gone through in case we can get a line on that telephone call, and Fenn and that fellow Slade to be followed up. And we'll need to send someone down to the Venturers' Club to make sure there aren't any holes in the story Masters gave us just now.'

Tremaine turned back from his study of the downs.

'And we'll need the files on the murder of Patrick Marton,' he said quietly.

'The seaman?' Boyce studied him reflectively. 'You still think there's a connection?'

'I still think there *might* be one.'

They drove by a roundabout route that enabled them to drop Parkin at the big, white-stoned building near the centre of the city that was the local police headquarters before setting out to contact Sergeant Witham at the empty house where Hardene's body had been found.

Both Boyce and Tremaine were silent after Parkin had left them; there was, indeed, plenty to occupy both their minds. It was not until they had once more reached the road bordering the downs that Boyce roused himself to study his companion with a quizzical smile.

'Well, Mordecai, where's it getting you?'

'Nowhere,' Tremaine told him ruefully. 'But I'd like to know,' he added, 'what else was on Parkin's mind.'

Boyce looked at him in surprise.

'Parkin? What else? I thought Masters was the bee in his bonnet.'

'It was *one* of the bees,' Tremaine said. 'But there's something else as well. And I think it must be something important. So important that it scares him.'

Boyce started to smile benevolently and then changed his mind. It didn't do to laugh where Mordecai Tremaine was concerned. He had a disconcerting habit of sometimes arriving at the truth a long way in advance of other people.

7

THE CHIEF CONSTABLE PRESIDES

THE *Evening Courier* was a very creditable production for an evening newspaper with limited resources. Mordecai Tremaine, who had a weakness for newspapers and journalists, surveyed its early edition appreciatively.

Rex Linton's story, with suitable headlines, held the leading position on the front page. He was relieved to find that there was no mention of his own name; the account was, in fact, quite clearly the opening gambit.

Linton was keeping one or two tricks up his sleeve; stripped of its biographical details concerning Hardene and its references to previous unsolved murders—Tremaine thought he detected the reporter's sense of mischief—it gave nothing more than the bare facts of Hardene's death.

Tremaine read it in a few moments and then turned his attention to the rest of the paper. It was possible to glean a great deal of knowledge of a city and its inhabitants from the contents of its local journal.

He was sitting in an inexpensive restaurant near police headquarters to which Boyce and he had repaired for a belated lunch, awaiting Jonathan's return from making a telephone call to Sergeant Witham, now posted at Hardene's surgery.

The day had, of course, begun early, but even so he felt that they had accomplished a good deal—including arranging for accommodation at a seventeenth-century inn that had once been built against the ancient city wall and was now near enough to the modern centre to be a convenient base for operations.

A touch on his shoulder made him look up to see that Boyce had returned.

'Everything's under control. Witham's still busy sifting and there've been no visitors worth noting. Plenty of telephone enquiries though from people who've seen the papers. I've asked Miss Royman to take all calls and I've put a man in with her to keep a record of everybody who rings up. She'll have her work cut out for a while but it'll save her from brooding—if she has anything to brood about.'

There was the faintest of undercurrents in his voice. Nervously Tremaine pushed back his pince-nez. It was a disturbing thought that such an attractive young woman as Margaret Royman should have shown a furtive interest in the items that had been locked in Graham Hardene's desk, but it was also a fact there could be no disputing.

Jonathan Boyce did not, however, say anything more about the girl. He nodded towards the newspaper Tremaine was still holding.

'That Linton's report? Anything there?'

'Nothing we didn't know—except for a few notes about Hardene.'

Boyce glanced over the headlines and then looked down at his watch.

'H'm. Time we were moving. Chief Constable's waiting for us and I don't want to start off on the wrong foot by keeping him waiting too long the first day.'

A few minutes brisk walking brought them to police head-quarters and they were shown up to the Chief Constable's room—a long, official-looking apartment just above the main entrance to the building.

'Come in, gentlemen, and find yourselves chairs.'

Sir Robert Dennell turned from the window at their entrance and indicated the round, polished conference table that held the centre of the floor. With the light from the window falling upon him from behind he looked older than Tremaine had imagined him to be that morning. His tall, spare figure showed signs of stooping and there were lines of fatigue in his grizzled countenance.

Not that there was any evidence of weakness in either voice or manner as he took his seat with them at the table.

'Now, Parkin,' he said incisively, to the inspector who had accompanied them, 'you first. Let's have your report.'

Briefly Parkin detailed the morning's activities, including the visit to Jerome Masters. The Chief Constable listened intently to what Parkin had to say and then looked significantly across at Boyce.

'Masters, of course, is an obvious suspect. I take it you already know about the trouble with Hardene?'

'I know about it, sir, in the sense that I've heard that Hardene and Masters were at daggers-drawn over certain accusations Hardene had made. What I don't know is how much truth there was in them and therefore how much real motive Masters might have had.'

'Neither does anybody else,' the Chief Constable said drily. 'It rather looks as though we're going to have the unpleasant job of looking for dirty linen. It's always a distasteful business when things go wrong in local politics. Even a city like this is really quite a small place. Before you know where you are you've got down to personalities and the mud that's stirred up takes years to settle down again.'

'I think you're being a bit gloomy, sir,' Boyce put in. 'Naturally, if we're forced to decide that Masters is the chap we want we'll have to see about getting a watertight motive, but there's nothing definitely pointing his way as yet apart from his upset with Hardene. And if he *is* in the clear over the murder we'll have no call to go probing into anything else.'

The Chief Constable nodded.

'I'm certainly not anxious to get his back up if he's innocent. Masters can be an ugly customer. What was your impression?'

'I'm inclined to agree, sir—up to a point. He *could* be a very ugly customer, if he thought he could get away with it. But my feeling this morning was that he wasn't altogether sure of himself. And whatever else he may be there isn't much doubt that he isn't master in his own house.'

A shadow crossed Sir Robert Dennell's face.

'We needn't hold that against him. Plenty of men are in the same boat—if they were honest enough to admit it. Very often it's the man who feels most sure of himself who has the least cause to boast.'

There was a note of bitterness in his voice and Tremaine gave him a thoughtful glance. But the Chief Constable did not elaborate what he had said. He glanced down at the note he had made on the pad in front of him and when he spoke again it was in the authoritative tone in which he had opened the proceedings.

'So far it seems that although there are one or two likely leads you haven't been able to arrive at anything definite. Not that I'm concerned about that. It didn't look like an open and shut case, otherwise I wouldn't have called in the Yard, and I hardly expected you to have anything concrete to put forward at this stage.'

He glanced across the table, and his eyes, blue and hard, the eyes of a man used to having his instructions obeyed without question, rested upon Jonathan Boyce.

'Any assistance you need, Chief Inspector, is at your disposal. In return I want to be informed of every development as soon as it takes place. As soon as it takes place,' he repeated, with a slight emphasis.

'I quite understand, sir,' Boyce returned, without expression, and the Chief Constable gave a wintry smile.

'I wonder whether you do? People don't like unsolved murders and we've had two in the last eight months. It becomes a little difficult when the Chief Constable has to refuse dinner invitations because it's embarrassing to be asked awkward questions by leading citizens. I'll be available to you at any time, and any request you make to Parkin here will be dealt with without delay. I want this case broken and I want it broken in the shortest possible time.'

'I'll do my best, sir,' Boyce returned quietly. 'You're giving me all the advantages you can. The scent's still warm. I won't let you down.'

For a moment the Chief Constable's gaze held, then he relaxed with something like a little sigh.

'I don't think you will,' he said. He reached out to a pile of documents and files and pushed them across the table. 'I understand you wanted these. You'll find everything there about Marton and the pawnbroker Wallins—everything we were able to find out, that is. I think, quite frankly, that you're off on a wild-goose chase because my men didn't leave much undone, but if you think you can dig up anything fresh, well, there's the whole bag of tricks.'

Someone coughed, a trifle nervously. It was Parkin.

'I haven't had an opportunity yet, sir, of checking back to make sure, but I've an idea that Doctor Hardene's name was mentioned at the time of the Marton case.'

'The deuce it was!' The Chief Constable's stare alighted challengingly on his subordinate. 'I don't recall it.'

'It didn't amount to much, sir,' Parkin explained. 'I've been thinking it over since Mr. Tremaine here first put the idea into my head this morning. As far as I remember this chap Marton was supposed to have made some remark at the Seamen's Mission about going to see Doctor Hardene. Quite a few men from the Mission went up to him at different times—he was supposed to be interested in welfare work.'

'Wasn't Hardene asked about it?'

'He was interviewed, sir, but he said that Marton hadn't called on him and that he knew nothing about him. There wasn't anything to connect and it just looked like a dead end. Hardene had a good reputation; there was no reason to suppose that he was hiding anything so naturally the thing was left there.'

'H'm. Doesn't sound as though there was much to it.' The Chief Constable pushed back his chair. 'I've a Committee this afternoon and it's time I was off. Use this room if you want to—I doubt whether I'll be back much before half past five.'

'That's good of you, sir,' Boyce said. 'I'll be glad of a chance to run through these files and sort things out. My sergeant's still at the house and I'll be joining him later on. If there should be anything fresh I'll contact you.'

The Chief Constable nodded and left the room, leaving the three of them still seated round the table.

'Masters again,' Tremaine observed. 'There seems to be a general feeling locally that he must be behind it.'

He was looking at Parkin, but the inspector left it to Boyce to reply.

'You mean all that stuff about the complications attached to finding a motive?' he mused. 'It did sound a bit as though Sir Robert was taking it for granted that our chief job's going to be pinning it on Masters. Still, that may be due to the fact that he doesn't want a third unsolved killing on his hands and is in a hurry to get things cleared up.'

Boyce reached for the files on the table in front of them and sorted rapidly through them.

'Here you are, Mordecai, you take the Marton affair first, since it seems to be your particular pigeon. I'll take the pawn-broker. I don't pretend I can see any daylight, but Hardene must have had some reason for keeping those cuttings.'

For some while there was silence as they studied the accumulation of reports, statements, and photographs. At last Boyce put the last item aside and leaned back with a frown.

There was no doubt that the local police had been thorough, but it was equally clear that in each case they had been presented with the kind of problem that is an investigating detective's nightmare. He glanced at Tremaine.

'Not so good,' he observed.

'On the other hand, Jonathan,' Tremaine remarked, 'a challenge is always stimulating. After all, when a murder is committed by a member of the criminal classes or when you can narrow it down to a person belonging to a fairly small group of suspects who must have known the victim intimately, detection becomes a mere matter of humdrum routine. All you have to do is to look through your *modus operandi* records until you find all the known criminals who leave the sort of traces you've found at the scene of the crime and then start in to break down their alibis. If the person you're after isn't a regular criminal, but belongs to a small group of the victim's relatives or acquaintances, there isn't much trouble as a rule in deciding who might have done it; the real job is to get hold of the proof, which generally means that it's in the science laboratory where most of the detecting is done. The policeman is just an office boy, collecting nail filings, or dust, or odd fibres of cloth.'

Boyce made a grimace.

'Sometimes it isn't a bad thing to be an office boy. It saves a lot of wear and tear on the nerves. This kind of thing is calculated to make the plodding type like me wonder whether it's worth while hanging on for the sake of the pension. Look at them!' Boyce brought his palm down on the topmost pile. 'Wallins had no near relatives and precious few acquaintances—certainly there's no sign of anybody who could have had a motive for killing him—and every one of the known crooks who might have done the job has a cast-iron alibi. Some person unknown just walked in out of nowhere, did for the old chap and walked out again. With fifty million people to choose from it's some outlook, isn't it!'

He pushed the papers from him and leaned back with a gesture of despair.

'As for this other fellow, Marton, there isn't even a place to begin. It isn't even certain who he really was. Enquiries in the West Indies where he joined his ship drew a blank and nobody here in Bridgton seems to have known anything about him.'

Inspector Parkin was looking disturbed. Tremaine glanced at him over his pince-nez, his eyes twinkling.

'Don't take it to heart, Inspector. He doesn't mean it, you know. It's just his way of letting off steam.'

Boyce pushed back his chair and rose to his feet. He paced restlessly about the room, hands thrust into his pockets and his brows drawn together in a frown.

'I suppose he *could* have had those cuttings just because he was interested in them as cases. As a doctor he might have found something worth studying from the medical point of view. I suppose there was a good deal of comment locally at the time about the murders.'

'There was,' Parkin agreed. 'A murder in the city naturally gets talked over quite a lot—we don't get all that number, fortunately—and a murder that seems just a bit out of the ordinary is usually given a fair amount of space in the newspapers, even in these days.'

Boyce stopped in front of the window, staring down into the street below for a moment or two, then he swung back to face his companions.

'Well, we can't afford to go running into dead ends,' he said decisively. 'The Chief Constable's expecting results, and there doesn't seem to be anything here that ties up with Hardene. Sorry, Mordecai, but you see how it is.'

'That's all right, Jonathan,' Tremaine said quietly. 'It was just a feeling I had. After all, there was really nothing to go upon.'

He was gathering up the files and documents they had been studying when there was a knock at the door and a uniformed constable came in.

'Beg pardon, sir,' he said, approaching Parkin, 'but these have just come for you. The lab said they were urgent.'

Parkin took the photographs and the typewritten sheet the constable had brought. He studied them intently for a moment or so and then he gave a low whistle of excitement.

'Take a look at these!' he exclaimed, and held them out to Boyce.

The photographs were enlargements of revolver bullets and they showed the markings made by the gun from which they had been fired. Whoever had prepared the photographs had marked various points in red ink.

Boyce raised his head from the prints and looked across at Tremaine, a sudden keenness in his grey eyes.

'It looks,' he said, 'as though your hunch wasn't so wide of the mark, after all. The bullet that killed Marton did come from the gun Hardene was carrying around in his little black bag!'

He handed the photographs across the table for Tremaine, trying to preserve a decent modesty, to examine for himself.

There could be no doubt about the points of resemblance. The Chief Constable was going to be presented with his first development in excellent time.

8

HINT OF A SECRET ROMANCE

SERGEANT WITHAM had evidently been both busy and methodical. Books and papers were arranged neatly upon the late Doctor Hardene's desk, and in the notebook in front of him the sergeant had made a number of careful entries.

He sprang up as Boyce and Tremaine came in.

'I think this is the lot, sir. As far as I can take it, anyway.'

'Good man,' Boyce said. He sat down at the desk and flicked the pages of the note-book. 'You seem to have done the job thoroughly—as usual, Witham. I'll see it's mentioned in the right quarters.'

'Thank you, sir.'

Boyce sat down. A note had been despatched by special messenger to Sir Robert Dennell at his Committee meeting, informing him of the result of the tests made with the gun in Hardene's bag; it should allow him at least a limited breathing space in which he could gather up any further threads.

'H'm. Investments about four thousand. Income—not too bad; if he was honest in his income-tax returns. He seems to have been comfortably enough off. Anything to show where the money came from?'

'No, sir. I haven't been able to find anything going back more than four or five years—that's about the time he came here. As far as it goes it's all straightforward enough. He kept an account of his dividends as they came in—all his money was in good class industrials and he doesn't seem to have done much buying and selling.'

'Anything particularly interesting?'

'There's this,' Witham said. He reached towards the desk and picked up a small, blue-covered book. Tremaine recognized the diary Boyce had earlier found in the desk. 'Seems to have been with his personal papers, cheque book and so on. It's not so much a diary as an appointment book.'

'Sounds all right,' Boyce remarked. 'I did glance at it as a matter of fact.' He took the book from his subordinate's hand. 'As a doctor he'd need to keep some record of the people he was due to see. Miss Royman, I daresay, would keep the ordinary list of appointments, but he might have liked his own reminder of the more important patients. You didn't happen to notice,' he added, balancing the note-book thoughtfully, 'whether Miss Royman seemed at all interested in this? I left it with several other items on the desk as I mentioned over the 'phone.'

'Everything seemed to be where you left it, sir,' the sergeant returned. 'I can't say I noticed anything in that way about Miss Royman. In fact, I don't think she came in here at all.'

Boyce pursed his lips.

'She didn't, eh? Still, I'm sidetracking you. What was it you were going to say about the book?'

'It looks as though he used it to jot down notes about different affairs he had to attend—dinners, lectures, and so on. But I did spot something I thought you might like to have a look at.'

Witham leaned over and turned the pages of the diary. He indicated an entry and then flicked over a page or two more and pointed out another.

'He seems to have been in the habit of seeing quite a lot of the lady, doesn't he?' Boyce remarked. He quoted from the diary. '*Elaine—eight-thirty. Meet Elaine—Elm Tree.* Does he give her any other name anywhere?'

Witham shook his head.

'No, sir. It's always just Elaine. The entries begin in January and go on right up to a day or two ago. Generally there are about two entries a week, sometimes only one.'

'Just the name and a time?'

'A time or a place. I had a word with Miss Royman—didn't tell her anything, of course. Elm Tree is a place on the downs—there's an old elm tree there that's a local landmark. The only unusual entry,' Witham finished, 'is this one.'

He indicated a date in the diary about a fortnight previously. The name and a time appeared as in the other entries, but right across it Hardene had scrawled the word *Trouble.* The letters were thick as though he had been in a state of emotion at the time so that the nib of his pen had spread more than usual.

Boyce closed the diary and passed it across to Tremaine with a twinkle.

'This looks as though it might be right in your department. A secret romance. Hardene and the mysterious Elaine.'

Tremaine looked disapprovingly over his pince-nez.

'I don't know,' he said, 'that I am in sympathy with clandestine meetings—unless there are good and sufficient reasons for them.'

He spoke a little primly. Boyce was aware of his weakness for *Romantic Stories* and was sometimes given to pulling his leg. Where lovers and romance were concerned Tremaine had a blind spot; he was a sentimentalist and he disliked there being no happy ending. He also disliked any note of the sordid being introduced into what he saw as something fundamentally beautiful in the best of all worlds.

The Yard man saw the effect he had produced and turned with a chuckle to the remainder of the items on the desk.

'What about his bank statements?' he asked. 'Everything in order?'

'Apparently,' Witham said. 'Decent balance in his current account and no large outgoings. Bills were all paid by cheque. The only cash withdrawal was a regular one of fifty pounds, drawn on the first of the month and payable to self.'

Boyce nodded acceptance.

'Well, I suppose he'd need a certain amount of cash to keep going. To pay his housekeeper and so on.'

'She was paid by cheque, sir.' Witham's voice showed that he was puzzled. 'I thought fifty pounds was rather a lot since everything was settled by cheque and not cash. He even had an account for his tobacco and cigarettes that was cleared monthly through his bank.'

'Petrol? Being a doctor he must have got through quite a bit on his rounds.'

'Same way as the rest. He had a monthly account with a garage round the corner. I've been scratching my head about it, but I'm blessed if I can see where he got rid of fifty quid a month.'

'Maybe it brings us back to Elaine. The high cost of women,' Boyce remarked.

'I did think of that, sir, so I checked back. There are references to Elaine right back in January, and I got the feeling that if we could find his diary for last year there'd be entries there as well. But the fifty-pound withdrawals don't start until May. Before then he just drew odd amounts on different dates as though he put in a cheque whenever he was short of money.'

'H'm.' Boyce stared up at the ceiling for a moment, frowning. 'Miss Royman's gone, of course, but the housekeeper's still around, and she's probably the best bet for this job anyway.' He brought his eyes down. 'Ask her to come in, will you?'

A few moments later, shepherded by the sergeant, Mrs. Colver appeared in the doorway. Boyce rose and put out a chair for her.

'Sit down, Mrs. Colver,' he invited. 'I only want a friendly chat and we may as well make ourselves comfortable.'

The housekeeper brushed a wisp of grey hair from her forehead and took the proffered chair uneasily.

'I know you think I'm a confounded nuisance,' Boyce went on cheerfully, 'and no doubt I am, especially if I've just interrupted an important operation in the kitchen. But we're making progress and we've come to a point where we need your help.'

The housekeeper sat forward on the edge of her chair. Her face looked suddenly startled.

'Progress?'

'Yes,' Boyce said, as though he had noticed nothing significant in her manner. 'We're feeling quite pleased with ourselves. Now, Mrs. Colver, you may think that my questions are a little, well, indelicate, shall we say, but I can assure you that they're not being put without good reason.'

Tremaine stared suspiciously at his friend. It was unlike Jonathan Boyce to take so long to get to the point.

Then he glanced at the housekeeper, her plump, middle-aged form seated uncomfortably on the edge of her chair, and apprehension growing in her face, and he thought he could see what Boyce was aiming at.

'We've been looking into the doctor's affairs,' Boyce went on, 'and it seems that he was in the habit of paying all his bills by cheque. He even, in fact, paid your own salary that way.'

'Yes, that's right. He said it made things much easier if everything was done through the bank.'

She spoke in a precise, artificial manner. She was anxious to give a good impression and yet did not want to make it obvious what she was doing in case it aroused curiosity as to her reasons.

'The only cash drawings we've been able to trace,' Boyce continued, 'are various amounts of fifty pounds each which were drawn on the first of the month, commencing last May. For a man in Doctor Hardene's position, of course, it wouldn't normally seem anything unusual, but it does seem rather a large sum for him to draw since he dealt with all his obvious expenses by cheque. Can you suggest any reason why he might have wanted so much in cash?'

The housekeeper held his steady gaze. She shook her head.

'No,' she said firmly. 'No, I can't give you any reason. Everything for the house was ordered on account. When the bills came in I gave them to the doctor and he paid them. It was only when anything unexpected happened that he gave me any money.'

'You mentioned this morning that the doctor went out now and again socially although he did very little entertaining here. When he did go out where did he usually spend his time?'

'Sometimes he went out to dinner. With friends—or perhaps when there was some special affair on with other doctors. After he began to get interested in council work he went out more often, but as a rule it was only to see people he thought he ought to know or to go to political meetings.'

'He was a bachelor, of course,' Boyce remarked casually, 'but because a man isn't married it doesn't mean that he can't have any friends among the ladies. Did he ever give you any cause to think he might decide to marry one day?'

The housekeeper's lips met in a thin line. For the first time she seemed unable to keep her feelings firmly under control.

'He wasn't the marrying kind,' she said, and there was a waspish note in her voice.

Boyce glanced at her from beneath his eyebrows. It was always a good thing from the point of view of really finding out things when a witness allowed emotion to show.

'But he was—interested—in the ladies?'

'Doctor Hardene's private life wasn't any concern of mine. I was paid to act as his housekeeper.'

'I'm looking for an explanation for that fifty pounds a month,' Boyce said quietly, and waited.

Tremaine watched the changing expressions in the house-keeper's face. She said, at last:

'I—I suppose I ought to tell you. He's dead, anyway, and it's your job to find things out. I didn't say anything about it while he was alive. He was always kind to me and it wasn't any of my affair. But there were things I didn't like—things no self-respecting woman could agree with.'

'We've found a note-book of the doctor's, Mrs. Colver—a diary, to be accurate, which he seems to have used for his personal appointments. Did you ever hear him mention anyone called Elaine?'

'Elaine?' The housekeeper looked puzzled. She frowned, and then shook her head slowly. 'No, I never heard him speak of anyone of that name.'

'He was seeing a good deal of her all through the year. At least once a week and more often it was twice.'

Understanding came into her face then.

'Oh, so that was her name!'

'You mean he never told you?'

'No. I knew what was going on, of course. I knew that he was going out to see a woman—it was obvious enough, the trouble he took, more than he usually did. But he never said who she was.'

'I take it in that case that she never came here to the house?'

'There was something funny about it. That's why she was never here. I knew from the start that there was something that wasn't straightforward and he gave it away once. He got to talking seriously when he came back one night—he did sometimes; he knew that he could talk to me. Well, I—I said what was in my mind about all his goings-on. I asked him why he didn't get married, and it was then that he told me she was married already.'

'Married, eh?' Boyce pulled at his chin. 'So *that* was the reason for all the secrecy. He had to take care he didn't get mixed up with any scandal, naturally. Being a doctor it was more important to him than to most.'

'He knew what he was doing,' she said, with just a trace of vindictiveness in her manner. 'He'd always take the car and they'd meet somewhere quiet and then go out of Bridgton.'

'Risky, though. Never know when there's somebody about who'll recognize you even though you may not realize they're anywhere in the neighbourhood.'

'He was the sort to take risks. If he wanted something he'd go after it and wouldn't trouble about what it might cost.'

She stopped and bit her lip, as though she had been led into saying more than she had intended. Boyce shrugged.

'Sometimes it pays, sometimes it doesn't. As a rule that's where *we* come in. That's all, Mrs. Colver. I'm sorry you can't tell us any more about this rather elusive lady called Elaine, but I'm obliged to you for your help. I think we can make a guess as to where some of that fifty pounds a month went. I don't know what your personal plans are,' he added, 'but I take it that you'll be wanting to stay on here at least for a day or so until things are sorted out. After that—'

He broke off, leaving it to her to finish.

'It's all been so sudden,' she said. 'I haven't had time to think out what to do. Of course, I shan't be able to stay here long. I suppose the house will have to be sold.'

'That will depend on the will—if he made one.' Boyce looked enquiringly at his sergeant. 'What about it, Witham? Any note of his solicitors?'

'Yes, sir. I've got the address and telephone number. As a matter of fact, I believe they rang up today—must've seen the news in the paper. One of the local men's still standing by, although it's pretty quiet now. You saw him when you came in, of course. He's got the full list.'

'Tomorrow will do for the solicitors—probably gone home now, anyway, and there don't seem to be any relatives to go into a panic about whether they've been left anything. We're keeping a man in the neighbourhood all night, Mrs. Colver,' Boyce went on, turning. 'Not that we're expecting trouble, but under the circumstances I daresay you'll be glad to feel you aren't being left completely on your own.'

'You needn't worry about me,' she told him, a little bitterly. 'I'm used to looking after myself. A widow soon has to get used to doing that.'

When she had gone the Yard man swivelled in his chair to face Mordecai Tremaine.

'Reactions, Mordecai?'

'Speaks well, Jonathan. Sounds rather as though she's known better days. It's made her—hard.'

'That was my verdict, too. She didn't like Hardene as much as she's tried to make out.'

Boyce's next move was to go out to the reception room where the local detective was still waiting by the telephone in case any further calls should come through. He ran quickly down the list; most of the enquiries seemed to have been made by various organizations, either medical or political, with which Hardene had been associated. The time the call had been made had been added in each case.

He glanced at his watch.

'Nothing in the past hour and a half, I see. You might as well knock off. The housekeeper can deal with anything else that comes along. We're past the point when we might have picked up something useful anyway. The news is cold now.'

He was on the point of folding the list to place it inside his note-book when he noticed that one entry differed from the others. The time had been written in, as also the fact that the call had originated from a public-box, but no name was given.

'Hullo, what's this? Couldn't you find out who rang up?'

He put his finger on the entry in question, indicating it to the detective.

'She wouldn't give her name, sir.'

'A woman, was it?'

'It was a woman's voice. She started asking what had happened to the doctor but when I tried to find out who she was she wouldn't answer—just said that she was one of Doctor Hardene's friends.'

'What was her voice like?'

'Wouldn't like to be certain about it, sir,' the man returned slowly. 'You know how difficult it is to place people on the telephone, but I'd say she was young. Educated, too—by the sound of her.'

Boyce raised his eyebrows in an unspoken question and the other explained.

'Local accent's pretty strong, sir. Daresay you've noticed it already. *She* didn't have it. She was pretty worked up though— frightened, I'd say. I tried to keep her while I got the call traced, but she was wise to me and rang off. I got the address of the call-box she was using and one of our patrol cars went there right away, but there was no sign of her by then. Sorry about it, sir.'

'You did the best you could,' Boyce said. 'No fault of yours. Corner of Prince Avenue and Kinley Gardens. That far from here?'

'About a mile I'd think, sir. In Druidleigh but getting in a bit towards the city.'

Tremaine had been following the conversation. He touched Boyce on the arm.

'What time was the call put through?'

'Couldn't have been long after we'd left this morning,' Boyce told him. 'About ten-thirty. Are you thinking what I'm thinking?' he added.

'Elaine?'

'Mysterious lady,' Boyce said. 'Could be.'

They went back into Hardene's surgery and they were still there some twenty minutes later, Tremaine with the blue diary in his hand and Boyce studying the bank statements, when they heard the telephone ringing and after a short interval Witham put his head around the door.

'Call for you, sir,' he said to his chief.

Boyce went out. Tremaine heard his voice, muffled by the intervening wall, speaking to the person at the other end of the wire. The conversation lasted several minutes and when at last Boyce returned his face bore the excited expression of a man who had important news to tell.

'That was Parkin,' he announced. 'His men have been checking up on Masters. It's true enough that he didn't get home until eleven o'clock—a constable on patrol happened to see him turning into his gateway—driving his own car—but the rest of his story just falls apart. He didn't go anywhere near the Venturers' Club last night.'

Tremaine's eyes widened. He put up a hand to straighten the pince-nez now perched precariously indeed on the end of his nose.

'Dear me, Jonathan, that sounds as though it might be very awkward for him.'

'It certainly does,' Boyce said grimly. 'If friend Masters *wasn't* at the Venturers' Club at the time when somebody was busy knocking Hardene on the head with a lump of rock, just where was he?'

He sat down at the surgery desk and took out his note-book. Tremaine watched him as he entered methodical comments on the next available page. When next Chief Inspector Boyce paid a call upon Jerome Masters that gentleman was in for a bad time.

9

DISTURBING INCIDENT BY NIGHT

A LONG time ago Mordecai Tremaine had read somewhere that Haroun Al Raschid, the great caliph of Bagdad, had been in the habit of wandering incognito at night through the streets of the city he ruled in order that he might the better become acquainted with his people. Tremaine, in whom there dwelt both a strong sense of romance and an intense interest in people and things, had ever since then regarded the caliph as a man whose example might well be followed—at least in that one particular respect.

One of his pleasures was to stroll idly through the crowded places of any city in which he might happen to be, studying the men and women whom he passed and wondering what they might be and whither they might be bound.

There was, of course, little danger of his identity being unmasked by an awestruck bystander, despite the embarrassing fame that had attended his excursions into crime detection; in that his adventures had perforce to differ from those of the caliph.

It was a harmless enough entertainment, and if sometimes his deductions led to his giving the most innocent of citizens the most horrifying of intentions, his victims were blissfully unaware of the characters he had bestowed upon them.

A strange city—or at least a largely unfamiliar city—offered opportunities which were irresistible. Tremaine left Chief Inspector Boyce wrestling with his reports at their hotel and set out in search of excitement of the soul.

The thought was not consciously with him as he walked down the narrow cobbled street in which their place of lodging was situated; he knew better than to allow sentiment to intrude upon the grim business which had brought him to Bridgton. But nevertheless, it was Tremaine the romantic, rather than Tremaine the relentless man-hunter, who made his way towards the bright lights and the crowds of the city's centre.

There was, perhaps, another reason that took him abroad, although this also he would not openly have admitted. Murder was an ugly, furtive affair of twisted passions and evil motives; when you were pursuing it you came inevitably upon blackness of heart and mind.

This was a kind of antidote; something that helped to restore the balance in favour of sanity and goodness. In the lights, restricted though they still were in these days, there was something with which to oppose the dark forces of evil, just as the wand of the fairy confronted and discomfited the demon; the sight of young lovers, hanging upon each other's arms and with happy smiling faces, even though they might be within his vision for no more than a brief instant before they had passed him for ever, did something to lift the despair from his heart. They were a blessed reminder that the world was not made up of dark places and evil deeds.

He walked on, without a fixed purpose save that of absorbing the saving atmosphere of humanity living and moving around him. He passed the bridge where the ships came into the heart of the city and went on along the road at the side of the ornamental gardens that had recently brought a whisper of the countryside and a restful splash of colour into the midst of dust, grey buildings and gyrating cars.

Just ahead of him he saw a neon sign running along the top of a tall building in which several lights still blazed, although the ground floor was in darkness. He quickened his steps despite the fact that there was nothing more to see.

So this was the office of the *Evening Courier*. Tremaine could never pass a newspaper office without an absurd surge of emotion and a hastening of his pulse that belonged to idealistic adolescence rather than to a sober and experienced citizen of his years.

When he drew level with the building he stopped in the shadows by the wall. The presses were silent now; the last edition had long since come hurtling to the despatch room to be distributed by motor-cycle, van, and train to the corners of the region of which Bridgton was the hub.

He looked up at the lighted windows. It was strange to think that into this quiet, almost empty building, news might be coming at this very moment of happenings in far-off places of the world.

There was a movement near at hand. Two figures emerged from the darkened entrance. He heard the door close behind them.

They stood on the pavement for a moment or two after they had come out and he was able to see that one was a girl and the other a man. He heard the girl speak in a low, troubled voice. He could not distinguish what she was saying, for she was turned partly away from him, but there was something familiar in her tone that made him peer at her more closely.

He recognized her then. It was Margaret Royman. A match flared briefly as her companion lit a cigarette, and Tremaine, who had been on the point of approaching her to make himself known, instinctively held back. The man was Rex Linton!

They moved slowly away from the doorway and he heard her voice quite plainly.

'You don't think they'll find out?'

'Of course not,' Rex Linton returned confidently. 'There isn't a chance of it.'

'But the Chief Inspector—the one from Scotland Yard—looks as though he won't let anything slip past him. And there's the other man with him—Mr. Tremaine. Isn't he the same man who's solved a lot of other cases?'

'It's the same Tremaine all right. There couldn't be two of them. He must be the innocent-looking old bird who was with the Chief Inspector when I was talking to him this morning. His name wasn't mentioned.'

Mordecai Tremaine felt a prickle of indignation. Innocent-looking old bird indeed! This young man needed to watch his manners or he would be finding himself in difficulties!

'I'm frightened,' Margaret Royman was saying. 'I know it's stupid of me, but I can't help it—I just am.'

Rex Linton put an arm around her.

'You're letting it get you down, darling. There's nothing to worry about—absolutely nothing. Everything's going to turn out all right.'

They turned together, Linton's arm still around the girl's waist, and moved off along the pavement—fortunately in the opposite direction to the anxious Tremaine, now pressing himself back against the wall in the shadows, anticipating discovery and feeling far from happy. His relief as he watched them go was mixed with the feeling that his evening had been ruined and the mood of contentment destroyed beyond recall.

The knowledge that Margaret Royman and Rex Linton were apparently in love with each other should have pleased his sentimental soul; they were a presentable young couple and he should have regarded it as a highly desirable discovery. But the air of secrecy, of conspiracy even, was too much a confirmation of his doubts earlier in the day to enable him to find any pleasure in what he had seen.

Margaret Royman had not told all she knew. She had something to hide. Tremaine shook his head sadly and pushed back his pince-nez. It was all very distressing.

His depression must have been evident in his face, for Jonathan Boyce, looking up from his work, gave him a meaning glance when he returned to the hotel.

'What's the trouble, Mordecai? Didn't the night air of Bridgton agree with you? Or couldn't you find any evidence of love's young dream?'

'That's just it,' Tremaine returned. 'I did find some. I saw Miss Royman.'

'Very nice, too.' Boyce nodded appreciatively. 'I admire the lucky man's taste. Who is he?'

'Rex Linton,' Tremaine said, and Boyce sat up with a low whistle.

'Our dashing young reporter, eh! The plot thickens.'

'I'm afraid it does,' Tremaine said unhappily. 'I saw them coming out of the *Courier* office. I couldn't help hearing something of what they were saying to each other, and it was clear that Miss Royman at least is worried about your finding out too much.'

'And Linton?'

'He acted as though he wasn't so concerned, but that might just have been because of the girl.'

'I suppose it *is* a case of young love?'

'Oh yes. He put his arms around her and it was obvious that they're on very close terms.'

'Well, I'll certainly accept your evidence in a matter of that sort! It looks,' Boyce said, 'as though we're going to have yet another line of enquiry—as if we didn't already have enough to be going on with. The trouble with a case like this is that the more you dig the more digging you find you've given yourself to do.'

Boyce was still very much engaged with his report, as was obvious from the papers scattered around him. Tremaine sat down on the other side of the gas-fire and tried to take his mind off Margaret Royman by thinking about all the other people whom he had met or heard about during the day.

It was quite a list. He took paper and pencil and jotted down their names, allowing his thoughts to drift around each of them as he wrote it down.

First, of course, there was the principal character in the drama, who, although no longer moving upon the stage was the mainspring of the entire piece. Graham Hardene. A middle-aged medical practitioner with a comfortable practice in a pleasant suburb of a provincial city. Unmarried, no financial worries as far as could be ascertained; in fact, no troubles of any kind except possibly the fact that he'd been carrying on an affair with a married woman—although it didn't look as though it had been causing him any qualms of conscience.

Hardene had been called out late at night, apparently to one of his patients who hadn't so far been traced. That seemed reasonable enough; what wasn't so easy to understand was why he'd thought it necessary to take a revolver with him and why he'd been found in an empty house.

Was it still possible that he'd made a mistake in the dark with the address and been killed in a moment of panic by a tramp whom he'd disturbed?

No, it wasn't. Tremaine shook his head with a regretful sound that made Boyce glance up from his work. It would certainly be a nice, neat solution that would avoid uncovering all sorts of unpleasantnesses, but it just wouldn't fit. It wouldn't explain, for instance, why Hardene had been carrying a gun that had killed a man.

The unpleasantnesses were there and pretending they weren't wouldn't help in the long run. It was going to be necessary to dig them all out, and some of the digging was likely to be distasteful.

Not all they would find would be of direct assistance. There were always all kinds of other threads mixed up with the one main thread you were trying to trace in affairs like this; the tricky job was to decide which was the one that really mattered and go after it never mind what it cost.

Determinedly he returned to his task of checking the members of the cast he had encountered thus far.

There was Martin Slade. One of Hardene's patients, sometimes at loggerheads with him, but crippled and in pain—a great many things could therefore be forgiven him that might appear as graver faults in other men.

Anything against him? Only the fact that he'd been a little too anxious to admit to his near-rows with Hardene. He'd visited the surgery for a perfectly normal reason—to see the doctor by appointment—and Margaret Royman had confirmed that he'd left his house before she could warn him by telephone not to come.

Tremaine frowned as a memory crept naggingly into his mind, a memory of Slade's clumsily moving figure stopping for a moment or two as he'd been about to climb into his car. He wondered whether Hardene had been an efficient doctor and whether Slade had been satisfied with the treatment he had been given.

Who next? Obviously, Fenn, the seaman who had arrived at the house just after Slade's car had been driven off.

A sailor looking for a shore job who'd come to Hardene because he'd heard that Hardene would very likely give him a helping hand? Well, why not? It was sound enough; plenty of tramps, sailors, and down-and-outs had apparently been known to go to Hardene.

It seemed to have been part of his stock-in-trade, to put the lowest valuation on it. He'd been setting himself up as the champion of the oppressed, although that kind of thing was getting a bit out of date. The real oppressed in these days usually wore neat if shabby suits and struggled to keep up an appearance of respectability under the weight of a mortgage and a frustrating degree of education acquired in easier times.

Anything to be noted about Fenn? Rather an ugly-looking chap, accent from the other side of the Atlantic—otherwise little that was worth putting down.

His attitude had been antagonistic, although he'd answered Jonathan's questions. Had he been hiding anything? Or had his manner been due to the fact that he didn't believe in being on good terms with the police on principle?

On the face of it there was nothing against him. He hadn't reached the house until long after Hardene's death and the news of it had appeared to surprise him.

But Fenn was a seaman. And Patrick Marton had been a seaman. And Patrick Marton was dead.

Oh, well. Tremaine gave it up and passed on to Mrs. Colver. At first she'd been rattled but she'd settled down all right and she'd appeared to talk openly enough even if she hadn't been exactly brimming with speech. Seemed to have looked after Hardene on the domestic side but she'd had little to do with his private life.

Unless, of course, she knew more about the intriguing Elaine than she'd said.

Elaine. Just what kind of woman had been attracted by Hardene to the extent of deceiving her husband? It was annoying that there was so little to go upon; it might have thrown a useful light upon Hardene's character to have had a description of Elaine.

Who else had there been? Ah, yes, Jerome Masters. *There* was an interesting development, at least. So far Masters held the major role as the person who appeared to have possessed the greatest dislike for Hardene—and with good reason. He had given himself an alibi for the time of the murder, but it was an alibi that had folded up under the first examination.

Odd, that. After all, Masters wasn't a fool, even if he was a blusterer. He must have known that enquiries would be made at the Venturers' Club to test his story, and that as soon as that happened his lie would be obvious.

Why had he behaved so stupidly? Was it because he had panicked and said the first thing that had come into his head without giving himself time to think out a convincing story that would stand up under pressure?

But if he *had* killed Hardene he had had long enough to decide what he intended to do. Jonathan Boyce hadn't paid his call until more than twelve hours after the discovery of the murder; surely that had been time enough for Masters to have rigged up a more substantial alibi?

After all, his enmity with Hardene had been open enough to do away with any hope that his movements wouldn't be questioned. He must have known he'd have to face enquiries. His wife had certainly made no secret of the feud.

His wife. Tremaine stared at the steady flame of the gas-fire. A woman of character, undoubtedly. He wondered whether there was much that Masters did without consulting her.

The thought brought a queer little doubt to his mind. Had he dismissed her too lightly? Had she played a much more important part than he had imagined? She wasn't the kind of woman to wait unobtrusively in the background when there were grave issues at stake. She was too strong a personality to be overlooked, despite her frailness of form; Masters himself had given them evidence of that.

That was it. That was the complete list. Except, of course, for Margaret Royman and Rex Linton—and he'd purposely left those two out of the running. He wanted to know a little more about them; he didn't want to go rushing to any rash conclusions.

And then he frowned. No, that wasn't the complete record, after all. He'd forgotten something. Somewhere, during the day, he'd seen someone, or heard something, that was important.

He was sure of that. But he'd forgotten it. He'd allowed it to slip out of his mind and out of his reach. He concentrated, trying to recall what it was, but persistently it eluded him, although it came near enough to tantalize him with the sensation that he had almost recaptured it.

Deliberately then he gave up the attempt. It was no good trying to force it. He might end by destroying the moment of intuition and remembering the wrong thing altogether.

Better by far to put effort aside and wait for it to return freely in its own good time. Because it *would* come back.

10

THE LADY RECEIVES A LEGACY

JONATHAN BOYCE had a long list of things it was essential to do. He looked down at it and shrugged resignedly.

'We're going to have a busy day. Come on, let's face it.'

But despite the Yard man's doleful air Tremaine knew that he was not really depressed. Boyce was at grips with a problem, and if he was faced with a mountain of work, with a solution to the murder nowhere in sight, he was nevertheless a contented man.

The first task was to ring Inspector Parkin, find out whether he had any further news for them, tell him their own immediate plans, and arrange to confer with him later. The next step was to visit the offices of Messrs. Cunnam, Cunnam, and Darymple, Solicitors and Commissioners for Oaths.

A narrow street, running from the accepted city centre, was the scene of Bridgton's banking and legal life. The main branches of the leading banks were scattered along both sides, in company with stock-broking firms, insurance offices, and a liberal sprinkling of solicitors.

'It looks,' Boyce commented drily, 'as though everybody here is either busy taking in other people's money or is drawing a living from seeing that it's all done lawfully.'

Cunnam, Cunnam, and Darymple had their entrance in a somewhat dingy lane leading off the street in the shadow of one of the banks.

Boyce climbed the steep and dark flight of stairs to the rabbit warren of offices in which clerks and typists worked in what appeared to be an impossible confusion of files, conveyances, and ledgers, some so dusty and neglected that it seemed unlikely they were ever consulted, and presented his card. Almost at once they were shown into an inner room in which Mr. Horace Cunnam, the senior partner in the firm, was seated.

He rose from his chair as they came in and held out his hand in greeting.

'Good morning, gentlemen. Your chairs are ready for you.'

Boyce gave him a glance of enquiry.

'So you were expecting us, Mr. Cunnam?'

The solicitor, an elderly, grey-haired man with a wrinkled and humorous face that appeared to have little in common with the forbiddingly titled and soberly bound legal text-books on the shelves behind him, gave a smile.

'I've been expecting you ever since I read the news in yesterday's *Courier*. As a matter of fact, I rang up the house in case you might wish to get in touch with us—but no doubt you've been informed of that.'

'Yes, Mr. Cunnam, the message was passed on to me. It was extremely thoughtful of you. This is Mr. Tremaine, by the way. He is accompanying me during my investigations.'

Cunnam darted a quick glance at Tremaine, clearly intrigued but hesitating to ask questions.

'I trust you had no difficulty in finding us? I'm afraid we solicitors have a reputation for hiding ourselves away, especially here in Bridgton.'

'Well, I won't say you aren't a bit off the beaten track, Mr. Cunnam,' Boyce observed, and the solicitor smiled.

'It wasn't always the case, you know,' he said, and it was clear that he was seizing the opportunity to ride his hobby. 'At one time the boundary of the ancient city ran through here. The lane outside actually follows the line of the wall of the Middle Ages. Sometimes—particularly when I'm looking through an old lease—I can feel ghosts at my shoulder.'

'Not always a comfortable business, sir,' Boyce returned, with an answering smile. He cleared his throat as a sign that the preliminaries were over. 'Since you've been waiting for my visit there's evidently no need for me to do any explaining. You acted as Doctor Graham Hardene's solicitors, I believe.'

'Yes, that is correct.'

'Did you carry out much work for him?'

'As a matter of fact, very little.'

'How did he happen to come to you?'

'We've acted for Doctor Reedley for many years—it was Doctor Reedley from whom Doctor Hardene bought his house and the practice, as you may know. Hardene had no objection to using the same solicitor as the vendor and we acted for both parties. After that, I suppose, he came to us as a matter of habit. I advised him about one or two investments, acted for him in a quite trivial matter concerning a right of way at the back of his house—actually it was a matter left over from Doctor Reedley's time—and drew up his will. Beyond that we had no contact with each other.'

'Ah yes, his will. I take it you have a note of the provisions, Mr. Cunnam?'

'I have the will itself,' the solicitor replied. 'That is, unless you happen to have come across a later one at his house, which I'm inclined to doubt. He had no near relatives and he was quite unconcerned about what happened to his property after his death.' He picked up a blue document from a pile lying on the side of his desk and opened it out. 'Here we are. A bequest of a thousand pounds to Miss Margaret Royman, his receptionist, if still in his employ, and the residue to various local charities which are enumerated. Shall I read them to you?'

'Any unusual ones mentioned?'

The solicitor shook his head.

'No, they're all perfectly sound charities and well respected in the city.'

'And that's all?'

'That,' said the solicitor, closing and refolding the will, 'is all, Chief Inspector.'

'H'm. Not very exciting, is it?'

'As you say, not a very exciting will. Except, of course, from the point of view of Miss Royman who will, I imagine, have rather a pleasant surprise.'

Boyce shot him a glance from under his bushy eyebrows, looking for any significance in the other's face.

'Do you know her?'

'No. I never had any occasion to visit his house and on the rare calls he made here he didn't speak very much either about himself or his staff. Even when the will was drawn up he was quite off-hand about it as if he didn't really care one way or the other.' The solicitor tapped the document in question enquiringly. 'Do you wish to take it with you?'

'No, thank you, Mr. Cunnam,' Boyce said, rising. 'Clearing up Doctor Hardene's estate is going to be your job. Mine is to find out who killed him.'

'I'll wish you luck, Chief Inspector. I liked what I saw of him. It's a dreadful business. I hope that you and Mr. Tremaine here are soon able to get to the bottom of it.'

'We'll do our best,' Boyce told him. 'I'm obliged to you for your help.'

'Not at all.'

Cunnam shook hands with them and a few seconds later they were going back down the narrow stairs.

'One of your fans, Mordecai,' Boyce observed, as they reached the street. 'I was expecting any moment that he was going to start asking questions. If he hadn't been a solicitor and naturally cagey he'd have opened up before. Your fame is spreading abroad.'

'I'm sorry, Jonathan,' Tremaine said contritely. 'I don't want to make things difficult for you with the Commissioner—especially now, with your promotion due. If you think I ought to go back to town—'

He looked downcast. He, too, had noticed the solicitor's inner excitement and had been expecting some open comment on his presence.

And it would be upsetting if there was any unfortunate publicity to put Jonathan in an unfavourable light. For this case was important to him. He was in line for promotion to superintendent's rank; if all went well the news might be through on their return.

But Boyce did not seem to find any cause for alarm in the situation. He gave his companion a reassuring clap on the shoulder.

'Nonsense! You don't suppose the Commissioner didn't realize that people were going to recognize you after all the headlines you've had! Provided the newspapers don't make too much of a song—and you're not the fellow to encourage them to do it—he won't worry. Nor,' Boyce added, 'shall I. It's a relief to think that you'll be somewhere around if I get to feeling that I'm butting at a brick wall with the case!'

'The newspapers,' Tremaine said slowly. 'Yes, we'll have to see they don't print anything that might be embarrassing.' A harder expression came into his usually benevolent face. 'I think,' he went on, after a moment or two, 'I can see a way of doing that. In fact, I'm sure I can.'

They strolled slowly down the street in the direction of the police headquarters building where they were to meet Inspector Parkin.

'What did you think of the will?' Boyce remarked. 'Pretty dead end, eh?'

There was a significant note in his voice. Tremaine looked uncomfortable.

'I know what you mean, Jonathan. Except for Miss Royman. Very well, I'll agree. You're right.'

'Am I?'

'She might have known about it. And if she did it gives her a useful motive. A thousand pounds is big enough bait for anyone in her position, even in these days.'

'Especially,' Boyce put it, 'if she wants to get married. I must admit I can't quite see her picking up that rock and letting drive at her employer's head. But—'

'I know. Rex Linton. She could have told him. And he's a reporter, used I daresay to being in tough places. They could have been in it together.'

Boyce made no further comment and they finished their journey in silence. Inspector Parkin was waiting for them. So, too, was the Chief Constable.

'You seem to have got things moving pretty fast already, Chief Inspector,' Sir Robert Dennell said. 'Good work. Are you going after Masters this morning?'

'No, sir,' Boyce said. 'I see it this way, sir,' he went on, as he met the Chief Constable's stare of surprise. 'We've got Masters where we want him at the moment. We know his story's a phoney one but he doesn't know we know, and as far as he's aware there's no reason to go doing anything silly like making a dash for it. I'd like to let him ride for a little while. I agree that it's looking pretty black against him, but there are a lot of things I'd like to get cleared up before I make a definite move in his direction.'

The Chief Constable clearly did not relish what he had been told. There was a cold, set look in his face. It was a look both of disappointment and of suppressed anger.

'Very well,' he said, in clipped tones. 'I promised you a completely free hand and I don't propose to go back on my word. But I must confess I find your attitude a little difficult to understand. I trust you have an adequate reason for it.'

He went out of the room, disapproval in the rigid lines of his soldier's back. Boyce grimaced at Parkin.

'Seems off-colour this morning. What's eating into him?'

The inspector made a deprecating movement of his shoulders. He hesitated for an instant or two.

'It's nothing to worry about. He's been overworking a good deal lately,' he said loyally. 'He's bound to be feeling the strain a bit. Besides—'

He broke off. Tremaine looked at him.

'Yes?'

'Oh—nothing,' Parkin said. 'There's quite a bit of news to pass on to you,' he went on, just a trace of hurriedness in his manner. 'I suppose I'd better get down to it.' He pulled a sheaf of papers towards him. 'Here's the full report on Masters—daresay you'll want to go through it yourself. And this is what we've been able to dig up about Fenn so far.'

'Does it say how—if at all—Hardene's name came to be mentioned at the Seamen's Mission?' Tremaine asked, and the inspector shook his head.

'Some doubt over that. Seems that nobody was quite sure just how his name did come up—or if it ever did. Fenn did come from the *Altiberg* all right—captain gives him a clean sheet—and he did say at the Mission that he was after a shore job and wanted to get in touch with somebody in Bridgton who could give him something in the caretaker line. My man couldn't get a really good idea of how the doctor came into it. Seems that he was fairly well-known in the place by name and that other people had gone up to see him from the Mission so that it's possible that somebody *did* mention him to Fenn. On the other hand nobody actually remembers doing it.'

'And nobody remembers Fenn doing it either. That the position?' Boyce said, although more as a statement of fact than as a question.

'That's it. We're still working on it though. My man naturally had to go carefully in case Fenn got alarmed—not that he isn't likely to smell a rat in any case now—and with a place like the Mission, with men coming and going all the time, there's always the chance that whoever did tell him about Hardene has already left Bridgton.'

'What about the rest of his story?'

'Same thing. Could be true or could be phoney. He spent part of the evening in the Mission playing billiards and he slept in the hostel at the back of the building—that's what he told you, of course. We couldn't give him an alibi to cover the whole time. He might have been around, as he says, until he went to bed, but on the other hand there's no definite proof that he didn't slip out at some period during the evening.' Parkin shrugged. 'With so many strangers about and men constantly coming in and going out it's next door to an impossibility to be certain about him.'

'All right,' Boyce said. 'We'll leave Mr. Fenn still with his big question mark. Anything more?'

'I've wired a description to Halifax and asked them to let us know if they've anything on him, but I daresay it'll take time to get their reply.'

'And in the meantime Sir Robert is champing at the bit. I know,' Boyce said. 'A policeman's life is a dog's life. What about friend Slade? Any skeletons in his cupboard?'

'If there are we haven't found 'em so far.' Parkin selected another report from the papers in front of him. 'Lives at a place called Red Gables on the other side of the river. Good class house but a bit isolated. Means you either have to cross by the toll bridge or go right down into the city and cross the river by one of the main bridges. Slade's been living there about three and a half years—came from up north. He's a sleeping partner in a small wholesale grocery firm in the city—he bought his interest shortly after he came here—but apart from that he doesn't seem to have any business connections. No directorships or anything of that kind. Bank says he's solid and he's never been in the news for any reason. Doesn't go in for politics or public work. His being a cripple probably explains that.'

'Maybe. What's the trouble with him?'

'Had a fall of some kind. Injured his spine and has had partial paralysis ever since.'

'Before he came here—or after?'

'Before. Tried various specialists it seems but without getting anywhere. Got fed up with being pushed from one doctor to another and stuck to Hardene after coming to Red Gables.'

'Did Hardene do anything for him?'

'To cure him?' Parkin shook his head. 'No, I gather there isn't a hope of anybody doing that. But he's always given Hardene a good name as a doctor. Told his servants that Hardene was the one man who understood him and that he wouldn't go to anyone else whatever happened. He's a bachelor—lives with an old couple who combine the jobs of housekeeper and gardener and generally do anything he needs.'

'What about his car?'

'He can't drive himself because of his disability, so he hires a chauffeur from an agency whenever he needs to go out. But he hasn't made much use of his car lately, apart from his visits to Hardene. Funny thing,' Parkin mused, glancing down at the papers in front of him, 'both the servants said that Slade thought a good deal of Hardene and was always praising him up. Yet he was so rattled when we talked to him yesterday and made a point of telling us that they'd had violent arguments.'

'A man who's in constant pain,' Tremaine said, 'sometimes does behave in what seems an irrational manner. He might have had what sounded like strong disagreements with his doctor and yet he might really have been satisfied with him all the time.'

He looked up at the wall behind Parkin's head, upon which was placed a large-scale map of the city and its immediate surroundings. He pushed back his chair.

'I wonder if you'd point one or two things out to me, Inspector. Whereabouts, for instance, is Martin Slade's house?'

The inspector rose to his feet in turn and picked up the long wooden pointer that stood against the wall at the side of the map.

'Here's the river, of course, and here's the toll bridge. Red Gables would be about here. The scale isn't big enough to show the actual house but I'd say it was about three hundred yards beyond the bridge itself.'

'I see. And Hardene's house and surgery?'

The pointer moved searchingly and stopped.

'Here.'

Tremaine peered over his pince-nez, standing on tiptoe, a frown on his face.

'Did Hardene have any other patients who live on the far side of the river?'

'Couldn't say off-hand. Miss Royman will have the list, though.' Parkin peered at the map and a frown came into his own face. 'Yes. See what you mean,' he said slowly. 'Bit off the beaten track.'

'I shouldn't have thought Hardene's practice would have stretched so far.'

'It didn't,' Parkin said. He moved the pointer. 'This strip right against the river and these houses up by the bridge are served by a couple of doctors who live in Lancaster Crescent here. I'd have thought that most people across the bridge—at least in its immediate neighbourhood—would have gone to one of them rather than to Hardene. His practice was mostly the other way.'

He swept the pointer over the map and Tremaine nodded.

'It ran in the direction of the house where he was found. That's what I thought was likely to be the case. I wonder what made Slade choose him?'

He did not continue that particular line of thought, however, but remained staring at the map.

The bridge was near the top left-hand corner and the road serving it ran in a fairly straight course right across the map and on to meet a trunk road curving around the northeastern suburbs of the city. Most of the area above the road, apart from the exclusive extension of Druidleigh in which Jerome Masters lived, was taken up by the open downs.

'Which is Elm Tree?' he asked.

Parkin indicated a point on the downs about half-way between Hardene's surgery and the eastern edge of the map. It was a lonely spot. A narrow road that was an off-shoot of the main artery from the bridge twisted around it, but there were no houses in its immediate vicinity.

'Lovers' Corner is the local name for it,' the inspector said, and Tremaine gave a distressed cough.

Jonathan Boyce was gathering his papers together.

'I'll be glad of a car,' he observed. 'I'm making a call on Doctor Reedley, the fellow who sold Hardene the practice, and then I'm going up to the surgery. If I haven't run into you before I'll either ring you or meet you here at three this afternoon. That suit your plans?'

'Quite all right, sir,' Parkin returned. 'I've still quite a bit of routine checking-up to do.'

Boyce drew a finger along his chin.

'Reminds me,' he said. 'I'll have to ask you to add a bit more to the list. Sorry to be loading the donkey work on you like this. But I'd like you to find out what you can about Miss Royman and that fellow Linton—the *Courier* reporter.'

'Linton?' Parkin looked puzzled, but he nodded. 'It ought to be easy enough—*Courier's* editor will give us all we want. But I don't—'

'You don't see what it has to do with anything,' Boyce put in, smiling. 'As a matter of fact, neither do I—not yet, anyway. You'll have to thank Tremaine for that particular job. Did you know young Linton was sweet on the girl?'

'No, I didn't know that. Is it—certain, sir?'

The inspector had become subtly more official in his attitude. Apparently he was feeling that he had allowed his enthusiasm too free a rein during their earlier conversations and had not been giving the Yard man the deference which was his due.

'It seemed to be certain enough when Tremaine saw them together last night,' Boyce told him. 'And this morning we picked up another interesting little item of news from Hardene's solicitors. He's left Margaret Royman a legacy of a thousand pounds.'

'A thousand!' Parkin whistled. 'It's quite a sum!'

'Worth picking up if you want to get married and your only source of income is a few pounds a week you're making out of your job,' Boyce said drily. 'It'll be news to me if provincial reporters get paid a princely wage. So you see we can't overlook it.'

'No, I can see that, sir,' Parkin said, his hand on the door. 'I'll get things moving in that quarter. But first I'll fix up your car.'

Tremaine's head was in a whirl as he went down the stairs at Boyce's side. This was only the second day of the investigation, but already so much had happened and so many things had come to light concerning so many people that he was beginning to feel that he must have lived in Bridgton all his life.

It seemed a very long time ago when he had walked along the platform at Paddington Station at the side of a burly detective-sergeant who had been carrying a murder bag. He wondered whether he would have stepped into the train if he could have foreseen the complications to which his journey might lead.

But as he left the building and walked towards the waiting police car he knew that there was nowhere else he would rather be. Despite its horror, despite the nausea and the fear that clutched him sometimes at the thought of what he might be called upon to do, the excitement of the greatest hunt in the world—the hunt for a human being—held him firmly in its grip.

He climbed quickly into the car and huddled himself into a corner of the rear seat, not looking at Jonathan Boyce. He had a sudden paralysing sensation of guilt; he felt that he ought to be ashamed of himself.

11

THE PROWLER VANISHES

CHIEF INSPECTOR Jonathan Boyce, for all his abrupt manner and his air of stocky aggressiveness, was both a wise and a compassionate man. One glance told him what Tremaine was feeling and he made no attempt to draw him into conversation.

They travelled smoothly through the traffic and out of the city on its southern side. After forty years as a hard-working but unspectacular general practitioner Doctor Meredith Reedley had taken down his plate and settled himself in a modernized cottage situated on a fertile ridge from which there was a magnificent view over twenty miles of rolling country beyond.

He was pottering about in his half an acre of garden, pipe in mouth, when the police car drew up outside his gate. He stuck the trowel he had been using into the earth and came slowly towards them.

Boyce handed his card across the gate.

'Good morning, Doctor. I wonder whether you could spare me a few minutes?'

The older man raised his eyes from the card to Boyce's face, and pulled open the gate.

'Scotland Yard! What have I been up to?'

'The question of an innocent man, Doctor!' Boyce told him. 'If you'd really been up to anything you wouldn't have dared to ask!'

'You should have been a doctor yourself, Chief Inspector. Your bedside manner is irreproachable. But come inside, gentlemen, and tell me what I can do for you.'

They went into the comfortably furnished interior of the cottage and Boyce looked about him appreciatively.

'You've certainly picked a delightful place for your retirement, sir.'

A touch of sadness came into Doctor Reedley's face and he turned away for a moment or two, gazing out of the window at the distant line of hills.

'For nearly forty years,' he said slowly, 'I dreamed of somewhere like this. I always wanted to live in the country—I never did want to be a townsman. But after I'd qualified it seemed like suicide for a young man to bury himself in the country—the end of ambition in a rustic backwater—and so I decided that I'd start with a town practice and when I'd gained enough experience and made my name I'd come and settle down like the country gentleman.'

'Judging by what I've seen up to now, sir,' Boyce said, politely, 'it seems to have been well worth waiting for. I rather gather you stuck to the town after all until the time came for you to give up your practice?'

'Yes,' Reedley said, with a sigh. 'I stuck it for forty years. At first you don't notice how the weeks and the months are slipping by—anyway, you tell yourself, there's all the time in the world; you're still a young man. And then you find that you aren't a young man any longer and that you're fast in your little groove with no more hope of becoming the great success you once imagined than you have of flying to the moon. Five years ago I made up my mind that it was time to cut loose. I knew that although my wife hadn't made any complaints she'd been pining all the time to get away into the country where there wouldn't be a surgery bell or a telephone to ring at any hour of the day or night. We found this place, had a few alterations made, and moved in. It was just what we'd always wanted. I told myself that at last I'd be able to make amends to my wife. But I'd left it too late. In six months she was dead.'

'I'm—sorry,' Boyce said, feeling his own inadequacy. 'It must have been a bitter blow.'

'I suppose I earned it. If I'd had the sense to do what I ought to have done years ago it might not have happened.' The older man stared unseeingly through the window, over the green fields stretching away beyond the cottage. 'Well, it's over now and regrets aren't of much use.'

Boyce cleared his throat gently. He thought he saw his opening.

'It's about your leaving your practice in Bridgton that I wanted to see you, sir.'

Reedley nodded.

'It's about Hardene, is it? I saw in yesterday's *Courier* what had happened. Terrible business. I don't see, though, how I can be of any help to you.'

'In cases like this we naturally have to follow up every possible line of enquiry, even if at first sight there doesn't seem to be much connection. I'm wondering whether you can tell me anything about Doctor Hardene that may link up.'

Reedley drew his brows together in a frown.

'I'll do what I can, naturally, but it was five years ago and I'm not going to pretend that my memory's as good as it might be. What is it you particularly want to know?'

'I'm not so much following any special line as trying to find out as much as I can in a general way,' Boyce said. 'It'll be a help if you can just tell me anything you remember about your association. How did Doctor Hardene come to do business with you in the first place, for instance?'

'That's easy enough, anyway. Apparently he'd been abroad—Canada, I think. He'd just come back and was looking for somewhere to settle down. Whilst he'd been in London he'd met an old acquaintance of his student days—they took their finals together—and I suppose he must have mentioned his plans. Anyway, the point is that the father of this friend of his happened to be one of my own contemporaries who knew that I was thinking about getting rid of my practice. Hardene and I belonged to different generations, of course. They gave Hardene my name. He came down to see me, said he liked the place and the job, and agreed to take over.'

'Did he make any bones about it? About the price, for example. Did he give you the impression of being short of money?'

'He certainly didn't give me the idea that he was hard up, although I'm not in a position to give you any real information about it. He didn't haggle at all—accepted everything lock, stock, and barrel at the first valuation. The whole business, in fact, went off amicably.'

'Did he carry the whole thing through himself?' Boyce hesitated as if searching for the right phrases. 'I daresay you knew he wasn't married. Did he appear to be completely on his own? You didn't happen to meet or even hear him mention any relatives or close friends?'

'On the contrary, I gathered he was pretty much a stranger in a strange land. He'd been abroad for so many years that he'd lost touch with his friends over here. It was just by chance that he'd run into his old student acquaintance I spoke of—you know how these things do turn out sometimes. Now I come to think of it, I do seem to remember his telling me that he had no near living relatives.'

'That was why, no doubt, he advertised for a housekeeper as soon as he took over?'

'Yes. I was able to recommend someone to look after him on a temporary basis for a week or two, but he engaged a permanent housekeeper very soon after he settled in.'

'I suppose you kept in touch with each other, sir?'

'Well, we did at first. If a query came up regarding the practice he might get in touch with me—but that was only at the beginning, while he was finding his feet so to speak. But we were never on what you might call social terms. He never came out here and I never went in to see him at the old house.' The doctor shrugged. 'You know how these brief acquaintances gradually die off—like the friendships you make on a seaside holiday. We did exchange Christmas cards for a year or two but that was all. In fact, until I saw the report in the *Courier* yesterday I hadn't given him a thought for a long time. I'm afraid this isn't very helpful,' he finished apologetically. 'I'm sorry I can't be a great deal of use to you.'

'That's all right, sir,' Boyce said, with a cheerfulness he didn't feel. 'It means that we know where we are. The position is then that you hadn't seen him for several years and that you didn't have enough real contact with him when you did meet to learn very much about his private life.'

'That's a fair summing up, Chief Inspector.'

'I don't think there's any need to take up more of your time, sir,' Boyce said, rising. 'I'm much obliged for your help.'

Doctor Reedley looked mildly surprised.

'I wasn't aware that I'd been able to give you any. I daresay you already knew what little I've been able to tell you about Hardene before you came.'

'It isn't always the things you hear that are important, sir. Sometimes it's the things you don't hear.'

Boyce was on his way to the door when he turned.

'Oh, there *was* just one more thing, Doctor. I don't suppose you happen to know where Doctor Hardene qualified?'

'As a matter of fact, I do. Glad to be of some service, anyway,' Reedley said. 'It was Edinburgh.'

Walking back to the car Tremaine turned to gaze back at the cottage, admiring its natural setting and the lawns and flower-beds surrounding it, so clearly set in order by loving hands.

'It's a delightful spot, Jonathan. Poor devil, losing his wife like that. Must have made everything a mockery.'

'Hasn't got much to do with what we came for,' Boyce observed, 'but I hadn't the heart to stop him.'

'What was the meaning of the cryptic remark?' Tremaine asked, as they passed through the gate. 'I mean the bit about the things you don't hear.'

'What do *you* think?' Boyce raised his eyebrows quizzically. 'A fellow comes back to England after a long time abroad. No relatives and apparently no friends. It seems reasonable to me to suppose that he might have opened his heart now and again to a nice old couple from whom he was buying his practice. But did he give anything away? No, sir, not on your life. By not telling us anything that very fact tells us something. Hardene didn't *want* to talk. And a man who doesn't want to talk usually has a very good reason.'

Tremaine nodded.

'I see what you mean, Jonathan.'

They drove back to Bridgton and went straight to Hardene's house. Sergeant Witham was waiting for them.

'Nothing to report from my end, sir,' he said, in answer to Boyce's question. 'But I daresay you'd like to have a talk with the housekeeper. Seems that she had a bit of a nightmare. Local man told me about it when I got here.'

'A nightmare?' Boyce regarded his subordinate enquiringly. 'Sounds a bit personal. Where do *we* come in?'

'She thought she heard somebody outside the house, sir—trying to get in, she says. Anyway, she pushed up her window and called for the man on duty and then went downstairs to let him in as soon as he reached the door.'

'What happened then?'

'Nothing, sir. There was no sign of anybody in the house or in the garden and no trace of any attempt to force an entry.

I've had a good look around myself, and I must say everything seems to be in order.'

'Just a bit of reaction, eh? I'll have a word with her, though, to see what she has to say about it. Ask her to come in. Oh, before you do,' Boyce added, as Witham turned to go upon his errand, 'what's she been like this morning? Upset? Signs of being off-colour?'

'Well, I wouldn't say so. Seems pretty level-headed to me. Not likely to start hearing things or go into hysterics—if that's what you're after, sir.'

'Yes, that's more or less what I'm after,' Boyce said. 'All right, ask her if she can spare a minute or two.'

Mrs. Colver, when she came in, certainly showed no sign of being so far overwrought that her nerves were beginning to play tricks with her. There were shadows under her eyes and her face had lost a little of its former high colour, but it was clear that she was perfectly self-controlled.

'Good morning, Mrs. Colver,' Boyce said pleasantly. 'I hear you had a rather disturbed night.'

'Someone tried to break into the house,' she told him levelly.

Boyce appeared to be considering the point. He stared up at the ceiling for a moment or two and then brought his glance back to her face.

'I suppose you're quite certain? Don't think I'm trying to doubt your word, but you've had rather a difficult time and it's bound to have upset you. And sleeping in the house alone under such circumstances couldn't help but make you—well, not quite yourself. You probably wouldn't be sleeping quite as soundly as usual. Any slight noise outside the house might have awakened you and you might have thought it to be much nearer than it actually was.'

A slight twist appeared at one corner of her tight lips.

'Do I look the kind of person to imagine things, Chief Inspector?'

'I'll admit,' Boyce said, 'that you don't. But even a person with the strongest nerves, waking up suddenly in the dark, is quite likely to be mistaken about the source of an unexpected sound.'

'Someone tried to break in,' she repeated firmly. 'I'm as certain of it as I am that I'm talking to you now. The mistake I made was in hearing him too soon. When I pushed up the window and shouted I scared him and he was able to get away before the detective came. I ought to have waited until he was inside the house before I let him know I'd heard him.'

'Both the local detective and my own sergeant have had a thorough look around but they haven't been able to find any trace of anyone.'

'I told you,' she said stubbornly, 'I called out too soon. He was at the back of the house, and if he'd walked down the garden path he wouldn't have left any footprints. Your men *wouldn't* have found anything.'

'All right,' Boyce said. 'We'll keep looking. How do you feel about things now?' he added. 'I mean as far as sleeping in the house is concerned?'

Her lips came together even more determinedly.

'I'll stay.'

She looked at Boyce, clearly asking whether he wanted her further, and when he nodded an indication that he had said all he wished to say, she moved towards the door.

Mordecai Tremaine said:

'One moment, Mrs. Colver. I wonder whether you can help us a little more with this unwelcome visitor?'

A glint of antagonism came into her eyes.

'How can I? I've told you all I know. I didn't see him. I only heard him.'

'Quite so. What I meant was that possibly—without perhaps being aware of it—you may know something that will provide us with a clue. Have you, for instance, ever noticed anyone taking an unusual interest in this house? Not just within the last twenty-four hours but before Doctor Hardene's death.'

She turned slowly away from the door and came back into the room; there seemed to be a distinct hint of unwillingness in her manner.

'Yes' she said slowly. 'Yes, I have.' Her eyes left Tremaine's face for an instant or two. She appeared to be searching in her memory for the answer to his question. 'There *was* someone—a man—about two or three days ago. It was about ten o'clock at night. Doctor Hardene had had to go to a political meeting and I was in the house on my own. I had to go out into the garden—I wanted to go to the coal store—and when I opened the back door of the house I saw a man on the path. As soon as he heard me he ran out through the gate that leads to the lane behind the house. I was too surprised to do anything at first and by the time I started to go after him it was too late. I went as far as the lane but by that time he'd gone.'

'What did you do then?'

'Doctor Hardene came back not long afterwards and I told him about it.'

'What action did Doctor Hardene take?'

'He said we'd have to make sure that everything was securely fastened in case we had burglars, and we went over the house together.'

'Did he notify the police?'

'I don't think so. Not as far as I know, anyway.'

'Did Doctor Hardene make light of the incident or did he seem disturbed by it?'

'He was upset by it,' the housekeeper said. 'I could tell that. But he didn't say anything to me except to be sure and see that the doors and windows were shut every night just in case there was anybody prowling around the neighbourhood.'

Tremaine pushed back his pince-nez; they had been slipping towards the end of his nose with a relentlessness of purpose that had been fascinating Jonathan Boyce.

'Could you recognize this—stranger—again, do you think, Mrs. Colver?'

'I—I don't know,' she told him, hesitatingly. 'It was very dark, and I was taken by surprise. I didn't have a really good look at him.'

'But you did get a general impression of him, no doubt—his height, build, and so on. Could it, for instance, have been Mr. Rex Linton?'

Her eyes widened. She stared at him without replying, her expression difficult to read.

'I believe you know Mr. Linton,' Tremaine went on. 'A reporter on the *Evening Courier*. The young gentleman who's been very friendly with Miss Royman.'

'Yes, I know Mr. Linton,' she said at last. 'But it couldn't have been him I saw. This man was taller and I think he was a lot older.'

She stopped. But it was clear that there was something else she wanted to say. Tremaine gave her a lead.

'Yes?' he said gently.

'It's about Mr. Linton. Now that you've spoken about him.' The words came slowly at first, as though she was feeling her way, and then with a rush. 'I *have* seen him near the house. He's been up here several times.'

'To meet Miss Royman?'

'Sometimes. But not always. I've seen him about after Miss Royman had gone home. Once he came in to see Doctor Hardene. I heard them in the surgery. They had words.'

'Was it a—serious—argument?'

'Mr. Linton seemed very excited. I heard Doctor Hardene say something about it not being any of his business and he'd better keep out of it, and Mr. Linton said that it *was* his business and that he was going to make Doctor Hardene pay. I didn't hear very much of what they actually said, of course—I didn't go too near the surgery.'

'Were they still on bad terms when Mr. Linton left?'

'Yes. I heard Mr. Linton shout something as he came out of the surgery and he slammed the door hard when he went out of the house as though he wasn't in a good mood.'

'When did this quarrel take place?'

'About a fortnight ago.'

'Did Mr. Linton come again afterwards?'

'I don't think so. Not when I was here.'

Tremaine rubbed his chin. He glanced at Boyce over the pince-nez. He seemed uncertain how best to phrase his next question.

At last:

'Have you any idea, Mrs. Colver,' he said, 'what the trouble between them was about?'

Once again the housekeeper's lips straightened into a thin, tight line.

'It was about Miss Royman. Mr. Linton considered that the doctor was becoming more friendly with her than he thought he ought to be.'

'And *was* that the case?'

'There's no smoke without fire,' she told him. 'But that's not for me to say. You'd better ask her yourself.'

'Yes,' Tremaine said, uncomfortably. 'Yes. Quite so. Thank you, Mrs. Colver.'

The housekeeper went out of the room in silence, giving Jonathan Boyce a backward glance as she did so. It was both speculative and faintly hostile. When the door had closed behind her Boyce looked at his companion.

'Well,' he observed, 'you brought her out. D'you think there's more to come?'

'I think she's hiding something, Jonathan,' Tremaine said slowly. 'At first she wasn't anxious to say anything, and then she changed her mind and opened up. All that about Rex Linton coming here, for instance.'

'She certainly sounded as though she wanted to see him in trouble,' Boyce agreed. 'We'll have to take it up—especially in view of the legacy the girl's been left. There may be something in it.'

Sergeant Witham came back into the room. He glanced behind him into the receptionist's room before closing the door.

'Housekeeper seems a bit up in the air, sir,' he said to his chief. 'Looks as though you might have rattled her.'

'Did she say anything?' Boyce asked.

'No. That was it, sir. She just went by as if she couldn't get past me quick enough. Funny. She's been quite matey up till now.'

'Has she been out of the house at all this morning?' Tremaine said.

'Not that I know of, sir,' the sergeant returned. 'Not since I've been here, anyway.'

'Has she had any visitors?'

'Couple of tradesmen—baker and milkman. Nobody that you might call social, though.'

'What about the telephone? Has she used it?'

The sergeant nodded.

'She put through a call about half an hour before you and the Chief Inspector arrived. As a matter of fact, she didn't seem to care for it much when I came through the hall while she was speaking. The door was open and I could see what she was doing. I'd been out in the garden and she gave me the feeling that she hadn't expected me to show up quite so soon. She made a point of not going on with what she was saying until I was out of the way again.'

Boyce stirred.

'What are you after, Mordecai?'

'I'm not sure myself,' Tremaine said. 'But I'd like to know a bit more about Mrs. Colver. And one thing I'd like to know about is her banking account—if she has one.'

'We'll see what we can do. Anything else?'

'Yes. I'd certainly like to know something more about her visitor of last night.'

'Then you don't think it was just imagination?'

'I think there *was* somebody outside the house. And I think she had a pretty good idea beforehand what was likely to happen. That's why she stayed here. She guessed you'd leave someone on the watch so that she wouldn't be in any serious danger.'

'You mean,' Boyce said, leaning forward, 'you think she was scared?'

'I mean that she seems to have raised the alarm without losing much time. Whoever it was didn't even have a chance to start getting into the house. It sounds to me as though she must have been lying awake expecting something.'

'In that case, why not tell us about it? Why didn't she say if she was scared of an attempt being made to get in?'

'Perhaps,' Tremaine said, 'she didn't want us to find out too much. She didn't want to risk anybody getting into the house but at the same time she didn't want to start too many enquiries. She's a clever woman, Jonathan. Or a determined one.' He stopped. He added, after a moment or two: 'It's love that makes a woman determined.'

'Love?' Boyce echoed the word, his surprise evident in his face. 'She must be well over fifty. You're not serious!'

Tremaine's expression was grave.

'Yes, Jonathan,' he said. 'Yes, I am serious.'

The tension was broken by the shrill ringing of the bell. Witham slipped unobtrusively from the room and was back a few seconds later.

'It's Miss Royman,' he announced. 'She's been making one or two calls this morning—had to go to the local hospital in the city about some talk or other the doctor was to have given, and see some of his political friends to return books and papers he'd borrowed. Do you want her in, sir?'

'Yes,' Boyce said. 'Yes, I do.'

The cold morning air had brought a flush to Margaret Royman's cheeks. She looked very pretty. Mordecai Tremaine felt his heart doing foolishly sentimental things.

Boyce gave no sign that he was being similarly affected. He pulled a chair forward, his manner precise and official.

'Good morning, miss. Glad you're here.'

'Good morning, Chief Inspector,' she said, seating herself. She gave him an enquiring glance. 'Your greeting sounded a little—ominous.'

'Did it, miss?' Boyce was bland. 'I'm sure I didn't mean it that way. As a matter of fact, all I wanted was to have a little chat with you about Mr. Linton.'

'Oh.' She could not repress the start she gave, although she controlled herself quickly. 'Mr. Linton? I'm afraid I don't quite understand, Chief Inspector.'

'My information, miss,' Boyce said, 'is that you and Mr. Linton are on what might be called friendly terms.'

'We are—friends,' she admitted. 'But I don't see what connection—'

She broke off. Boyce eyed her shrewdly, peering from under his bushy eyebrows.

'You don't see what connection there is between that fact and the business I'm engaged upon? That's just the point, miss. I'm given to understand that Mr. Linton and Doctor Hardene knew each other—and that they weren't exactly on the best of terms.'

'Who—who told you that?'

There was a gasping note in her voice and she had difficulty in keeping it steady.

'The real question,' Boyce said, 'is whether or not it's the truth. I thought that maybe you would be the best person to give me the answer.'

There was no mistaking his meaning and the girl made no attempt to hide that she was aware what was in his mind.

'All right,' she said quietly. 'I suppose you were bound to find out sooner or later. Yes, it is true. Rex came here to see Doctor Hardene. There was quite a scene. Rex told me about it. But that doesn't mean that he had anything to do with—with Doctor Hardene's death. In fact, I know he didn't.'

'You *know* he didn't?'

Her glance met the prolonged stare Boyce gave her without even the suggestion of flinching.

'Doctor Hardene's body was found at half past ten,' she said steadily. 'Rex and I were together all the evening. He saw me home and we didn't arrive there until almost that time. So Rex couldn't possibly have got all the way back to the downs and committed the murder.'

Boyce drew a finger thoughtfully along his chin.

'In other words, miss, you're prepared to give the young man an alibi?'

'I'm prepared to give evidence that Rex couldn't have been the person who killed Doctor Hardene,' she corrected him, 'because he wasn't anywhere near the place where it happened.'

'I see, miss.' Boyce cleared his throat. 'Would you mind telling me where you spent the evening?'

A slight flush came into her cheeks but she faced him steadily enough.

'Of course not. We went to the Empress—that's the big cinema in Queen's Parade. The new Academy Award film is on this week and we both wanted to see it.'

'And afterwards you went straight to your home?'

'Yes. You've already been given the address. It's on the other side of the city. You know it just wouldn't have been possible for Rex to have got back to the downs by half past ten after he'd left me.'

'I agree that seems to be the answer, miss.' Boyce did not rise to the bait. He looked at her quite mildly. 'I appreciate your being so candid with me. It always helps when people say straight out what there is to say. We always find out the truth in the end, of course, in any case, but it saves a lot of unnecessary fuss.'

She looked at him suspiciously but there was nothing in his tone to arouse a challenge. He went on, casually, as if he had nothing more in his mind than the clearing up of an odd minor matter or so:

'There's just one more point, miss. Could you tell me just why Mr. Linton and Doctor Hardene had this quarrel of theirs?'

'I thought you already knew the answer to that, Chief Inspector?'

'Well, I can—guess,' Boyce admitted. 'But it's always better to have confirmation of these things than to have to rely on guesswork.'

'It was because—because of me,' she said hesitantly. 'Rex thought that Doctor Hardene was—well, trying to pay me too much attention.'

'And was he?'

'He asked me to go out with him several times. I refused. I told him that whilst I enjoyed working as his receptionist I didn't want our relationship to go any further. I–I told him about Rex.'

'But Doctor Hardene,' Boyce interposed quietly, 'wasn't the man to take no for an answer. That it, miss?'

'That was it,' she agreed. 'He became rather–insistent. That was why Rex came here. I didn't want him to do it but he just wouldn't listen to me.'

'I suppose that after that things became a little difficult? I mean, working here as receptionist after what had happened.'

'Well, no,' she said. 'Doctor Hardene didn't refer to it and naturally I didn't.'

'You didn't think about giving up the job?'

'I thought about it–yes. Rex wanted me to leave. But I thought he was making too much of it and I told him so. I liked what I was doing and I didn't see that there was any need to be silly about things. After all, Doctor Hardene had always treated me quite properly–I hadn't any complaints.'

'So as far as you're concerned, miss, you'd found nothing to take exception to, but Mr. Linton–for very understandable reasons–was taking rather a jaundiced view of the matter.'

She met his glance with a hint of challenge.

'What do you mean by–understandable reasons?' she said, the colour in her cheeks.

Boyce shrugged.

'It's natural that a young man should be quick to resent someone else paying attentions to a young lady of whom he happens to be fond. Especially when that someone possesses rather a doubtful reputation where the ladies are concerned.'

'It still doesn't mean that he's likely to commit murder.'

'My experience doesn't lead me to agree with you, miss,' Boyce said soberly. 'And I've been concerned with quite a number of investigations in my time.'

The calmness of his manner clearly disconcerted her. Margaret Royman darted a glance at Tremaine, and that gentleman found himself wishing he was somewhere else. Beauty in distress always unhinged him when he knew that he was barred from offering aid.

She turned back to the Yard man.

'If you think that Rex had anything to do with it you're wasting your time. I've already told you that he couldn't have got to the downs in time. Is that all you wanted, Chief Inspector?'

'Yes, that's all, miss. Except that there's no need for you to start thinking I'm accusing Mr. Linton of anything. In my job I often have to ask a lot of questions that turn out not to have any real importance at all.'

She gave him a disbelieving glance and went out, ostentatiously closing the door behind her so that the reception room was sealed off from the surgery.

Boyce swivelled in his chair to face Tremaine.

'She was certainly defending that young man of hers, wasn't she? Almost as though she thought she had something to defend.'

'Oh, I don't know, Jonathan,' Tremaine returned uneasily. 'It's natural that she should want to see him cleared of any suspicions. And he *is* cleared anyway.'

'According to *her* story,' Boyce said drily. 'I wonder whether they can produce any witnesses to verify the time they got back to her home from the cinema?'

'Does she know about the legacy?' Tremaine asked, more from a desire to evade the issue than from any real eagerness to know the answer.

'Not as far as I'm aware. Odd, isn't it? Hardene seems to have made a pretty good pass at her and been content to take no for an answer—up to a point, anyway—and yet he left her a thousand in his will. A will, mark you, that doesn't seem to be outstanding for legacies to his fellow men.'

'Surely it was just a recognition of the fact that he was satisfied with her work for him?'

'Well, it might have been,' Boyce said, without conviction. 'What are your plans?' he went on. 'I'm here for a while as far as I can see. I'll need to take a look around and check on this story of our friend the burglar who didn't get any further than the back door, and then I want to go through Hardene's papers with Witham a bit more thoroughly. Will you be about, or is there anything you want to do on your own?'

Tremaine rose to his feet.

'I think I'll take a walk. If you haven't any objection that is, Jonathan. I want to sort things out for myself and I'd like to have a better look at the district—in a car you don't really get a chance to see what a place is like.'

'I daresay I'll be here for a couple of hours,' Boyce told him, glancing at his watch. 'After that we'll see about a late lunch, and then off to the Chief Constable—who's certain to want to know what I've done about Masters.'

He chuckled, but it was a wry sound with no laughter in it. He knew that it was unlikely that Sir Robert Dennell would receive the news of his inaction in that quarter with any satisfaction.

12

PANIC ON A CLIFF

TREMAINE let himself out of the house and set off in the direction of the downs, some two or three hundred yards distant. Boyce would quite clearly be engaged upon purely routine matters in which he could be of little assistance, and to stay would merely be to wander aimlessly about the house trying to avoid coming in contact with Margaret Royman.

When he reached the road bordering the downs he turned right and for a few minutes he kept to the pavement before crossing over and walking on the open grass. Although an occasional car went by there were few people about; he appeared to have the neighbourhood to himself except for a man, a small boy, and a dog away in the distance.

As he had already noticed during his drives about the city with Boyce, the downs consisted for the most part of a comparatively flat expanse of grass, but here towards the river the ground was uneven and broken up by hollows and by clumps of stunted trees and bushes.

It was clearly a popular strolling place, at least in more favourable seasons of the year, for seats, neatly painted, had been set out at intervals of a few hundred yards, as a rule discreetly screened by the rise of the ground or by the bushes.

He descended the gentle slope of a hollow that lay in his path. It was difficult to believe that he was in the midst of a great city; the houses lining the road behind him were out of sight now and only the sky and the grass remained within his vision. It occurred to him how easily murder might be done in such a place, with human life and activity so near at hand and yet so incredibly remote.

The far slope of the hollow was steeper. He climbed pantingly and halted for a second or two at the top to recover his breath. He saw that two or three hundred yards away across the grass a man was resting on a seat placed against a clump of hawthorns.

As he moved nearer he thought he recognized Martin Slade, and then the sight of the sticks lying against the edge of the seat at the man's side confirmed his first impression. Some distance beyond the hawthorns, where the road evidently took a wide sweep around a curve of the downs, the other's black saloon car was parked.

Slade stirred suddenly, and for an instant Tremaine thought the man had seen him. But it seemed that he had only been shifting to a more comfortable position, for his head remained turned away. It was not until Tremaine was no more than a yard or two from him, the sound of his approach now audible, that he looked round.

Slade's stare was blank as their eyes met, and then a hint of recognition came into his face.

'Good morning,' Tremaine said. 'Mr. Slade, isn't it?'

'Yes, that's right.'

'My name's Tremaine. We met yesterday morning—at Doctor Hardene's house.'

'Oh—of course. Remember you now.' Slade acknowledged him with a brief nod. 'You were with those police fellows.'

He did not seem particularly pleased at their encounter but he could not refrain from asking the obvious questions.

'What's happening? Have you found out who did it?'

'It's rather early yet,' Tremaine said, non-committally.

'Suppose it is.' Slade sounded a little sour. 'Can't expect miracles. Daresay you've one or two ideas though.'

'I think the police are working on certain lines of enquiry,' Tremaine said carefully.

The crippled man shifted awkwardly in his seat and glanced about him.

'On your own I see.'

'Yes, just taking the air. I thought I'd like a closer look at these glorious downs of yours. I must say I envy you Bridgton people, Mr. Slade.'

'Too many folk use 'em for my liking,' Slade remarked shortly. 'Not now, of course—weather keeps 'em away. But back in the summer the place was turned into a rabbit warren.'

His manner betrayed the fact that he wanted to ask questions, but he did not invite Tremaine to sit down nor did he try to prolong their conversation. He made a gesture beyond the clump of hawthorns.

'If you're out for a stroll I suggest you try that way—there's a path that takes you back towards the river. You'll find the best part of the downs over there.'

'Thanks,' Tremaine said. 'I wasn't going anywhere in particular. I'll take your advice.'

He nodded to the seated man, and walked on, taking the direction Slade had indicated. At first he kept determinedly facing the way in which he was going, despite the urge to turn his head, for he sensed that the other was gazing after him; but when he had gone a short distance he glanced around, as though taking casual stock of his surroundings.

The seat was just visible, but to his surprise he saw that it was empty. He looked for Slade, half expecting that he might see him beginning to make his way across the grass, and then he heard a car start up and when he turned his eyes towards the road he was just in time to see the black saloon moving away.

He went on thoughtfully. It was true that it was hardly the time of year to be sitting about for long in exposed places, but Slade had given no indication that he intended to leave. He must have started for his car almost as soon as they had parted company.

He had certainly seemed like a man who didn't know his own mind. He had wanted to find out just how much the police had discovered, but at the same time he had not been anxious to be drawn into conversation in case he had been tempted into saying more than would have been wise.

Perhaps that was natural enough. Tremaine recalled their first meeting on the previous day. Maybe Slade was having second thoughts; he was beginning to wish he had not been quite so outspoken and was anxious to keep out of the limelight whilst the investigations were going on.

Although his mind was thus active Tremaine still had eyes for his surroundings. Slade had been right when he had said that the path he had indicated would lead to the best part of the downs; the evidence of it was about him.

Away to the right a line of trees fringed the road leading to the extension of the suburb in which Jerome Masters lived, and through the trees, where the ground fell away, it was possible to catch an occasional glimpse of the sea several miles beyond. In front of him was the river valley, the path curving towards it and running for some distance along its upper edge.

When he reached the railings he saw that there was an almost sheer drop to the water; the cliff fell two hundred feet or more to the roadway that ran alongside the river. From his vantage point he could look up towards the docks and warehouses at the entrance to the city and down over the meadow land on the far bank that stretched towards the sea.

It was magnificent but it was also a little terrifying. The railings were widely spaced and they seemed to offer but little protection from that awesome drop. Instinctively, Tremaine drew back.

As he did so he saw that a man was coming towards him. At this point the main, paved pathway turned away from the river, following the line of the rocks; but the upper part of the gulley thus formed was dotted with trees and bushes and an earthen path ran through it, forming a short cut between the two arms of the curve.

It was this narrow path through the undergrowth that the newcomer was taking. Tremaine was walking slowly to meet him, unconcerned, when he saw that it was Fenn.

He stopped, and was surprised and a little annoyed with himself to find that he was feeling nervous. He tried to take himself in hand. Undoubtedly it was a lonely spot, and it was a long way down to the roadway bordering the river, but he was overworking his imagination. There was no reason at all to suppose that Fenn would adopt a hostile attitude.

He remained unpleasantly unconvinced. There was something menacing about the thick-set figure of the seaman plodding up the path towards him. And Fenn must have had a good look at him when he had been standing at the side of Jonathan Boyce outside Hardene's house—good enough, anyway, to enable him to recognize him now.

Tremaine measured the distance between them, glanced at the open downs on his left, and was on the point of breaking into an undignified run when Fenn suddenly left the path and disappeared into the bushes alongside it.

A moment or two later a brief glimpse of his form through the trees revealed that his purpose was simple enough—he was taking a short cut that would save him a hundred yards or so if, as now seemed the case, he intended cutting across the downs at right angles to the river, making for the heart of Druidleigh.

Feeling that he had been on the point of making a sorry exhibition of himself, Tremaine put a hand on the railing and stood staring down unseeingly at the river. He was relieved that there had been no one at hand to witness his momentary panic. Far from having any villainous intentions towards him Fenn had in all probability not even recognized him; the man had clearly been engrossed with his own errand.

Tremaine watched a remote toy barge moving slowly down the river, its wash rippling to either bank, and tried to set his emotions in order.

After all, what reason was there to suppose that Fenn had any interest in him? Had there been anything about that one brief meeting to cause suspicion or fear?

He turned slowly away from the railing. He was allowing his imagination to run loose; he was becoming too obsessed with seamen.

He would have to do something about it or Jonathan Boyce would begin to regret having invited him to accompany the murder bag.

13

THE CHIEF CONSTABLE DISAPPROVES

THE encounter, despite his efforts to dismiss it from his mind, had effectively dealt with his desire to roam about the downs. Tremaine walked briskly back to the main road and in twenty minutes had once more reached Hardene's house.

Boyce was still going over a number of papers with Witham but he had already got through the major part of his work.

'Any developments?' he asked, as Tremaine came in.

Tremaine shook his head. He thought that there was no point in mentioning Fenn.

'Nothing worth noting,' he said carefully. 'What about you, Jonathan?'

'Well, we didn't find anything to put us on to Mrs. Colver's visitor of last night,' Boyce returned, 'although she still swears she didn't imagine him. I'm nearly through now. It's just as well. I'm beginning to need my lunch.'

They left the house together, and after a brief but satisfying meal, were taken once more to police headquarters. Parkin and the Chief Constable were waiting for them in the austerely furnished room in which they had had their former conference.

Boyce began to apologize but Sir Robert Dennell cut him short.

'That's all right, Chief Inspector. The fact of the matter is that I'm early. Well, shall we have your report? I understand things have been opening out quite a bit.'

'They have that, sir,' Boyce returned.

Tremaine took one of the seats waiting for them at the table and glanced speculatively at the Chief Constable. His manner was decidedly more amiable than had been the case at their last meeting. He had a brisker, more cheerful air.

'That gun of Hardene's seems an obvious lead, of course. There's no doubt that it was the weapon used to kill Marton. Question is, how did Hardene come to get hold of it?'

'Question is, sir,' Boyce said, 'was it Hardene who *used* it?'

The Chief Constable frowned. His glance went around the table and came to rest upon Tremaine.

'I must say,' he commented, 'that it looks rather as though Hardene was the chap we were looking for. There's more to this than Masters, after all.'

There was no asperity in his tone and Boyce thought he saw his opportunity.

'I'm afraid I haven't been to tackle him yet, sir. I've been trying to get things sorted out a bit more clearly first.'

'H'm. Yes. Quite.' The Chief Constable coughed vigorously. 'All right, you know your own business best, Chief Inspector. I'm not going to be awkward about it. What's the general situation at the moment?'

Relieved, Boyce consulted his note-book.

'As far as we can tell, sir, Hardene didn't go out in response to a telephone call from any of his patients. We've checked on all the likely people and it's certain that none of them rang him up. It may be, of course, that the call came from someone outside his usual practice who wanted a doctor in a hurry. An appeal in the local papers might clear up that question, although since nobody's come forward to tell us about it I daresay it'll merely confirm what already seems certain—that the call wasn't from a patient at all but from someone else who wanted to get in touch with him. And someone who had enough influence with him to make him go out fairly late in the evening without wasting any time about it.'

Mordecai Tremaine pushed up his pince-nez and leaned forward.

'There is one other possibility,' he put in diffidently, 'and that is that Doctor Hardene didn't have a telephone message at all.'

The Chief Constable turned his sharp eyes upon him.

'What makes you think that?'

'The telephone isn't in Doctor Hardene's surgery; it's in the reception room, next to the hall. You'd think it could be heard by anybody in the kitchen almost equally as well as by anybody in the surgery. Mrs. Colver, the housekeeper, was quite used to taking calls after Miss Royman had gone and she was probably in the habit of listening subconsciously for the telephone whilst she was doing other jobs. But she says she didn't hear anything. The first she knew about it was when Doctor Hardene came out of the surgery into the kitchen and told her that he'd been called away.'

'Yes, that's right enough,' Boyce said. He looked at the Chief Constable. 'There's a point there, sir.'

Sir Robert Dennell's brows were drawn together. He looked a little less amiable, as though he was resenting the fact that the suggestion had come from the amateur.

'If he didn't have a call what made him go out?'

'He'd already made an appointment to meet someone. He didn't want to give the housekeeper the real reason for his going out at such a time so he used the excuse about having had an emergency call from a patient. I suppose,' Tremaine added, 'he could just as well have said that he was going out to a political meeting but if he'd done that there'd have been a chance that Mrs. Colver would have stumbled on the truth and he didn't want that to happen.'

'I daresay,' Boyce interposed, 'that he'd been in the habit of leaving his whereabouts with the housekeeper in case anything turned up that needed his attention. He'd need to tell her a convincing story. He couldn't be sure that a genuine call wouldn't come while he was away.'

'What you're saying,' the Chief Constable observed, his eyes still on Tremaine, 'is that Hardene deliberately went out to meet somebody and that the meeting was fixed up before-hand.' He hesitated for an instant or two. And then: 'Any ideas about who it was?' he asked, and there was a challenge in his manner.

'An idea—yes,' Tremaine returned, almost apologetically. 'It isn't any more, of course.'

'Well?'

There was an odd moment of tension before Tremaine's answer came.

'I think it might have been Fenn.'

The Chief Constable relaxed.

'H'm. Still trying to link it up with Marton, eh?' He looked at Parkin. 'Anything fresh on Hardene's past?'

'Not yet, sir.'

'Well, I suppose it *could* have been Fenn.' The Chief Constable's pencil traced idle designs upon the pad in front of him. 'His tale about spending the night at the Mission hasn't been corroborated yet. What about it, Parkin?'

The inspector was ill-at-ease, as though he had been hoping that this moment wouldn't come and yet had known that it was inevitable. A slight flush was beginning to rise from the region of his collar.

'As a matter of fact, sir,' he said awkwardly, 'there's been a bit more news about Fenn. Somebody at the Mission says he remembers him going out and that he's sure he didn't come back again until late. This chap says he was sleeping in the next bed in the dormitory and that he's certain about it because he waited for him to come in so that he could ask him about some money he was owed over a game of billiards they'd played earlier. It seems that he wasn't there when the first enquiries were made—didn't turn up again until this morning.'

Boyce turned to face the local man.

'That makes things look a bit different.'

'The news only came in a few minutes ago,' Parkin explained. 'I couldn't let you know about it before.'

'What does Fenn say about it?' Sir Robert Dennell asked. 'I suppose you've pulled him in?'

Parkin was looking very unhappy.

'Well, no, sir,' he admitted. 'The fact is—we've lost him.'

'Lost him!' The Chief Constable threw his pencil down with a gesture of irritation. 'Damn it, man, you were supposed to be keeping an eye on him!'

'I know that, sir. He must have got wise to it. He gave us the slip yesterday afternoon. Went into one of the big stores in King's Avenue and must have slipped out through a side entrance before our man could catch up with him.'

'Scared,' the Chief Constable said. 'Obviously. Must have known the balloon was going up and made up his mind to run for it. Well, you'd better get busy, Parkin. I want that fellow laid by the heels.'

'I've laid everything on, sir. We'll pick him up again.'

Tremaine looked thoughtfully over his pince-nez. The Chief Constable did not seem to be going to display any more than that momentary irritation, but he did not think it was an opportune time to mention his sight of Fenn on the downs.

Boyce cleared his throat tactfully.

'Sounds as though it could be that it was Fenn who was prowling around Hardene's house last night.'

The Chief Constable's gaze swung back from Parkin.

'Prowler?' he queried sharply. 'Man?'

'So the housekeeper says. She gave the alarm and whoever it was made himself scarce before the man on duty at the front of the house could get on to him.'

Sir Robert Dennell nodded.

'Daresay he made off down the lane behind. The house-keeper heard him, d'you say?'

'That's right, sir. It looks to me,' Boyce said, 'as though she was expecting something of the sort.' He darted a swift glance at the still discomfited Parkin. 'There's quite a promising list of suspects up to now,' he added. 'Might almost say a bit too promising, sir.'

The Chief Constable raised his eyebrows.

'You mean you think the housekeeper might have had something to do with it?'

Tremaine smiled inwardly at the way in which Boyce's red herring had accomplished its purpose. The Yard man's face, however, revealed no sign of elation.

'We've only her word for it,' he observed soberly, 'that she didn't go out after the doctor in order to see what he was up to. That doesn't make it certain that she *did* go, of course, but it does mean that we can't afford to leave her out of the picture.'

'What about motive?' the Chief Constable said.

'I'll admit that's the snag, sir. There doesn't appear to be one—not at the moment, anyway. With Miss Royman, though, it's a different story.'

He mentioned his visit with Tremaine to Hardene's solicitor and the legacy which had been left to Margaret Royman. Sir Robert Dennell's eyes narrowed.

'Seems a lot of money to leave to a secretary, or a receptionist,' he commented. 'If that's all she was.'

His tone was significant.

'As far as I can make out, sir, he wanted their relationship to become a little more—personal. But the lady wasn't having any—so she says.'

The Chief Constable looked unconvinced. He tapped the table softly with the end of his pencil.

'Hardene seems to have been quite a ladies' man. I suppose the girl's telling the truth?'

Boyce shrugged.

'There's nothing to say she isn't. On the other hand, I daresay they'd have been careful to keep it quiet if there was any—er—dalliance going on. When I tackled the housekeeper about it she said something about there not being any smoke where there wasn't any fire, but she didn't come out with any open accusations—not of that sort. What she did say was that Miss Royman's boy friend was taking a poor view of the doctor's attempt to poach on his preserves and that they'd had words about it.'

Watching him, Tremaine thought that he could see in the Chief Constable's face an odd reluctance, as though he realized that he was expected to follow up the line of enquiry Boyce had opened to him, but would have preferred not to do so.

'Have you discovered anything about him?'

'The boy friend, sir? Quite a lot,' Boyce returned. 'His name's Linton. As a matter of fact, he's the reporter on the local paper—the *Evening Courier*—who's been given the job of covering the story.'

Sir Robert Dennell's face registered surprise, but it was an automatic reaction with no real feeling behind it. He seemed distant and preoccupied.

'It's pretty clear that there's a great deal to be cleared up,' he said, with an obvious effort to bring his mind back to the conference table. 'Well, you go ahead in your own way, Chief Inspector. You seem to have things under control.' He hesitated. 'I don't like the sound of that legacy. Obviously you'll have to make sure about Linton and the girl. But unless we have to I don't think we need make too much fuss about Hardene's affairs with women. It can't do any good.'

He looked embarrassed. For an experienced man of the world he seemed to be making heavy weather of what he had to say.

'No need to start digging up any local scandal,' he went on, in explanation. 'The tidier we can keep things the better.'

'I understand, sir,' Boyce said, without a flicker of emotion. 'What I'd really like to get settled is this business of why Hardene was carrying the gun that killed Marton. And I've a feeling that it'll help us to get a line on things when we can find out something about what Hardene was doing before he came and settled down here in Bridgton.'

'Maybe so,' the Chief Constable said. 'Maybe so.' His voice rose a shade on a note of enthusiasm. He turned to Parkin with a trace of eagerness. 'What's the position?'

'We've done all we can this end, sir. Just a case of waiting for results.'

Tremaine had contented himself with following the exchanges between Boyce and the Chief Constable, but now he leaned forward.

'There's something else it might be interesting to learn,' he remarked quietly, and three pairs of eyes turned upon him.

'Yes?' the Chief Constable queried, amicably.

'The housekeeper said she saw a man prowling about at the back of the doctor's house a day or two before the murder. I'd like to know who he was and what he was after.'

'Did the housekeeper give a description of him?' Parkin asked.

'Well, not really. She was rather vague. She only said that it wasn't Rex Linton.'

'Pity,' Parkin said. 'Doesn't give us much to go on, does it?'

'No,' Tremaine said. 'No, I'm afraid it doesn't.'

He glanced up to find Sir Robert Dennell's eyes upon him. Just for a moment the other's feelings were plain, and he knew himself for an object of thorough dislike.

14

THE ATMOSPHERE TENDS TO IMPROVE

THE open spaces of the downs offered both a solace and an opportunity of uninterrupted thought. Tremaine paced slowly over the grass, hands clasped behind him and his pince-nez drooping ever lower.

There had been no developments of an active character since the conference with the Chief Constable and Inspector Parkin on the previous afternoon, but that did not mean that the case had been standing still. On the contrary, ideas and theories had been tumbling over themselves to find expression in his brain.

Tremaine sighed wearily. Crime detection could be an exhausting business even if one was involved in no physical violence.

He wondered whether today would bring any fresh information in answer to the enquiries Inspector Parkin had sent out. He glanced up at the empty, leaden sky of late autumn and around him at the lonely reaches of the downs, fringed by the grey roofs of the houses half a mile away.

It was an odd thought that a few thousand miles across the world people were consulting files and making telephone calls in order that the results of their activities might converge upon this place. For it did not seem that this quiet solitude had any connection with the world of violence and passion with which those activities were linked.

He realized that he was slipping into an unhealthy introspection that would reward him with nothing more desirable than an attack of depression and quickened his steps, trusting to exercise to prevent his brain from seeking forbidden channels.

A short distance ahead of him lay one of the paths that traversed the downs in the direction of the river. He came up the gentle slope that had so far restricted his view and saw the figure of a man moving along the path.

It was Martin Slade. He was leaning heavily upon his two sticks, his progress a painful shuffle.

Tremaine hesitated. Their previous meeting had not been marked by any great cordiality on the other's part and he was in no mood at present to spend any time in the man's company.

But there was no hope of avoiding the encounter with dignity, for Slade had already seen him. With an inward sense of resignation Tremaine went forward.

Slade had stopped. He was standing in the middle of the path, his weight bearing upon his sticks. He was breathing hard and his face bore signs of his exertions.

'Good morning,' he called, as Tremaine approached. 'I see you're making a habit of a stroll on the downs!'

'I thought the opportunity was too good to miss,' Tremaine returned. 'I see you had the same idea.'

'Oh, I do sometimes come out this way,' Slade told him. 'It's about the only real exercise I can get now—not that I can indulge in much even of this,' he added with a grimace.

He sounded a great deal more affable and he seemed ready to talk. Tremaine regarded him with a little more friendliness. It was possible after all, that yesterday he had caught the other at a bad moment—maybe he had been suffering a great deal of pain and it had naturally tended to make him unsociable.

Slade had turned and was beginning to work slowly along the path in the direction from which he had come.

'Got my car waiting over here,' he explained. 'Sage—my chauffeur—usually brings me to the end of the path and then turns me loose for half an hour or so. That's about as much as these confounded legs of mine will stand.'

Tremaine fell in at his side and adjusted his pace to fit in with his companion's awkward and painful movements.

'What happened?' he asked. 'An accident of some kind?'

'Yes,' the other returned briefly. 'My own fault. Ought to have known better. Too late now, though. No use kicking about it. Anyway, you can get used to anything in time—even to the knowledge that you're going to be a useless cripple for the rest of your life.'

'Isn't there anything to be done?'

'No.' The monosyllable was incisive. 'No good refusing to face facts. It doesn't help. I'm done for as far as walking again is concerned.'

'I thought maybe Doctor Hardene was hopeful about things. Wasn't he arranging for you to see a specialist?'

'Oh, he was doing his best—as far as he could,' Slade said. 'But a man knows without his doctor telling him whether there's any hope for him or not and I'm certain enough where I stand.'

'I take it you'll be keeping your appointment, though, despite what's happened?'

Slade shook his head with a determined gesture.

'No. I only agreed to it because I didn't want to let Hardene down. Not after the trouble he'd taken. But there wasn't a definite appointment made. We'd only got as far as my saying that I'd keep one if he made it. I don't suppose he was able to do any more about it. As far as I'm concerned the whole thing's finished.'

There was an undercurrent of bitterness in his voice and Tremaine did not pursue the question. It was a delicate matter, after all, to argue with a man who no longer had the normal use of his legs.

They went on in silence for a few moments, but it was clear from Slade's expression that he had something on his mind. He said at last:

'Your speaking of Hardene gives me a chance to say this. I'm afraid I haven't been as sociable as I might have been. I'm sorry. Put it down to the short temper of an old fool who's generally in pain and doesn't always know what he's saying. Besides, the shock rather knocked me over—I mean Hardene's being killed like that. We had our disagreements but I liked him. He did more for me than some of the others in his profession with a string of letters after their names and precious little inside their heads.'

The irascible note began to creep back into his voice. Aware of it, he tried to hold himself in check and searched for the right words.

'I just wanted to make my apologies,' he said, awkwardly for him. 'Bad business to act as I did.'

'That's all right,' Tremaine told him. 'I realize how you must have been feeling.'

'That's just it,' Slade returned with a sigh. 'I doubt whether you do. I've been wondering ever since what you must have thought of me.'

Tremaine automatically readjusted his pince-nez. It was an instinctive prelude to his posing a leading question.

'What I did wonder,' he observed, 'was why you were so anxious to make it known that you and Doctor Hardene didn't always get on together.'

There was no hesitation in the other's reply.

'Panic,' he said shortly. 'Sheer, stupid panic. You see, I didn't know anything then about where Hardene had been killed or when it had happened. If I'd stopped to think I'd have realized that there couldn't be any question of my coming under suspicion. Once I'm at home I'm a fixture unless I get Sage to come for me. But when the thing was thrust at me without warning I suppose I just lost my head. I knew that you'd find out sooner or later that we'd had arguments that were a bit heated and I wanted to get my say in first.'

'And now,' Tremaine said with a smile, 'you've had time to cool off and think it over, and you can see that all you did was to make matters worse. Is that it?'

'Well, I've been able to find out one or two things I didn't know at that time. When I discovered that Hardene had been found in an empty house facing the downs and that he'd been killed somewhere round about half past ten I realized what an idiot I'd been.'

'People often do lose their heads on such occasions,' Tremaine said, with the worldly air of one of wide experience in matters of the kind. 'I suppose your mention of Jerome Masters was another of the symptoms of your—er—distress?'

'That was my attempt to find a scapegoat,' Slade admitted frankly.

'I suppose you must have had a reason for picking on that scapegoat in particular?'

Slade looked at him in surprise.

'I thought you'd have discovered it by now. I certainly did have a reason. Hardene and Masters were at each other's throats. If anybody had a motive for the murder it was Masters. Not that I really thought he'd done it—any more than I do now. Masters wouldn't have been such a fool.'

But his glance was speculative, and somehow it belied his words.

Tremaine affected not to have noticed it. It was no part of his duties to allow Martin Slade to share the knowledge that Jerome Masters had put forward an alibi with a large-sized hole in it.

'In that case,' he observed, 'what *is* your theory? Somebody undoubtedly did kill Doctor Hardene, and if it wasn't Masters who did do it?'

Slade became diffident.

'It's only a theory, of course. I haven't as much knowledge of the facts as you have so I'm not in a position to have any hard and fast opinions. But it seems to me that the most likely thing is that he was killed by some tramp.'

Tremaine nodded.

'I understand there have been a number of tramps in the neighbourhood lately. The Chief Constable mentioned it.'

'At one time they increased the patrols around here, but I suppose the shortage of men made them give it up when nothing happened for a long while. The *Courier* report said that Hardene was hit on the head with a piece of rock that must have been lying somewhere near the house. I'm no policeman but it seems to me that there's proof enough that the thing wasn't premeditated.'

'What do you imagine happened?'

'Hardene was unlucky enough to disturb a tramp who'd broken into the house for shelter. There was a bit of a rumpus —Hardene was inclined to be a hasty sort of chap—and the fellow lost his head and picked up that piece of rock and hit him with it. I don't suppose he meant to kill but in his panic he struck a bit too hard. When he realized what he'd done he made himself scarce.'

'It's certainly a sound enough theory,' Tremaine remarked. 'But there's still the question of the house to be settled. What made Hardene go there in the first place?'

Slade lifted his shoulders.

'Made a mistake in the dark and picked the wrong house. Easy enough to do.'

'But what was he doing out at that time in any case?'

The other looked surprised. He raised his eyebrows.

'He had his bag with him, didn't he? I'd say that he'd been called out to see a patient. Haven't the police checked on that? I'd have thought it was one of the obvious things.'

'I'm playing the innocent abroad,' Tremaine said hastily, sensing troubled waters ahead. 'I just wanted to see how it struck someone on the outside.'

'Oh, I see.' Slade's face cleared. 'Well, that's *my* view—based on what little I know.'

'The weak point,' Tremaine said slowly, 'is how he came to make a mistake over the house. After all, you'd expect him to be familiar with where his patients lived.'

'His practice covered a lot of ground. And maybe it wasn't one of his usual patients. He might have had an emergency call from somebody he hadn't seen before. It wouldn't have been difficult to go to the wrong house in the dark.'

Tremaine pursed his lips. His companion regarded him with a hint of a twinkle.

'I know it's full of holes, but fortunately it isn't my job to work out a solution. I can do it for exercise and it doesn't matter if I'm wrong. I can see plenty of difficulties right enough. For one thing, you'd think that even if it wasn't one of his regular patients who rang him up, whoever it was ought to have come forward by now. Although,' he added, as another thought occurred to him, 'they might have called in another doctor when Hardene didn't turn up, and I suppose it's possible that if there was something badly wrong—a person seriously ill, for instance—they might not be aware of all this business in the newspapers. And if they didn't say anything to the doctor about having tried to get Hardene he naturally wouldn't see any connection.'

'It may not be your job to work out a solution,' Tremaine said, 'but you seem to be putting things together admirably.'

For a few moments they went on in silence. Slade stumbled on an uneven section of the path. Tremaine instinctively put out a hand to assist him, realized the other's dislike of having attention brought to his infirmity, and sought for a topic that would occupy his mind.

'By the way, Mr. Slade,' he observed, 'I understand you live over on the other side of the river. It looks rather an attractive spot from this part of the downs. I must try and get over there before I leave Bridgton.'

'It's pleasant enough,' Slade agreed. He added, 'Look here, if you're thinking about crossing the bridge some time why not drop in at my place?'

'I'd be delighted. Let me see, Red Gables, isn't it?'

'That's it. You can't mistake it. Detached place, about half a mile down the road from the bridge on the right. Name's on the gate.'

'You must find it a rather lonely spot—especially at this time of the year.'

'It's well enough. I'm not the type who likes noise and people fussing around anyway.'

They had almost reached the point where the path joined the roadway. The black saloon was parked ahead of them, the chauffeur sitting at the wheel, a book in his hands. He glanced up as they approached, and climbed down to open the rear door for his employer.

'Can I drop you anywhere?' Slade enquired.

'I was going back to Doctor Hardene's house. If that wouldn't be out of your way—'

'Not at all. We've got to pass the end of the road in any case. In you get. Don't worry about me. Sage'll give me a hand.'

Tremaine seated himself in the rear of the saloon, and Slade, aided by the chauffeur, clambered pantingly in at his side.

'Now, this visit of yours,' Slade said, as they moved off. 'When is it to be?'

His tone made it plain that he was not merely being polite. Tremaine reflected for a moment or two and then made up his mind.

'Would this afternoon be inconvenient?'

'Capital. I'll send the car for you. Where would you like to be picked up?'

'No, don't do that,' Tremaine said. 'I'm a little uncertain what time I'll be able to get away and I'd rather make my own way over—gives me more opportunity to get to know places.'

Slade did not demur and a few minutes later they had turned away from the downs and were running smoothly down the road in which Hardene's house was situated.

15

THE LADY IS INDIGNANT

TREMAINE pushed open the entrance gate and walked up the short path towards the house, self-consciously aware of the big car as it moved off.

'I see,' Jonathan Boyce said, as he opened the door, 'that you're beginning to make the acquaintance of the local inhabitants.'

'That was Martin Slade,' Tremaine said defensively. 'You remember he was here the other morning. Cripple, one of Hardene's patients.'

'I remember,' Boyce said. 'I've seen his car running around the neighbourhood this morning. Anything interesting come of it?'

Tremaine described his meeting of a short while before and Boyce gave a little nod.

'Sounds as though he's had second thoughts. I had an idea he might be trying to undo that first impression and give us a more flattering edition.'

'It sounded logical enough, Jonathan,' Tremaine said.

There was no doubt that Slade had been in a much more friendly mood. He had been altogether less prickly—even, in fact, ready to make the approaches.

Tremaine followed Boyce into the house. Margaret Royman had arrived and was working in her room. He greeted her as he passed the open doorway. She returned his good-morning pleasantly but her eyes went down almost immediately to her task; she clearly did not wish to be drawn into conversation.

He saw that she was very pale and that the hand resting upon the papers on her desk was not quite steady.

When they were out of earshot he looked at Boyce.

'Has she heard?'

'About the legacy? Yes. Seems to have shaken her. She's been very off-colour this morning.'

'Good,' Tremaine said cheerfully, and the Yard man eyed him in surprise.

'What, no romance in the air today?'

'If she's upset it sounds as though she didn't know anything about that thousand pounds. And if she didn't know anything about it where's the motive?'

'There *have* been accomplished actresses,' Boyce rejoined, a trifle morosely, but Tremaine did not take up the challenge.

The late Doctor Hardene's residence was not remarkable for its air of cheerfulness. If Margaret Royman was reluctant to talk, the housekeeper proved to be even less willing to indulge in conversation.

Tremaine found her disapproving and tight-lipped, ostentatiously busying herself with tasks in the kitchen which even his untutored eye could see were unnecessary. He wondered what, indeed, she had to do now that her employer was no longer in existence to give his orders.

'I'm sorry to trouble you again, Mrs. Colver,' he began mildly, 'but I know how willing you are to help clear up this dreadful affair.'

'I've told you all I can,' she said frigidly. 'You and the Chief Inspector.'

'I'm quite sure you have,' he told her conciliatorily. 'It's just that sometimes—quite inadvertently—things slip one's memory. I'm wondering whether there is any further way in which you can help to throw some light on what happened to Doctor Hardene. What I'm chiefly concerned with at the moment,' he went on, before she could voice an objection, 'is the doctor's social work.'

She relaxed at that, as though she had been on her guard against something quite different.

'His social work? You mean his politics?'

'Well, not quite. Politics and social work don't always mean the same thing. No, I mean the interest he took in helping people who came to see him when they were in difficulties. I believe he was especially interested in helping seafaring men, wasn't he?'

Her guard was back again now, unmistakably.

'I don't know anything about that,' she told him. 'He never said anything to me about what he was doing and I didn't ask him. It wasn't my place.'

'But I expect you saw the people who came to the house?'

'Not always.' There was a sullen, obstinate note in her voice. 'If I was working in the kitchen I might not see them.'

'You mean Doctor Hardene would have answered the door himself?'

She saw the trap and drew back from it.

'Miss Royman might. Like she sometimes did for patients. I wouldn't see who it was calling then.'

'Oh, I see. It's a pity. I was hoping you might have been able to throw some light on things. Still, it can't be helped.'

Tremaine was wandering about the kitchen, peering at the cupboards lining it, as if his mind was not really on what he was saying at all.

'I suppose you'll have made up your mind now about what to do,' he observed casually. 'Will you be leaving Bridgton altogether?'

'No,' she said shortly. 'Why should I?'

'I must say it's a pleasant city,' Tremaine agreed. 'Very pleasant indeed. But I thought you might have been going to live nearer your son.'

It was a shot in the dark but it went home. She gripped the edge of the table.

'My—son?' she said falteringly.

'I happened to see his photograph in your room. He's in hospital, isn't he?'

'How—how did you know?'

'The background of the photograph looked like a hospital or a sanatorium building, and he was in a wheeled chair. Has he been a patient long?'

'Five years,' she said. She had recovered a little now, although she had still not regained her former attitude of rigid defence. 'It was an accident—his spine was injured. The doctors say that he'll always have to have treatment and that he'll never be able to work.'

'I'm sorry,' Tremaine said quietly. 'It must make matters very difficult for you.'

'I manage,' she said, hard-voiced, and he knew that the armour was back in position, even more forbidding now because of her chagrin at her brief, involuntary weakness.

The arrival of Jonathan Boyce extricated Tremaine from what was becoming an uncomfortable situation. The Yard man put his head around the door.

'Oh, there are you. Like to come?'

Tremaine, grateful at the rescue, did not ask questions until the door had closed behind them.

'Masters,' Boyce said, in response to the enquiry he made when they were outside. 'It's time we asked him to explain that shaky alibi. He's sure to know that we've been checking on him and he'll have had time to make up his mind whether he's going to come across with the truth or not.'

'Does he know you're on the way?'

'No. But Parkin's been keeping an eye on him. He's been avoiding his office—found that too many people were asking awkward questions apparently. We'll find him at home all right.'

The police car which had been placed permanently at their disposal took them across the downs and into the select neighbourhood in which Jerome Masters lived. Boyce gave his name to the maid who answered his ring and they were shown into a lounge overlooking the trim lawns that ran down to the roadway.

They were not kept waiting long.

'Mr. Masters is in his study,' the maid said to Boyce as she returned. 'Will you come this way, sir.'

There was an undercurrent of excitement in her manner. Boyce glanced significantly at Tremaine as they followed her out of the lounge.

Jerome Masters was seated at the desk where they had seen him on their earlier visit. He raised his head as they were shown in and they saw that his eyes were bloodshot and that his big form was sagging; evidently he had been enduring no quiet time in the interval.

'I've been expecting you back before,' he told them, without preliminary. 'You've been long enough in coming.'

His tone was ungracious. Boyce, appraising the situation, saw that the man had decided upon attack and his own manner hardened.

'Why should we have come back at all, Mr. Masters? I believe I made it quite clear the other day that our visit was purely a routine one.'

'You did,' Masters growled. 'Maybe that's why your confounded plain-clothes men have been going around asking questions about me ever since.'

'You must realize, sir,' Boyce said imperturbably, 'that all statements made have to be checked before they can be accepted. It's a matter of course.'

'What I want to know,' Masters almost snarled, 'is when it's going to stop! The whole place is talking. I've had to give up going to my office and stay here like a monk because I can't put a foot out of doors without some fool wanting to ask questions.'

'I'm sorry if you've been inconvenienced, sir.'

'Inconvenienced! I tell you, Chief Inspector, I'm tired of it and I don't propose to put up with it much longer. We'll see whether the Chief Constable can do anything about it. Your attitude's been infernally high-handed.'

'The Chief Constable, sir? You don't appear to have seen him yet,' Boyce observed gently.

Masters put his elbows on the desk and leaned forward threateningly, his jaw thrust out.

'What d'you mean by that?'

'I mean that it's time we got down to business, Mr. Masters,' Boyce said quietly. 'You haven't been to Sir Robert Dennell with any complaints so far, nor are you likely to go to him—and for a reason we both know very well.'

The glare left the other's eyes. He sat back, the truculence oozing out of him, like a boxer who had just taken a shrewd, scientifically aimed blow to the body that had turned his legs to water.

'What—reason?' he got out reluctantly.

'You told me, sir,' Boyce said dispassionately, 'that on the night of Doctor Hardene's death you were at the Venturers' Club in the city and that you didn't leave until late in the evening—some time not far short of eleven o'clock, to be precise. You're quite right about enquiries being made, but I'm afraid they haven't been very satisfactory from your point of view—or from mine. We haven't been able to find anyone who remembers seeing you in the club at all on that particular night.'

Masters was breathing heavily.

'Are you trying to tell me I wasn't there?' he demanded.

'All I'm saying, sir, is that we haven't been able to find anyone who'll confirm it. You're a prominent man in Bridgton and you're well known at the Venturers' Club. It seems rather—odd—that no one seems to be able to say that you were there.'

'Plenty of people make use of the place. Nothing very strange about nobody being able to remember me in particular out of all the others who were there.'

'The queer thing is, sir,' Boyce went on levelly, 'we can account for every night in the preceding week. It's only that one night that seems to be giving trouble.' He paused. His grey eyes rested on the other man's face. 'You wouldn't care to reconsider what you told me the other day, sir? After all, mistakes do occur and when you're suddenly asked to account for your movements it's very easy to say the wrong thing.'

Tremaine saw the emotion struggling for expression in the coarse, fleshy face. He thought for a moment or two that Boyce was going to produce results, and then Masters brought his fist down with a thump on his desk.

'I'm not the kind of man to forget where I was, Chief Inspector! What're you driving at?'

'Am I to take it then, sir, that you persist in your statement that you were at the Venturers' Club that night?'

'Whether anybody remembers seeing me or not,' Masters said thickly, 'that's where I was. If you're prepared to take the word of a pack of addle-pated idiots in preference to mine, Chief Inspector, that's your affair. But if that's the way you're going to conduct the case you'd better look to your job.'

Boyce rose to his feet.

'I realize that you're not quite yourself, Mr. Masters, and that's why I'll say no more about it. But I think you'd be well advised not to repeat the remark you've just made.'

He left it at that but his tone was curt enough to strip Masters of his bluster. They left him glowering at his desk, in an ill temper but well aware that he had gone as far as he dared.

As they passed through the hall the frail, grey-haired woman who was the builder's wife came forward to meet them, briskly in spite of the stick on which she leaned.

'I was told you were here, Chief Inspector,' she said, 'and I decided to have a word with you before you left.'

Boyce stopped.

'Yes, Mrs. Masters?' he said enquiringly.

'I imagine you've just come from my husband,' she said, in an incisive tone that contrasted oddly with her slight form. 'How did you find him?'

'I don't quite understand,' Boyce said, playing for time.

'My dear Chief Inspector, they don't appoint fools to jobs like yours. You understand me perfectly. Did my husband strike you as a man who is behaving normally?'

'He seemed rather—distressed,' Boyce told her cautiously. 'But, after all, that's only to be expected under the circumstances.'

'Nonsense! Jerome isn't a weakling. D'you think he'd have got where he has if he was anything of the sort? He hasn't been to his office for two days—won't take any telephone calls. It's all over this business of Doctor Hardene's murder. Because they didn't like each other people have started whispering things about Jerome. They'd accuse him openly if they dared.'

Boyce searched the determined face looking challengingly up into his own.

'Assuming all this to be true—and I'm not by any means agreeing that it is—what action do you suggest that *I* should take?'

'The police can do a great deal. For instance, they can let it be understood that there's no suspicion attached to my husband. A hint or two in the right quarter will soon get around. In a city like this it doesn't take long for things to become known. You've seen for yourself how upset he's getting and you know that he couldn't have had anything to do with Doctor Hardene's death.'

'Do I?' Boyce said quietly.

'Surely my husband told you that he spent that night at the Venturers' Club and that he came straight home?'

'Yes, he told me that.'

'Then your duty is quite plain, Chief Inspector,' she told him. 'I shall expect to hear that you've taken the necessary steps to see that my husband's name is cleared. Good day to you.'

She did not wait to find out whether Boyce intended to make a reply. She crossed the hall to press a bell and in a moment or two the maidservant who had admitted them made her appearance.

It occurred to Tremaine that the girl looked disappointed. He wondered whether she had expected to see her master escorted from the house in handcuffs.

Walking down the drive Boyce drew a deep breath.

'Not much doubt about where we stand with that good lady. I don't remember the last time I was shown the door so pointedly.'

'She's more on top of the situation than her husband seems to be,' Tremaine observed. 'All that bluster of his was a sign that he's on edge about something.'

'He means to bluff it out, anyway,' Boyce said. 'Well, we'll see. Our Mr. Masters is riding for a fall.'

Tremaine noted that Jonathan seemed unperturbed by the act that Jerome Masters was making things difficult. He was, in fact, humming a light-hearted little tune.

16

AFTERNOON CALL

IT WAS a fine afternoon, although cold with a hint of winter to come, and Tremaine decided to walk the comparatively short distance to Red Gables rather than wait for an uncertain bus.

Boyce raised his eyebrows when he mentioned his destination but made no comment.

The way led over the bridge spanning the river. Tremaine stopped for a few minutes when he reached the centre of it and gazed out over the city stretched below him, with its factories, houses, railway sidings, and its network of docks and waterways, looking from this height like parts of a child's expensive toy.

Turning, his eyes followed the steep face of the rock that rose up from the water to the point where he had been standing when he had encountered Fenn. From the bridge, one's view unhindered, it was possible to appreciate the full grandeur of the gorge through which the river had cut its way.

The sight was also inclined to make one a little dizzy. He moved back from the rail that protected the edge of the bridge and walked slowly towards the far side. The road here ran through a wooded area bordering the river, with a sprinkling of detached houses each set in its own small clearing around which the trees and bushes gathered.

Red Gables proved easy enough to find. As far as he could tell without walking on it was the last house in the road and was isolated from its neighbours by a strip of ground, overgrown with bushes, which had seemingly been reserved for an intervening residence that had never been built.

He gave his name to the pleasant-faced elderly woman who answered his ring and was shown into a comfortably furnished lounge in which Martin Slade was resting upon a couch.

'Hullo, Tremaine! Glad you took me at my word and decided to come!' Slade pulled himself into an upright position. 'Forgive my not getting on my feet. I'm afraid it's rather a tricky business with these legs of mine.'

'I quite understand,' Tremaine said. 'Please don't let me disturb you.'

'Find yourself a chair,' Slade told him. He glanced at the elderly woman who had shown his visitor into the room. 'I think a cup of tea is indicated, Mrs. Sheppard.'

As the door closed behind her Tremaine lowered himself into a big easy chair facing the couch and looked about him appreciatively.

'You've a very inviting place here.'

'It's adequate,' Slade returned. 'It's adequate. I try to make myself as comfortable as I can. No point in doing otherwise.'

'That was your housekeeper who went out just now?'

'Yes. Mrs. Sheppard. Don't know what I'd do without her. She and her husband run the place for me between them. He looks after the gardens and sees to things that need doing on the outside, and she handles the internal affairs.'

'It sounds a very convenient arrangement.'

'It is. Especially for an awkward individual like me. I'd find it difficult to get hold of ordinary servants who'd be willing to take me on. That's why I give them a fairly free hand. As long as everything's being run smoothly I don't bother them much. It suits me and *they* seem to like it.'

'From what I saw of Mrs. Sheppard,' Tremaine observed, 'she struck me as being the right type from your point of view.'

Slade did not make a direct reply. He shifted himself into an easier position on the couch and regarded his visitor shrewdly.

'Well, all right, now that we've got the introductions over, go ahead.'

Tremaine looked puzzled.

'Go ahead?' he asked, and the other smiled.

'We both know that you didn't come here just to make a social call. You're out on business. What is it you'd like to know?'

Tremaine hesitated, a little disconcerted by the frontal attack, and Slade's smile grew wider.

'I'm not offended, man! Far from it. I knew that if you came you'd want to make the most of it and I don't blame you. In fact, I've been rather hoping you'd have some leading questions to ask. After all, I knew Hardene and I'm as interested as anybody in finding out who killed him. If there's anything I can tell you that'll make the job easier, don't hesitate to ask me about it.'

'I appreciate your attitude, Mr. Slade,' Tremaine said, his manner relaxing noticeably. 'I must confess that when I decided to take advantage of your invitation and call on you I did have in my mind that a chat with you might be useful.'

'I'm not going to pretend that there isn't any ulterior motive on my part, too,' Slade told him. 'Because there is. The chance of getting in on the inside of a murder investigation is too good to miss. Especially when someone like yourself is involved. You *are* the Tremaine who's been mentioned in the newspapers in connection with other cases, aren't you?'

'Yes, I'm afraid I am,' Tremaine admitted. 'But you won't spread the news, I hope?' he went on anxiously. 'You see, I'm here more or less unofficially. I don't mean that the Commissioner and the local Chief Constable don't know anything about me, but I don't want the newspapers to print anything that might make things awkward. You know what they are for exaggeration.'

'Don't worry, I'll not give you away. If you want to keep your light under a bushel you can rely on me not to say anything.'

'Thank you,' Tremaine said gratefully. 'I'm sure you understand that publicity wouldn't be at all welcome.' It was, he thought, time for a change of topic and he embarked upon the first line of enquiry he had mentally prepared. 'I'm right in saying that you didn't see a great deal of Doctor Hardene outside your professional contacts?'

'You'd be right in saying that I didn't see *anything* of him. I believe I mentioned that our politics weren't the same and in any case I don't lead much of a social life—for obvious reasons.'

'*His* social life seems to have been somewhat—involved,' Tremaine said carefully.

'You mean because of his getting mixed up with women?' Slade nodded. 'Yes, I did get to know something about that. Always struck me that he was running a lot of unnecessary risk—being a doctor.'

'I wonder,' Tremaine said ruminatively, 'who the women in question were?'

'That's rather out of my depth, I'm afraid. Although I had a feeling that he was interested in that receptionist of his—Miss Royman.'

'Did she seem to reciprocate?'

'Not to my knowledge. Anyway, I fancy she has a young man already and I don't suppose he'd be likely to take kindly to the thought of Hardene cutting in on him.' Slade broke off suddenly and eyed his visitor with a new shrewdness. 'You're not trying to tell me that something of that sort *did* happen?'

Tremaine drew a deep breath and took the plunge.

'Would it surprise you to learn that Margaret Royman was left a considerable sum of money in Doctor Hardene's will?'

The expression on Martin Slade's face answered the question plainly enough.

'You're not serious? I can understand a nominal legacy, of course, but you don't mean it was something more?'

'Something very much more—considering the total size of the doctor's estate, that is. Something that certainly makes it appear as though their relationship was closer than that of employer and secretary.'

'It does make things more complicated, doesn't it? Perhaps I was wrong in thinking that she didn't give him any encouragement. It might have been just an act of hers to put everybody off the scent. After all, she and young Linton might even have been in it together.'

Slade sounded as though he was going to develop the theme, and then he frowned and shook his head determinedly.

'No, I just can't believe that. It's too fantastic. She's always seemed to me to be too nice a girl for anything of that sort. The whole business was just an unlucky accident. Hardene ran across some tramp who lost his head, as I said this morning. That *must* be the explanation. The other is too—too unbelievable.'

'Nothing is unbelievable,' Tremaine said, 'when it comes to murder.'

'No, I suppose not. You've had the experience, of course. But still—'

Slade relapsed into silence. Tremaine said, after a moment or two:

'Does the name Elaine mean anything to you?'

'No,' Slade returned slowly. 'No, I can't say it does. Should it?'

'Not necessarily. Hardene was evidently the type who believed in keeping his private affairs to himself. But Elaine is the name of a lady with whom he seems to have been on very special terms at the time of his death.'

'Oh—I see.' Slade wrinkled his brows. 'It doesn't convey anything to me. I suppose it couldn't have been a code-name?

If he wanted to keep his business as secret as all that he might have used the wrong name deliberately, just in case somebody heard it.'

'That's a possibility, of course, although I somehow don't think that he did.'

'I'm afraid I'm not being of much help to you,' Slade said ruefully. 'I did point out, though, that Hardene and I weren't exactly on intimate terms.'

'It helps just to talk about things,' Tremaine told him. 'Discussing it with someone else is a way of sorting a case out in one's own mind even if it doesn't lead to anything new. Just one last question. Do you happen to know a man called Fenn?'

Slade shrugged his shoulders helplessly.

'A blank again. What does he look like?'

'Thick-set sort of fellow. Gives you the feeling he's seen plenty of rough spots in his time.'

'Is he supposed to have had something to do with Hardene?'

'He landed at Bridgton a few days ago and asked for Doctor Hardene at the Seamen's Mission.'

'Did it go any further than that?'

'That's just the trouble,' Tremaine said with a sigh. 'We don't know.'

Slade looked puzzled.

'But surely the police can clear up a problem of that sort without any difficulty? If this chap Fenn's in Bridgton all they have to do is to ask him a few questions. They'll soon trip him up if he tries any fairy-tales.'

'Yes, I suppose that's true enough.'

Tremaine was feeling uncomfortable. He had taken a risk in telling his companion about the legacy to Margaret Royman; he shrank from passing on in addition the information that Fenn had given his shadowers the slip.

If the news got back to the Chief Constable that gentleman was unlikely to receive it with any favour. The thought of the jeopardy in which he might be placing Jonathan's promotion filled him with uneasiness.

Fortunately he was saved further embarrassment by the arrival of Mrs. Sheppard with the tea for which Slade had asked, and for the next ten minutes or so they talked on general topics and the subject of the murder was not raised again.

Slade was clearly doing his utmost to act the courteous host, and Tremaine felt that the situation demanded that he should respond to the other's friendliness. When the teapot was empty and the home-made cakes which had accompanied it had been disposed of, Slade regarded his visitor contentedly.

'I daresay you'd like to see something of the place before you go. I'm sorry I can't do the honours myself, but Mrs. Sheppard will be delighted to show you round. Nothing pleases her more—probably because she doesn't often have the opportunity,' he added with a chuckle.

'I hardly like to feel that I'm running away from you—'

'Nonsense! I'd like you to make the most of your visit now that you have come to see me. After all, I don't suppose you'll be staying long in Bridgton once you've cleared up this business, so it's a case of getting in as much as you can.'

Under the housekeeper's direction Tremaine was given a comprehensive tour of the premises. It was evident that she had been primed beforehand; Slade was clearly proud of his house and had intended that his visitor should be impressed.

Duly—and with honesty—Tremaine produced the opinion required of him.

'It's ideal,' he said enthusiastically. 'Big enough to live in and not so large that it's uncomfortable.'

They were standing in the garden, where the housekeeper's husband, a grizzled, cheerful-faced man of about her own age, was engaged in tidying the hedges. He nodded as Tremaine spoke.

'Aye, it's a rare good spot, sir. Mr. Slade not being able to get about like ordinary gentlemen it makes him take more of an interest in things like.'

Tremaine glanced around him. The roadway leading to the bridge was just visible beyond the hedge bordering the garden.

'I suppose the only difficulty from your point of view is that it's rather isolated. I haven't noticed any buses passing since I've been here.'

'Bless you, we don't find it lonely, sir,' the housekeeper said. 'There's plenty enough to do to keep the both of us busy.'

'Isn't shopping rather a problem?'

'Everything gets delivered, sir. And if we want anything in a hurry like there's always the telephone, or maybe Mr. Slade'll get himself driven into Bridgton.'

Lying on top of a heap of garden rubbish that had been gathered together at the side of the path was a crumpled poster. Stooping, Tremaine read the announcement of a social and amateur dramatic performance advertised for three nights previously.

'I see there's a chance of an evening's entertainment without going over the bridge into the city. That's if you can get away, of course. Seabury village hall,' he quoted from the poster. 'Seabury isn't far from here, is it?'

'About five miles, sir. Mr. Slade's a very easy gentleman to get on with. Never complains if we want to go out. Not that it's often. We aren't ones for the pictures. But the social was something special—Mr. Slade knew we'd been looking forward to it.'

'I see it went on until quite late. Rather awkward for the buses, I expect, being a country service.'

'Bless you, that was all arranged, sir. All of us had coaches back to where we lived. Had it all in style, we did.'

As he walked back into the house Tremaine studied his companion's good-tempered features.

'I must say Mr. Slade seems very lucky in his choice of housekeeper and gardener,' he observed.

'It's a pleasure to work for a gentleman like him, sir. Never makes a fuss. And you might expect him to more than most, him being a cripple and suffering all the time.'

'Yes, it must be a dreadful trial for him.'

When he re-entered the lounge Slade looked up at him with an expectant smile.

'Well, what's the verdict?'

'I think you already know. I envy you both the house and Mr. and Mrs. Sheppard. They seem a really genuine and simple-hearted old couple.'

'Yes, I'm well looked after,' Slade agreed. 'You must come and call on us again. Don't forget I want to keep in touch with the way things are going.'

'I won't forget,' Tremaine promised.

He went away from the house with the feeling that he had seen a new and kindlier Martin Slade and that despite his physical limitations the other had succeeded in making himself very comfortable.

He did not think his visit had been wasted. Although he had learned nothing unmistakably new that bore upon Hardene's death, he had nevertheless garnered a certain amount of food for thought concerning it.

17

EXPLANATION FOR AN ALIBI

HE HAD recrossed the bridge and was walking briskly along the road bordering the downs not far from the turning that led to Hardene's surgery when he saw Margaret Royman in front of him. He quickened his pace still further and then saw a man step out from the shelter of the gateway of one of the big houses fronting the road and walk to meet her.

It was Rex Linton. The reporter plainly had no eyes for anyone but the girl and did not even glance in his direction.

Automatically Tremaine slackened his stride. He came almost to a standstill and then, having made up his mind, moved forward again.

As he drew nearer both of them turned at the sound of his footsteps on the pavement and he saw sudden recognition and dismay in their faces.

He felt a sense of disappointment but he did not allow it to show in his expression.

'Good afternoon.'

There was a sullen flare of antagonism in Linton's eyes and he did not return the greeting.

'So you haven't caught the murderer yet.'

Tremaine ignored the sarcasm behind the words.

'Not yet,' he returned mildly. 'But we have hopes.'

'Indeed?' Linton stared at him challengingly. 'That's interesting. News is getting short. Your friend the Chief Inspector hasn't been very helpful up to now.'

'I'm sure you'll find him reasonable enough when there are developments to report.'

'Maybe. It's beginning to look as though I'll have to find my own developments. I daresay, for instance, that the *Courier*'s readers will be glad to know about *your* being here. It'll give them something to talk about.'

The girl instinctively put a hand on his arm.

'Rex—please.'

Linton did not respond to her gesture. He stood facing Tremaine with more than a little of the pugnacious in his attitude.

'It'll make quite a story, won't it? Well-known amateur arrives in Bridgton. Working with Scotland Yard because neither the Yard's men nor the local police know what to do.'

'Dear me,' Tremaine observed mildly, 'you do sound an aggressive young man.'

Margaret Royman made an attempt to retrieve the situation.

'I'm sorry, Mr. Tremaine. Rex is upset. He doesn't really mean it.'

'I rather think he does, my dear. And as a matter of fact he's made quite a point. I'm not anxious to have any newspaper publicity. There are good reasons why I should stay in the background.' A much sharper note came into his voice and his eyes held the younger man's. 'If I were you, Mr. Linton, I'd think very hard before making use of my name in your newspaper. For Miss Royman's sake if not for your own.'

A watchful expression came into Linton's face.

'What are you getting at?'

'At the moment both Miss Royman and yourself can be included under the heading of suspected persons—for reasons I needn't remind you of. I wouldn't like matters to go any further—just because my name found its way into the columns of the *Evening Courier* through a misunderstanding.'

Rex Linton's lips curled slightly.

'In other words it's blackmail. I keep quiet or else.'

'It's a precaution,' Tremaine said. 'Just to make sure you don't do anything regrettable before I've had the opportunity of a really effective talk with you.'

'Just what might an—effective—talk be?'

Tremaine did not make a direct reply.

'Suppose the three of us make an arrangement to meet for coffee at a quarter to eleven tomorrow? I daresay you'll know how to deal with your editor—especially if you tell him that you've the prospect of learning something interesting about Doctor Hardene.'

Linton had lost something of his guarded manner. He was looking puzzled. He glanced at the girl and she gave a slight nod of agreement.

'All right,' he said slowly. 'If that's what you want. Where do we meet?'

'At the Elm Tree. I understand that it's a favourite place of assignation in Bridgton. I'll leave it to you to decide where we go from there. As long as we can talk without being disturbed for a while I'll be quite satisfied. Now I don't doubt that you've a great deal to say to each other so I'll not detain you. I'll look forward to our meeting tomorrow.'

He nodded and turned away before either of them could make any further comment. He knew that both of them were wondering what he had in his mind and he did not wish to face a cross-examination just then.

When he reached Hardene's house he found Jonathan Boyce on the point of departure and they returned to the city together.

In their hotel room that night Boyce lay back on his bed and contemplated the ceiling. He pursed his lips as though in the act of whistling a tune but he gave forth no sound.

'What's on your mind, Jonathan?' Tremaine enquired.

Boyce grinned and twisted to look at him.

'The same that's on yours,' he returned. 'The question of who killed Doctor Graham Hardene of Bridgton and why. Plus a few rather more personal thoughts about how useful a superintendent's pay would be.'

'You haven't given very much away up to now,' Tremaine went on slowly. 'But I suppose you've a few theories?'

'Nasty things—theories,' Boyce said. 'Don't like 'em. Never did. You now, you're different. Amateurs can afford to take a chance or two because there's nobody to stand them on the carpet if they happen to be wrong.'

Tremaine considered the implications of this last sentence for a moment or two.'

'All right,' he said at last. 'What is it that Mrs. Colver knows that she hasn't told us?'

Boyce nodded approvingly.

'Full marks. She's holding out on us right enough. If I *was* given to having theories—which I'm not—I'd say that she had something on Hardene and that she knows quite a bit about that fifty pounds a month he used to draw.'

'You knew that she has a son?'

'Yes. I saw that photograph in her room.' A smile touched Boyce's lips fleetingly. 'Sanatorium in the background, wasn't it? I noticed you were having a good look at it. She couldn't do much to help him on a housekeeper's pay and the prospect of a little extra something, even if there was a risk attached to it, must have been very tempting. Problem: what was it she knew that made Hardene pay up?'

'Suppose we speak to her about it tomorrow?' Tremaine said, tentatively, and Boyce stroked his chin thoughtfully.

'It's an idea. Maybe we will.'

There was silence for a while and then Tremaine said:
'What about Masters?'

'I'm expecting to hear from him at any moment now. He
was sweating this morning if ever I saw a man sweat. I've an
idea it won't be long before something cracks.'

Boyce sounded unconcerned and Tremaine regarded him
a trifle reproachfully. For a man anticipating promotion, and
therefore with everything to gain by doing himself justice,
Jonathan seemed to be displaying surprisingly little emotion.

He knew, however, that appearances were deceptive. If the
taciturn Jonathan was apparently at peace with the world it
was because he was satisfied that he was beginning to see
daylight. He was, in addition, expecting something to turn
up—not in the Micawber-like manner, out of the blue, but
as a result of certain activities he had himself caused to be
carried out.

Something did turn up. Inspector Parkin, when they met
him in accordance with routine at police headquarters, was
labouring under an excitement he was doing his utmost to
hold in check for the sake of his dignity.

'I imagine there's been news of Hardene,' Boyce said, eyeing
him with an amused smile.

'There has that, sir,' Parkin announced. 'I tried to get you
at your hotel but you'd just left. Not that it mattered, since
you were coming here anyway, but I thought you'd like to
have the news as soon as it came in.'

As they seated themselves around the now familiar table in
the Chief Constable's room, the inspector laid a closely typed
report upon it.

'There are still a few gaps—we haven't had time to cover
everything—but there's enough to give us a pretty sound line
on what Hardene was up to. I'll just give you the outline now,
sir; I daresay you'll be wanting to read the details for yourself
in your own time.'

'All right,' Boyce nodded. 'Go ahead.'

'It's confirmed that Hardene took his medical finals at
Edinburgh. After that he had a house surgeon's job for a time

at a hospital in Brum and then he went off to Canada. There was never any official action but it seems that he left under a bit of a cloud. Something about a shortage in the funds of a sports club he belonged to. Apparently the loss was made up by one of the other surgeons, but it was made plain to Hardene that it was a case of resign or else.'

'Hence Canada?' Boyce observed. 'So he started off on the wrong foot, eh?'

'That was only the beginning of it, sir,' Parkin went on. 'We sent his prints across as soon as we'd traced him that far. Hardene had a record on the other side; that's why we were able to get results so quickly. He didn't go under his own name—called himself Lacey. Seems there's quite a bit known about him. He did one twelve months' stretch for a bank job in Toronto and there's still a warrant out against him for a job that happened after he got out again.'

'Lone wolf?' Boyce said, and Parkin shook his head.

'No. He was mixed up with a gang that specialized in bank smashing. There were three of them in it. They did pretty well out of it, too, until an affair in Montreal that nearly put them all away. Something went wrong at the last minute and one of the gang slipped off a wall and broke his leg when they were trying to make a getaway.'

Parkin paused for a moment or two and flicked through the pages of the report.

'There's nothing definite about it,' he went on, 'but when this chap was sent down he swore that he'd been pushed from the wall and that it'd been Lacey who'd done it in order to slow up the chase and give himself and the third member of the gang a better chance of getting clear.'

'H'm.' Boyce frowned. 'A double-cross. Not very nice. I take it that Lacey—or Hardene—and the other fellow *did* manage to get away?'

'They got away all right and went to earth. As I said just now, sir, they're still on the wanted list over there, but Montreal says that Lacey was believed to have got out of the country a year or two back and they notified Scotland Yard. They knew he was English, although they didn't have his real name, and thought he might have made for his home ground.'

'In that case Records will have the full story,' Boyce said. 'We'll check back and tie up the ends. If Montreal didn't send to us until a couple of years ago it means that Lacey managed to get back into this country again without being spotted, changed his name to Hardene once more, and settled down to doctoring here as a respectable citizen. Daresay his share of the loot helped to set him up.'

'That's about it, sir. Nobody'd have any reason to suspect him, and he might have been genuinely trying to go straight. His only worry must have been over whether the pal he'd ditched was going to show up one day and make things awkward.'

Boyce lifted an eyebrow, sensing more in Parkin's words than their apparent meaning.

'Is that where Marton comes into the picture?'

'More or less, sir.' Parkin glanced at Tremaine, who had been closely following what he had been saying. 'In view of Mr. Tremaine's interest in him—and that business of the gun, of course—I thought it might be worth while checking on Marton at the same time. It came off. Marton wasn't a member of the gang, but it seems that he was doing a stretch at the same place as the fellow who was left behind by Hardene and the other chap. They must have got talking it over. Daresay it was a case of the one who'd been double-crossed not being able to keep his mouth shut about the revenge he was going to take when he got out. Marton was released first and came over here to find Hardene. He must have had some idea where to look and he knew Lacey's real name.'

'That might have come out before the bank job was pulled,' Boyce nodded. 'The three of them might have got confidential after a drink or two—talked about what they were going to do when they'd made enough of a pile.'

'Perhaps the Montreal job was intended to be the last anyway,' Parkin said. 'Things were beginning to get too hot for them, and they were planning to pull out. Daresay Hardene wished he'd kept quiet,' he added grimly.

'Yes. It looks as though Marton was bleeding him all right—that's why he didn't need to do any work. In the end Hardene took a chance and shot him. Maybe because Marton was going the way of all blackmailers and asking for a bit more each time, or maybe because he was scared that Marton intended to pass on the news of his whereabouts when the other merchant came out and that then there'd be an extra mouth to feed. What about Number Three, by the way? Is he out yet?'

Once more Parkin consulted the report in front of him.

'Came out just over two months ago.' He added, significantly. 'Last place he was seen was Halifax and he was believed to be trying to make his way over here.'

'Description?'

'Could be Fenn,' Parkin said ruefully. 'Fits him, anyway. Names aren't much good, of course—these gentry are the sort who pick a new one every few weeks. Prints would settle it—if we could get 'em.'

'Nothing new come in?'

'Not a thing, sir. Chap seems to have made himself scarce all right. We'll get him sooner or later, but in the meantime I don't fancy catching Sir Robert's eye.'

'I see what you mean,' Boyce said. 'In view of this latest piece of news he's going to expect Fenn to be laid by the heels before much more water has passed under that elegant bridge of yours. And if it doesn't happen he'll be wanting somebody's head.'

Tremaine leaned forward.

'You think it *was* Fenn who did the killing, Jonathan?'

The Yard man returned him the wily smile of the old campaigner.

'I'm not making any statements—yet. I'm only saying that the situation looks promising.'

'But there isn't much doubt about it, is there, sir?' Parkin put in anxiously. 'After all, there's plenty of evidence that Fenn was out for revenge; he didn't make any bones about it.'

'Assuming that Fenn *is* the third member of the gang.'

'I know it still remains to be proved, sir, but it makes everything fit. Either he had a good idea where to look for

Hardene already or Marton tipped him off before he was killed. He contacted Hardene after a few enquiries at the Seamen's Mission and the two of them arranged to meet somewhere quiet where they wouldn't be likely to be seen. Maybe Fenn rang up during the day and fixed it, even if he didn't actually call at the house. It might have given Hardene the idea of saying that he'd had an emergency call to explain why he had to go out.'

'It's sound enough,' Boyce admitted.

'Why did Hardene take that gun with him if it wasn't because he knew he might be running into trouble?' Parkin went on. 'It doesn't look as though he intended to use it deliberately, otherwise it wouldn't have been in his bag—he'd have kept it handy. He wanted it as a stand-by in case Fenn tried to be awkward, but my guess is that he wanted to avoid trouble and buy Fenn off if he could.'

'But,' Tremaine said, 'Fenn wasn't so easy to deal with. Is that what you think?'

'He wasn't willing to kiss and be friends, sir. Not just like that. Maybe Hardene didn't offer enough or maybe it was Fenn who was in an ugly mood. They got to arguing and Fenn picked up that piece of rock and landed him with it. We know about the tie-up between Hardene and Lacey; we know that Fenn signed off his ship when she docked; and we know that he hasn't an alibi for the time of the murder. It all seems to me to hang together.'

'On the face of it—yes. But it still might have been a tramp who did the actual murder,' Tremaine put in diffidently, 'and not Fenn at all. Suppose they *did* arrange to meet. Suppose Hardene was a few minutes early and Fenn was a few minutes late—he might easily have been in a strange city. Suppose Hardene disturbed a tramp who was using the house as a resting place for the night. There might have been an argument and an unlucky blow, and Hardene might have already been dead when Fenn turned up. As soon as he realized what had happened Fenn got out again in a hurry. All the facts still fit—but they don't make Fenn the murderer.'

Parkin opened his mouth to say something and then closed it helplessly. He looked at Jonathan Boyce.

'Don't make it more difficult, Mordecai,' the Yard man said wryly. 'Circumstantial evidence is as much as we're likely to get.'

Tremaine made an apologetic gesture.

'I'm sorry to sound awkward, Jonathan.'

Boyce did not make the reply that was on his tongue, for at that moment the door opened and the Chief Constable came in.

'No, don't get up.' He put out a restraining hand as they instinctively began to rise, and crossing the room joined them at the table. He seemed in a high good humour. 'Well, Parkin, they tell me your reports are through?'

'Yes, sir. I've just been giving the Chief Inspector and Mr. Tremaine the main facts.'

Briefly the inspector recounted what he had already told his earlier companions and the Chief Constable leaned back in his chair, beaming broadly.

'Couldn't ask for much more, could we! The whole thing ties up. Hardene a crook, eh? That'll make the tongues wag. Suppose I shouldn't be surprised at it, though, after finding out about that gun.'

'There's still some clearing up to be done, sir,' Boyce put in, and the other nodded.

'Quite, quite. A business like this always produces all sorts of loose ends that turn out to have nothing to do with the real job at all. Sort of thing you expect. But you won't find me asking questions about every small detail that's come to light. My concern is to see the murder question settled and as long as that's done I'll be satisfied. Between ourselves, the less mud that's stirred up the better.'

The Chief Constable cleared his throat with just a trace of self-consciousness and turned towards Parkin.

'Now, Parkin, that fellow's got to be found. As soon as Fenn's safely inside we can go ahead and let the newspapers have the story. I want every available man on the job.'

His tone was authoritative but without rancour. Parkin was clearly relieved.

'I'll get in touch with you the moment we find him, sir.'

There was a knock at the door and the constable who had previously acted as a messenger came in and spoke to the Chief Constable. Sir Robert Dennell brought the palm of his hand down upon the table.

'Bless my soul, I'd forgotten him! All right, Taylor, have him sent up.'

As the messenger went out on his errand the Chief Constable glanced at his companions, a smile on his lips, like a man who nursed a secret he knew would produce at least a mild sensation.

'I had a message from Masters this morning,' he announced. 'Rang me up at my house. Said he wanted to come and see me. You three had better wait and see what it's all about.'

'Masters, sir!' Parkin ejaculated. 'Wonder what *he* wants?'

'Probably wants to complain about being persecuted,' Boyce remarked. 'He didn't appreciate my call yesterday.'

The Chief Constable shook his head.

'No, it didn't sound to me as though he wanted to make a complaint. More as though he had something he wanted to get off his chest.' He made a rueful grimace as a thought occurred to him. 'Hope it isn't a confession he wants to make. That would put the cat among the pigeons again, wouldn't it!'

Tremaine's eyes flickered towards Inspector Parkin. The local man was regarding his chief in a somewhat doubtful fashion, almost as though he disapproved of his air of levity.

A moment or two later and the door opened again and the burly figure of Jerome Masters appeared in the entrance. The builder advanced into the room and then he hesitated and his expression changed as he saw that the Chief Constable was not alone.

'It's all right, Masters, I think you've already met these three anyway. Come in and sit down.'

Reluctantly Masters did as he was invited.

'I was hoping, Sir Robert,' he said awkwardly, with none of his earlier arrogance, 'I'd find you alone.'

'I take it,' the Chief Constable said, 'that you've come about the Hardene affair? That was the impression you gave me on the telephone, anyway.'

'Yes—that's why I wanted to see you.'

'In that case you can speak quite freely. These gentlemen are conducting the investigation, so they'll naturally be interested in anything you can say that will throw new light on things.'

Masters sat silent. He licked his lips and his gaze wandered away to the window. He looked very unhappy.

Mordecai Tremaine said quietly:

'I rather fancy that Mr. Masters has come *here*, Sir Robert, because he felt that what he had to say would be said easier here than at his home. You see, it's difficult for him to have visitors without his wife being aware of them.'

The Chief Constable looked blank, but Masters turned a suddenly grateful glance in Tremaine's direction.

'Yes,' he said. 'Yes, that's right.' He took a deep breath and then the words came quickly. 'I know what you're thinking, Sir Robert. You're thinking I had something to do with killing Hardene. That's why I've come—to tell you that you're wrong. I know I've been a fool—made things difficult for myself—but I swear I had nothing to do with it.'

The Chief Constable cleared his throat with an official sound. It was obviously a mannerism he employed when he wanted to gain time to phrase what he intended to say.

'Glad to hear you say so, naturally, Masters. I mean, a man in your position in the city. Don't want any scandal if it can be avoided—doesn't do any good to any of us. But things don't look too well, you know.'

'I know.' Masters sounded like a small boy caught out in some misdeed and ready to express penitence. 'I said I was at the Venturers' Club that night. I can see now that it was a stupid thing to have done.'

Jonathan Boyce leaned forward.

'Do I take it, Mr. Masters, that you're willing to admit that you *didn't* go to the club?'

Masters nodded glumly and the Chief Constable made a sound denoting exasperation.

'Then devil take it, man, what was the point in lying?' he said sharply. 'Surely you must have realized what the consequences would be! You must have known that you were bound to come under suspicion once you'd been found out.'

'I—I knew I had to have an alibi,' Masters said. 'Everybody had heard about Hardene and me being on different sides of the fence. When the Chief Inspector came to see me I said the first thing that came into my head and afterwards it was too late to take it back.'

Sir Robert Dennell frowned.

'The situation is then, Masters, that you haven't an alibi, after all?'

'No, I don't mean that,' Masters said, still more unhappily. 'I can prove I wasn't anywhere near the place where Hardene was killed that night.'

'Then what's all the mystery and argument about?' The Chief Constable's exasperation deepened. 'Why not say where you were and have done with it?'

'Perhaps,' Tremaine interposed quietly, '*Mrs.* Masters is the key to the matter.'

Once again Masters gave him a glance of gratitude.

'Yes,' he said. 'It was Sibyl—my wife. I couldn't risk her finding out where I'd really been.'

He was making very heavy weather now. Tremaine could not avoid a feeling of sympathy for the man. It was evident that it had cost him an effort to come.

Sir Robert Dennell was proving obtuse—whether wilfully or otherwise it was difficult to assess—and Masters was forced to elaborate his story in halting phrases.

It was a story that came oddly from the big man's lips; the story of the self-made builder, outwardly strong and ruthless, who was completely under the will of his frail-looking wife. It was Sibyl Masters who ruled, and the arrogant business man who dealt so hardly with his rivals deferred to her wishes.

As was perhaps inevitable he had sought for compensations—secretly, after the manner of a man who was not permitted to indulge his desires openly. His vices proved to have been simple enough—drinking and gambling parties with a group of male associates—but to Sibyl Masters, coming of a family rooted in the worst prejudices of the Free Churches, they would have been unpardonable.

The night of Graham Hardene's murder, unluckily for Masters, had been also the night of a particularly convivial gathering in a private room at a well-known bar in the city. To lie to the police had seemed to him in the first moment of panic easier than to risk his wife discovering where he had really spent his time.

The fact that he had lied in such a manner now provided paradoxical proof of his innocence of the murder. As far as Hardene's death had been concerned, his conscience had been clear; he had not imagined that serious enquiries would be made about him and he had failed to appreciate that to the police the fact that he was not the murderer was not self-evident but required to be established by careful proofs.

When the sorry recital was over Masters was huddled in his chair, his bombast utterly gone and in his face the drawn expectancy of a man who was waiting for the next blow to fall. Even Sir Robert Dennell's irritation had died.

'All right, man,' he growled, hiding his embarrassment with a roughness of tone. 'There's no need to look so doleful about it. We'll have to check what you've told us, but unless you've been making it all up again you won't hear any more of it.'

Masters lifted his head.

'You won't—you'll not let Sibyl know?'

'As long as she isn't mixed up in anything criminal, what your wife thinks or does isn't any of our concern and we aren't likely to go taking her into our confidence.'

'I—I'll appreciate anything you can do to keep things quiet, Sir Robert. She's—she's been very upset just lately because of all these enquiries.'

'All right. Well, if that's all you have to tell us—'

The Chief Constable half rose from his chair in an indication that the interview was over, and Masters followed suit. It was Mordecai Tremaine who introduced the jarring note.

'There's just one more matter,' he observed, 'that Mr. Masters may be able to clear up for us before he leaves.'

Masters turned towards him, an almost pathetic eagerness in his manner; he had clearly been regarding the benevolent-looking elderly man who was with the policemen as an unexpected friend.

'What I was wondering, Mr. Masters, is whether you can tell us what your wife was doing on that particular night. I mean the night of Doctor Hardene's murder.'

'My wife?' Masters stared at him, clearly at a loss. 'She was at home.'

'Are you certain of that?'

'Of course I am,' Masters said. And then he stopped, the doubt visible in his face. 'Well, no,' he admitted, 'I'm not certain. I wasn't there myself to see her. But I'm sure she would have said if she'd been out.'

He waited, expecting further questions, but Tremaine merely peered at him over his pince-nez, pushed them back into position, and smiled benevolently.

'That's all, Mr. Masters, thank you.'

Unwillingly, with a backward glance at the Chief Constable, Masters went out. As the door closed behind him three pairs of eyes turned upon Tremaine.

'What was all that about Mrs. Masters?' Sir Robert Dennell demanded.

Tremaine put the tips of his fingers together. He was wearing his most harmless expression.

'She gave me the impression of being a woman of strong character,' he observed. 'I'm not surprised to hear that Masters was dominated by her. She knew all about the trouble with Doctor Hardene and she wasn't afraid to make her opinion known. A woman like that can do surprising things. It might be interesting to find out whether she was at home on the night of the murder, and if she wasn't, just where she did spend her time.'

On Jonathan Boyce's face was the faint, surprised expression of a man who wasn't quite certain whether he had heard correctly; but it was the Chief Constable who seemed most affected. He made no comment but his fingers were drumming a tattoo on the arm of his chair. His irritation seemed to be a good deal more intense than was justified by such an apparently simple observation.

18

COFFEE WITH CONFIDENCES

WHEN Mordecai Tremaine arrived at the Elm Tree, a minute or so late for his appointment, Margaret Royman and Rex Linton were already waiting for him.

'My apologies,' he told them. 'I'm afraid I was detained with the Chief Constable a little longer than I expected.'

At his mention of the Chief Constable, Linton's eyebrows drew together in a sudden frown. He made no reference to it, however.

'We thought you might like to sample the coffee in the Canyon,' he observed.

'The Canyon?' Tremaine regarded his companions quizzically. 'It sounds rather like the Wild West.'

'You won't find it very wild,' Margaret Royman said, smiling. 'Except in the children's playground, and I don't suppose there will be many of them there at this time in the morning.'

The Canyon proved to be a natural valley in the rocks that lay on the far side of the main road running along the edge of the downs at this point. It was an attractive spot, with its harsh outlines softened by trees and undergrowth. An enterprising caterer had laid out the floor of the valley with flower gardens, a children's pleasure ground, and a restaurant.

The sun was out and was striking down with a stimulating warmth that was the more inviting after the cold air of the previous two days. They chose a table in the open and Linton went off to obtain the coffee.

There were few customers—no doubt the real season was now over as far as the Canyon was concerned—and he was back within a very short time. He set down the tray with a certain air of challenge.

'Now, Mr. Tremaine,' he began, 'let's get right down to it. Why did you want to see us this morning?'

Tremaine dropped a lump of sugar into his cup and stirred his coffee thoughtfully.

'I like young people. I think that's a good enough reason, don't you?'

'No,' Linton said bluntly, 'I don't. Let's cut out the pleasantries, shall we?'

'Rex is right, Mr. Tremaine,' Margaret Royman said. 'We both know what you're thinking. It's only fair to us to tell us what you're going to do.'

'That's easy enough to answer. I'm going to do my best to clear the innocent.'

He looked at the girl as he spoke. She wore no hat and the sunlight was glinting in her hair. She was obviously puzzled by his reply and the frown that wrinkled her forehead gave her an air of appeal that his sentimental soul found irresistible.

Linton seemed unimpressed.

'Does that mean,' he said calmly, 'that you've come to the conclusion that whoever killed Hardene, neither Margaret nor I had anything to do with it?'

'Precisely.'

'Rather sudden, isn't it? After all, I thought we were obvious suspects. Margaret's legacy gives us a really sound motive for wanting to get rid of Hardene before he could change his mind about his will. And if the legacy isn't good enough there's a version of the eternal triangle to put in its place. I didn't like Hardene's attitude to Margaret and knocked him on the head to prove it. Neither of us has a proper alibi. We say we went to the cinema, but if we were in it together we'd naturally stand by each other.'

Mordecai Tremaine took off his pince-nez, polished them carefully and put them on again.

'I like you, young man. I knew I wasn't wrong. You're inclined to be a little—ah—aggressive, but in a newspaper reporter I suppose that's rather a good thing. I don't think you killed Doctor Hardene for two reasons—one is that I'm a sentimentalist and it would upset my philosophy if two nice young people like you had stooped to such a sordid thing as murder.'

He stopped, regarding them benevolently.

Linton said:

'And the other reason?'

'I'm beginning to understand who did kill him.'

'This,' Linton said, 'is interesting. Who was it?'

Tremaine reached for his spoon and stirred his coffee for the second time, unnecessarily.

'I appreciate your anxiety as a newspaper reporter, young man, but for the time being I think it would be better to keep my theories to myself.'

Linton looked disappointed, and Tremaine smiled.

'You'll hear the news in good time. If I'm right, that is. In the meantime what I'm interested in is clearing up loose ends.'

'What is it you want to know about *us*?' Margaret Royman said, a little anxiously.

'Nothing that you can't clear up very quickly,' he told her. 'Let's get the unpleasantness over, shall we? On the morning after Doctor Hardene's murder certain things happened when you arrived at the surgery and I just want to make sure that I've found the right explanation for them.'

'Certain—things?' she echoed.

'When you arrived that morning and learned that Doctor Hardene was dead you were badly frightened. Why?'

'I—I was shocked,' she said. 'The news was so terrible. After all, he'd seemed quite all right the night before.'

'It was quite natural for you to have been shocked, but what I said,' Mordecai Tremaine observed gently, 'was that you were frightened. What was the reason for that?'

The girl's face had gone a little white but she faced him with steady eyes.

'I thought that he might have met Rex and that they might have quarrelled—as they'd done a short time before. I knew that Rex was still angry and I thought they might have come to blows. When I heard just how Doctor Hardene had been killed, of course, I knew that it couldn't possibly have been Rex. But just at first, before I knew the whole story, I was terribly afraid.'

Tremaine nodded in satisfaction.

'That was the way I summed up the situation, but I wanted to have it from your lips as well, just to be quite certain. No doubt,' he added, 'it was also your anxiety for Mr. Linton that made you go through the documents Chief Inspector Boyce left on Doctor Hardene's desk.'

She was startled.

'You—know that?'

'Oh yes. The Chief Inspector knows it, too. I'm afraid that the truth is that he set a little trap for you. He isn't really as careless as all that. He wanted to find out whether you had anything to hide, and you must admit that you gave him reason to think you had.'

'But he doesn't suspect me?' she said, a catch in her voice. 'Not now?'

'Naturally, I'm not in a position to say what the Chief Inspector is thinking,' Tremaine said gravely. And then he smiled. 'On the other hand I've known him a long time and I'm reasonably safe in saying that now that he's aware of your—interest—in Mr. Linton he understands the reason for your rather strange behaviour.'

He glanced shrewdly from the girl to Linton, who had been listening with a taut expression on his face. He thought that the atmosphere was favourable for the next stage in the operation.

'Suppose we just say that you took rather an uncharitable view of the police and tried to hide things from them when it might have been wiser to be quite frank about Mr. Linton and his relations with Doctor Hardene. That's all over now, but it still leaves us with the murder to solve. Now, Miss Royman, what can you tell me about Mrs. Colver?'

'What do you *want* me to tell you?' she countered.

Tremaine smiled across the table at her.

'I suppose it's a fair question at this stage,' he admitted. 'Doctor Hardene and his housekeeper were supposed to be on good terms with each other. Would you say that was true?'

'I can only speak for the times when I was at the house – and during the day I didn't see a great deal of Mrs. Colver. She saw to the household duties and it was my job to attend to the patients and Doctor Hardene's correspondence and so on. Although we were in the same house we didn't have much contact.'

'But you must have encountered her sometimes, and I daresay you would have heard Doctor Hardene speaking to her—or perhaps he might have referred to her when he was talking to you. What was your impression of the relationship between them?'

'Well, they appeared to get on all right together.'

'When you say they *appeared* to get on, do you mean that you had doubts about it?'

She was uncertain how to reply. She hesitated.

'It wasn't anything that was said,' she went on at last. 'It was just that sometimes there was an—an atmosphere. It was almost as though they really hated each other and were only keeping up a pretence of being on good terms. I used to think that I was imagining things because I never heard either of them speak sharply or saw any signs of a quarrel. It *must* have been imagination,' she added. 'If there had been any trouble, all that Doctor Hardene would have needed to do would have been to give her notice. I don't suppose he would have found it all that difficult to get another housekeeper.'

Deliberately Tremaine ignored the point.

'Did Doctor Hardene ever give you the feeling that he might be hiding something?'

The girl still hesitated; it was Linton who replied.

'Yes,' he said. 'There was something phoney about him. I can't put my finger on just what it was but I'll swear there was *something*. All that business about cleaning up local politics, for instance. It was just an act. He didn't really care about setting things to rights; what he was after was his name in the newspapers. Then there was the way he'd interview any down-and-outs who went out to see him. I don't believe he was genuinely anxious to give them a helping hand; he wasn't the sort.'

'What *do* you believe?'

'He was looking for somebody,' Linton said. 'That was the way it struck me. I daresay it sounds pretty crazy, but it seemed to me that there was somebody he badly wanted to meet and he had the idea that that was how he might do it.'

'You didn't,' Tremaine said, carefully, 'take any action about it?'

'As a matter of fact I did. When I saw what his game was with Margaret I decided that I'd do what I could to find out what was going on. I didn't have any real lead, of course; it was just that I didn't intend to take any chances where Margaret was concerned. I went down to the Seamen's Mission—made a few enquiries there; all very much on the quiet. It did occur to me that he might be mixed up in some sort of dope smuggling—plenty of ships put in here from the West Indies, and as a doctor it would be right up his street. But I drew a blank. If anything of that kind *was* going on it was being kept well under cover.'

Linton broke off. His glance held Tremaine's across the table.

'Look here, *was* Hardene a shady customer? Off the record, I mean. I'm not asking you so that I can print it. I'd like to know just for my own peace of mind.'

'I wouldn't be surprised,' Tremaine said, 'if it doesn't turn out that Doctor Graham Hardene was a very shady customer indeed.'

The reporter leaned back. There was a grim satisfaction in his face.

'Thanks. It's nice to know I wasn't following the green-eyed monster up a blind alley.'

Tremaine looked enquiringly at the girl.

'What about you, Miss Royman? Did you ever have any reason to suspect a skeleton in the doctor's cupboard?'

She shook her head.

'No, I can't say I ever noticed anything.'

'You're quite sure? There was nothing at all? What about those arguments with Mr. Slade, for instance? He's been quite frank with me, by the way—told me that sometimes he had quite high words with the doctor—so you needn't be afraid of telling me what's in your mind. I understand that some of the—er—disagreements—were connected with what Doctor Hardene was proposing to do about treating Mr. Slade's disability, but I rather gather that some of them may have touched upon non-medical matters. Mr. Slade told me, for instance, that he didn't like Doctor Hardene's politics and I can well imagine that he wouldn't mince his words!'

'I do seem to remember one occasion,' she said, frowning. 'It's not exactly to do with Doctor Hardene's hiding anything but it was about his getting himself into trouble or at least getting himself disliked. I'd been out—Doctor Hardene had asked me to go to one of the local chemists for something he wanted, and when I got back Mr. Slade was in the surgery. It was an appointment I'd made several days before. He must have arrived just after I'd left.'

'And the argument was in full swing?'

'Yes. They were both talking so loudly that I couldn't help overhearing them. Doctor Hardene said that it was nothing to worry about and that people couldn't see the wood for the trees and then Mr. Slade said that he was a fool and that he'd be sorry if he went on with it.'

'Did you overhear enough of what they were saying to gather any idea of what they were talking about?'

'I didn't exactly overhear it; Mr. Slade told me. A few moments after I'd got in the surgery door was opened and I heard Mr. Slade say that he'd get another doctor if Doctor Hardene didn't change his mind because he wasn't going to be made a laughing stock. Then he came out and when he saw me he said that Doctor Hardene was taking up politics and would I do something to stop it. He said that a doctor ought to stick to his profession and not go mixing with a lot of politicians and getting his name in the newspapers. I'm afraid he was rather—irate.'

'I don't doubt that he was!' Tremaine said. 'It sounds,' he added, innocently, 'as though he believed you had a certain amount of influence with Doctor Hardene.'

A flush came into Margaret Royman's face.

'Oh no,' she said hastily. 'It wasn't that. It was just his way of talking.'

'What about Doctor Hardene? What was *his* attitude?'

'He seemed—amused. He told me not to take any notice of Mr. Slade because he was a privileged patient and that in any case he didn't mean it.'

'Well, it looks as though Doctor Hardene *did* go into politics and Mr. Slade *didn't* change his doctor. They agreed to differ and that was the end of the matter, was it?'

'I suppose it was. They did have arguments, but I don't think Mr. Slade ever really was as fierce as he sounded. But he certainly did seem to believe that Doctor Hardene might run into trouble. You don't think,' she finished, looking at him seriously, 'that Mr. Slade was right and that his going into politics did have something to do with his death?'

'It mightn't be such a long shot at that,' Rex Linton put in. 'And I'm thinking of Jerome Masters,' he added pointedly.

'I don't think our different brands of politics in this country have reached the lethal stage,' Tremaine remarked. 'Not yet.' He took out his pocket watch. 'Dear me,' he observed, 'I'm afraid I'm dreadfully late. I'm supposed to be meeting the Chief Inspector. I really must ask you to excuse me.' He rose to his feet, extricating himself from the table. 'It's been a very pleasant little talk—very pleasant indeed. I'm always delighted when I'm able to satisfy myself that two nice young people couldn't possibly have had anything to do with a murder.'

He saw that Rex Linton was about to speak and he glanced at the girl.

'By the way, Miss Royman, do you happen to know the Chief Constable by sight?'

'Sir Robert Dennell?' She shook her head, clearly surprised by the question. 'No. At least, I don't think so.'

'Perhaps not,' Tremaine said. 'As far as I know he hasn't been to Doctor Hardene's house although he was at the house where the body was found. It isn't important.'

He smiled benevolently and turned away, leaving behind him two puzzled faces.

It must be admitted that he suffered no qualms of conscience but felt indeed very pleased with himself as he walked up the long winding path leading out of the Canyon. He had found out what he had wanted to learn and he had given little away in return.

It was unlikely, of course, that Rex Linton was as satisfied with the results of their conversation. The reporter had probably been expecting a story he could flourish before his editor, and the story had not materialized.

Still, the newspapers could wait a little while longer. The important thing was to clear the ground in preparation for the grand climax.

And he was doing that. Tremaine nodded contentedly as he came out upon the main road. Yes, he was certainly doing that.

19

THE LADY HAS SOMETHING TO HIDE

JONATHAN BOYCE was already at Hardene's house when Tremaine arrived.

'The housekeeper's here,' the Yard man announced. 'Haven't tackled her yet, though. Been waiting for you, since it was your idea.'

'Thank you, Jonathan.'

Boyce hesitated, his hand on the door handle of the surgery.

'How's the romance?' he enquired, suspiciously casual.

'It seems to be developing along the right lines,' Tremaine returned carefully, and Boyce grinned.

'No—difficulties? Such as one of the parties being arrested for murder, for instance?'

'I don't think so, Jonathan. And neither do you. Those two youngsters had nothing to do with the murder.'

'Case of the young lady getting scared on the boy friend's behalf, eh? Suppose it was natural in view of the general set-up. But you can't be too careful. Got to make sure there aren't any loose ends.'

Tremaine settled his pince-nez in position.

'Has he been found yet?'

'Fenn? No news so far. He's gone to earth all right and his scent seems to be giving Parkin's hounds some trouble. Well, let's see what we can do with our end of the problem.'

A few moments later the housekeeper was seated facing them in the surgery, a look of foreboding on her face although she seemed otherwise self-possessed.

'I had hoped, Mrs. Colver,' Boyce began, 'that it wouldn't be necessary to ask you any further questions, but I'm afraid it has become my duty to send for you again.'

'I don't see why,' she returned, sullenly. 'I've told you all I can.'

'The information in my possession,' Boyce said, 'doesn't confirm that statement.'

She flushed and looked up at him angrily, but he held up his hand before she could speak.

'Before you say anything, Mrs. Colver, I must point out to you that you are not compelled to answer my questions and that if you wish to obtain legal advice you are perfectly free to do so.'

The flush died away and her face became very pale. Her voice was unsteady.

'You're not—you're not going to arrest me?'

'That was not my purpose in calling you in here.'

'But what you said—it sounded—it was a caution, wasn't it? What the police always say before they arrest anyone.'

'It wasn't exactly a caution,' Boyce said. 'Not in that sense. But quite frankly I'm not altogether satisfied that you've told me everything and I considered it my duty to give you a warning before I questioned you.'

The treatment was having its effect. There was fear now in the housekeeper's eyes. She did not know what to do with her hands and her fingers were picking nervously at her dress.

'Among Doctor Hardene's private papers,' Boyce went on, 'we discovered a number of newspaper cuttings. Do you happen to know anything about them?'

'The doctor's private papers weren't any concern of mine.'

'In the ordinary way, perhaps not. But these cuttings were of particular interest. They dealt with two murders that took place in Bridgton at the beginning of this year. One of the victims was a seaman called Marton and the other was a pawnbroker whose name was Wallins.'

'Yes, I remember reading about them. There was a lot in the newspapers. The police never found out who did it.'

Despite her uneasiness there was a trace of sarcasm in her voice.

'Yes, that's right, Mrs. Colver,' Boyce said calmly, 'the police didn't find out who committed either crime—not officially.'

He stressed the last word and was rewarded by a nervous twitch in her face that she could not control.

'I don't see what it has to do with me.'

'Can you suggest any reason why Doctor Hardene should have wanted to keep those cuttings?'

There was a distinct hesitation in her manner before her answer came.

'No, I don't know of any reason. Except that he was a doctor and it might have had something to do with his work.'

'That's a possibility, of course. But I've been able to find nothing so far to support the theory that he might have been interested in murder from the medical or psychological point of view. In any case, why those two murders only and no others?'

'I've told you,' she persisted stubbornly. 'I don't know.'

Boyce nodded as though he was satisfied, and when he spoke again he seemed to be following an entirely different line of thought.

'I understand,' he remarked quietly, 'that there is very little hope of your son being cured.'

She stared at him for an instant or two, nonplussed by his change of front.

'There isn't any hope at all,' she said at last. 'The doctors have told me.'

'Keeping him in the sanatorium—even in these days—must be very expensive for you. I don't doubt that there are all sorts of little luxuries you try to get for him.'

Her manner softened and the hard, defensive lines of her face became almost gentle.

'I do what I can,' she said. 'After all, he's all I have left.'

Boyce was regarding her steadily.

'Mothers are notoriously ready to do a great deal for their sons. And the prospect of obtaining a regular income in addition to your housekeeper's salary would naturally be a great temptation.'

It was clear now where he was leading her. She sat upright, the earlier sullen antagonism replacing the brief softening of her expression. She waited for the direct accusation, but Boyce, seeing that he had accomplished his purpose, once more switched his attack.

'It's my opinion, Mrs. Colver, that Doctor Hardene had something to hide. Did you ever see or hear anything that might confirm that?'

'Something to hide?' she echoed. She drew in her breath. At first Tremaine thought that the denial was going to come, and then she hesitated as though she had changed her mind. 'I—I think there might have been something,' she said slowly, picking her words. 'He was strange at times—almost as if he was afraid. I didn't pay much attention to it. After all, it didn't seem likely that a man in Doctor Hardene's position would need to be afraid of anything.'

'Would it surprise you to learn,' Boyce said, 'that Doctor Hardene had very good reason to be afraid? That he had, in fact, a criminal record?'

She stared at him, her eyes wide and her expression one of blank innocence. It was a good performance, Tremaine thought, but rather overdone; it bore the marks of too careful a rehearsal.

'A—criminal record? Doctor Hardene? It isn't—*true?*'

'I'm afraid it's perfectly true, Mrs. Colver. It's also more than a possibility that Doctor Hardene knew something about the murder of the seaman named Marton who was found shot dead upon the downs.'

She appeared to be shocked and horrified.

'But surely—if the doctor knew something about the murder, wouldn't he have gone to the police?'

'He didn't go to the police,' Boyce said grimly, 'for the best of all reasons—because he killed Marton himself.'

She gave a gasp.

'Doctor Hardene a—a *murderer?* Oh no—'

'That's the way the evidence is pointing. You can see that it provides a very good reason why he should have kept at least one of those two sets of cuttings. What I'm interested in finding out now is why he kept the other set—the cuttings about the pawnbroker. That's where I'm hoping you'll be able to help us.'

'You mean—you think Doctor Hardene committed that murder, too?'

'Well, that's rather leaping ahead,' Boyce admitted. 'Let's say that all I'm looking for at the moment is a connection between the doctor and the pawnbroker.'

He waited, looking at her. She was breathing quickly.

'I don't know whether it will help you,' she said, breathlessly, 'but I did see him with a pawnticket once. I thought it was strange because I knew that he wasn't the sort who'd need to pawn anything. It was one day when I came into the surgery when he wasn't expecting me. He was looking at a cigarette case. I hadn't seen it before. I had a feeling that the pawnticket and the case were connected.'

'Did Doctor Hardene make any reference to it?'

'No. I don't think he was very pleased about my coming in. He put the case away in his desk, almost as though I'd caught him doing something wrong.'

'Did you ever see him with the cigarette case after that?'

'Not as far as I remember. That was strange, too, because I got to know most of his things. He was very fixed in his habits and I could always tell what he was going to wear or what he would carry in his pockets.' She was speaking more confidently now. Her words were coming more easily, as though some barrier had been broken down. 'I don't think it was the case that was important. There was something inside it. A letter I believe it was.'

'A letter, eh?' Boyce pursed his lips. 'Sounds interesting. Pity you didn't get a chance to have a look at it.'

She was clearly tempted but she did not rise to the bait.

'He put the case away too quickly. And he never spoke to me about it.' There was a reluctant note in her voice. It was as though she was aware of an opportunity that was slipping away from her and was loath to relinquish it despite its dangers. 'But now I come to think back it's true that he was afraid. There were all sorts of little things—like—like asking whether any strangers had called and being anxious sometimes when the postman was in the road and hadn't reached the house with the letters. Of course, I—I never dreamed there was anything like this.'

She broke off, looking up at Boyce from beneath lowered eyelids waiting for him to make the next move. He didn't make it, and although she made the effort she was unable to restrain herself.

'You said that the doctor had a—a criminal record. What had he done? Why should he have wanted to kill that man Marton?'

'That's a long story, Mrs. Colver, and I'm still trying to piece it together.'

She tried to conceal her disappointment and braced herself visibly to put the next question.

'Do you think the doctor's being killed had anything to do with his being a criminal?'

'It's a possibility we can't overlook. That's why I've been interested in finding out whether he had any visits from strangers not long before he was murdered.'

An expression that might have been relief crossed her face.

'You mean that someone who knew about him—someone like Marton—might have called here? I—I'm sorry. I didn't see anyone. But it doesn't mean that no one did come.'

'No,' Boyce said. 'No, it doesn't. In fact, it's very likely that Doctor Hardene did meet a stranger to the district, although the meeting may not have taken place here.'

His glance remained fixed upon her face, neither accusing nor unfriendly but at the same time offering her no encouragement.

'Is there anything else you can tell us, Mrs. Colver?'

'No,' she said, shaking her head. 'No, I don't think so.'

'You're quite certain?'

'Quite—certain,' she returned steadily.

'All right,' Boyce said. 'That's all, Mrs. Colver.'

He stood up. After a brief hesitation, she, too, rose to her feet.

'You don't want me—for anything else?'

'Suppose we say that for the moment I'd be glad if you'd arrange to stay in the house. Then if I should need to ask you anything further there'll be no difficulty.'

Boyce's tone was dispassionate but edged with authority. She looked at him doubtfully, but he added nothing to what he had said and she was forced to accept her dismissal.

When the surgery door had closed behind her Boyce thrust his hands into his pockets and glanced at Tremaine.

'She's still holding out on us.'

Tremaine pushed at his pince-nez.

'Yes, I know. At first you had her scared, Jonathan. She thought the game was up. And then she changed her mind and decided there was still a chance of getting away with it. So she told you as much as she dared without betraying herself. All that about the cigarette case was probably the truth.'

'Yes, that's the way I see it, too,' Boyce agreed. 'Marton came over and started blackmailing Hardene, either on his own or as part of a plan he'd fixed up with this chap Fenn who was still doing his stretch at that time. Hardene decided he'd had enough and shot Marton, but it didn't end his troubles because Marton had put down what he knew in writing and planted it where he'd thought it would be safe.'

'In a cigarette case,' Tremaine said, 'which he'd pawned. For a man who doesn't go in for theories, Jonathan, it's a neat little piece of deduction.'

Boyce grinned.

'Must be infectious. It's being with you so often. Daresay Marton told Hardene what he'd done—probably thought it was a kind of insurance policy to tell him. He didn't reckon on Hardene being so desperate. Anyway, that's where that poor devil of a pawnbroker came in. Hardene went after that cigarette case because he knew that as long as the statement it contained was in existence his neck was in danger.'

'It's possible that the murder of Wallins wasn't just an accident because he happened to hear Hardene break in,' Tremaine remarked. 'Hardene had the pawnticket but he didn't know just where the case was likely to be among all the scores of other unredeemed pledges. He might have awakened Wallins to make him get the case for him and when he was sure he'd found what he'd come for he picked up that statue and struck the old man down to make sure he didn't talk.'

'And then,' Boyce said, 'the housekeeper found out what he'd been up to and put the black on him. She was playing with fire all right. With two murders against him he wouldn't have troubled much about a third.'

'He wouldn't have hesitated if he'd thought it was necessary. But it wouldn't have been quite as easy as the others.' Tremaine pursed his lips. 'With Marton and Wallins there was nothing to link Doctor Hardene of Druidleigh with the murders, but with his own housekeeper concerned he would be bound to become the subject of enquiries, and once the police had their eyes on him he couldn't be sure how much they'd uncover. Besides, Mrs. Colver doesn't seem to have been too exorbitant in her demands. He probably thought his best policy was to pay up, although it might have been a different story if she'd tried to squeeze him.'

Boyce nodded.

'Once she'd taken his money she was in it as deep as he was and he was the sort who wouldn't have forgotten that. She isn't really the blackmailing type—that's the devil of it from our point of view. It's clear enough, of course, what made her do it. That was what you meant, wasn't it, when you said that it was love that made a woman determined?'

'Yes, that's what I meant, Jonathan. What are you going to do about her?'

'I don't know,' Boyce said, frowning. 'I know what I ought to do, of course. She's an accessory after the fact. No doubt about that. But with her son like he is—' He broke off, almost savagely. 'Why the devil is she still holding out on us? It isn't just that she's trying to save her skin. There's more in it than that.'

Tremaine eyed his friend reflectively. Jonathan was on the right track; as usual he had not missed the significant point. But he wondered just how far along that track he had progressed.

'Maybe we'll get somewhere when the locals lay their hands on Fenn,' Boyce was saying. 'He might talk—if there's anything for him to talk about. We'll just have to wait for news of him, that's all.'

The Yard man's tone implied that the wait was likely to be a long one, but it proved to be of no more than ten minutes duration. At the end of that time the telephone rang. Boyce went to answer it and Tremaine heard him speaking in clipped phrases and curt monosyllables.

The door opened. Boyce stood there, a wry expression on his face.

'Well,' he announced, 'it seems that they've found him. But he won't be doing any talking. He's dead.'

Without apparent emotion he passed on the information he had been given. The body of the man who had called himself Fenn had been discovered by two trespassing small boys lying among the tangle of bushes at the foot of the rocks where the cliff fell almost sheer to the river.

From the appalling nature of his injuries he must have fallen the whole distance of that terrible drop and in the opinion of the police surgeon he had been dead for some forty-eight hours.

20

THE CHIEF CONSTABLE GOES OUT TO TEA

IT WAS Tremaine who suggested a conference over a cup of tea and it was Inspector Parkin with his local knowledge who suggested the setting. He led the way to an attractively designed restaurant of sun verandahs and coloured awnings built on the edge of the downs and almost overlooking the bridge.

In summer it was no doubt a popular rendezvous, but as had been the case with the Canyon, at this time of the year it was occupied only by a handful of people. They chose a table on the upper floor, from the wide windows of which it was possible to look out over the river valley, and in a far corner where it seemed likely that they would be able to talk undisturbed.

Parkin waited until the tray was set in front of them and then he leaned back and faced Jonathan Boyce. He seemed in a contented mood, like a man from whom the cares had rolled away.

'This seems to be it, sir. Just a matter of clearing up the odds and ends and the job's over.'

A smile crinkled the corners of the Yard man's eyes but he did not offer agreement.

'All right, let's begin the inquest. How did it happen?'

'He knew we were after him, of course,' Parkin said, 'and he was hiding out on the edge of the downs—plenty of rough ground there for a man to sleep out, especially over by the river. It looks as though something startled him—might have been one of our men on patrol—and he went too near the edge, lost his footing in the dark and went over. There was nobody about to see what happened and he might have been lying in the bushes still if those boys hadn't been playing around where they had no business to be.'

'Isn't that part of the cliff a well-known place for suicides?' Tremaine said.

'Yes, that's right,' Parkin returned. 'There've been quite a few. Suicide Corner we call it.' He stopped suddenly and his eyes narrowed. He gave Tremaine a sharp glance. 'What made you ask?'

'You don't think it could have been suicide in this case?'

'I suppose it could have been. There's nothing in the doctor's report against it. But why *should* he have killed himself?'

'He might have thought the game was up. He knew he didn't have a hope of getting away and took the easiest way out.'

Parkin gave a nod.

'That might have been it. Although I'd have thought he wasn't the kind to put himself under. After all, he'd been on the run before.'

'But not for murder.'

'I see what you mean,' Parkin admitted. He grinned. 'As a matter of fact, I'd like to believe it *was* suicide. It would tie everything up. Fenn came over after his revenge, murdered Hardene, found he couldn't get away with it, and chucked himself over the cliff before we could catch up with him and hand him over for the hangman.'

'You think it's certain,' Boyce said, 'that Fenn was the chap who was double-crossed?'

'We'll have to get his prints checked, of course, but I think that's who he was all right. Don't you, sir?'

'Yes,' Boyce agreed, 'I do.'

He sounded convinced but not satisfied. Parkin regarded him doubtfully. He thought for a moment or two.

'I look at it this way, sir,' he went on, painstakingly, as though he was desperately anxious that the Yard man should be persuaded. 'We've cleared the ground now—or rather, *you* have. We know that it wasn't Masters, and neither Miss Royman nor young Linton had anything to do with it. I've run the rule over Linton and he comes out all right. Nothing against him, except that he took a poor view of Hardene's making up to the girl—and I can't say I blame him for that. There isn't much choice left except for Fenn, and he *does* fit with everything we know about Hardene.'

'There's Mrs. Colver,' Tremaine observed.

'The housekeeper?' Parkin looked taken aback. 'You don't mean you think that *she* did it?'

'We don't know,' Tremaine countered gently, 'that she didn't.'

He glanced out of the window. A grey saloon car was drawn up outside the restaurant. It stirred his memory and he frowned.

Parkin's voice brought his attention back.

'Why the housekeeper?' he was saying. 'What motive could she have had?'

'She might have had a disagreement with Hardene—about something that hasn't yet come to light. And after all, she hasn't a real alibi.'

'I suppose not. Nothing to say that she didn't go out after him.' Parkin sounded disappointed, almost like a man seriously disturbed. He made a determined effort to bring the cheerful note back to his voice. 'But she doesn't fit the whole story—not like Fenn. She doesn't explain what Hardene's car was doing with its lights out, where he'd obviously parked it himself, as though he'd gone to meet somebody. You're just having your little joke, sir, aren't you? The only thing that's still really doubtful is whether it was an accident or whether it was suicide, and I don't suppose we'll ever be certain about that now.'

Tremaine did not appear to be listening to him. He glanced around the room like a man to whom memory had suddenly returned, and then, as if he had failed to find something for which he had been searching, he rose to his feet.

'If you gentlemen have finished, shall we go?'

Jonathan Boyce looked up at him in surprise, but the urgent note in Tremaine's voice stifled the question that came to his lips. He pushed back his chair, and Parkin, equally surprised but feeling himself in the minority, followed suit.

The bill had been paid when their tea had been brought to them. Tremaine made for the staircase leading to the ground floor and went down briskly, his companions close behind.

At the foot of the stairs he paused. His glance travelled over the sprinkling of people occupying the room, and then went to the door. A tall, soldierly man, accompanied by a woman, was just going through to the pavement.

Tremaine hurried forward and reached the pair just as the man's hand was going out to the door handle of the grey saloon.

'Good afternoon, Sir Robert.'

Sir Robert Dennell turned. He recognized the speaker.

'Oh—good afternoon.' He saw Boyce and Parkin coming out of the restaurant, and his expression became both frigid and wary. 'I see you aren't alone.'

'No,' Tremaine said, as if he was completely unaware that he was being shown that his presence was unwelcome. 'We've been in conference. Following the news about Fenn,' he added, after the slightest of hesitations.

'Fenn,' the Chief Constable said. 'Yes, of course.' He looked at Boyce. 'Well, it looks as though you're nearly through, Chief Inspector.' His grasp tightened on the handle of the car and then relaxed. 'Congratulations. You haven't taken long.'

It was a palpable afterthought. Boyce met it coolly.

'A certain amount of luck, Sir Robert. In any case, although Fenn's turned up it isn't *quite* over yet.'

A flush of antagonism showed in the Chief Constable's face. His voice betrayed the irritation of a man not used to being thwarted who suspected opposition.

'No? I would have said that there wasn't any doubt.'

Tremaine was looking at the Chief Constable's companion. She was a good twenty years or so younger, still pretty in an immature doll-like fashion. There was a trace of weakness in the over-full, too heavily made-up lips, and there were shadows of strain under her eyes. She was standing nervously at the side of the car, clearly anxious to be gone but hesitating to assert her own personality.

Sir Robert Dennell noticed his significant glance. His lips tightened and he frowned. But there was little he could do about it now.

He half turned and placed a hand on his companion's arm.

'This is my wife,' he said, reluctantly. 'You know Inspector Parkin, of course, my dear. These two gentlemen are Mr. Tremaine and Chief Inspector Boyce.'

She did not say anything, but her eyes darted to Boyce in a frightened fashion. Sir Robert Dennell released his light hold on his wife's arm and opened the car door with a significant gesture.

'I daresay you're busy, Chief Inspector. I know Parkin is. I'll arrange to see you when I've checked my engagements and we'll discuss the final details. Come along, Lin.'

He ushered his wife into the car and slipped into the driving seat. He nodded and the car moved off. The three of them watched it until a left-hand bend in the road took it from their sight. Boyce pursed his lips.

'Not the most friendly of meetings. Your boss seems off colour again this afternoon.'

He was addressing himself to Parkin. The inspector was looking worried.

'Yes,' he said uncomfortably, 'he does.'

Boyce glanced at Tremaine.

'You knew he was in the restaurant,' he said. 'That why you dashed off in such a hurry?'

'Yes, I saw his car outside. I thought we might be in time to meet him if we went out straight away.'

'What was the idea? I didn't notice that you got very far with him.'

Tremaine did not make a direct reply. Instead he looked at Parkin.

'I noticed that the Chief Constable called his wife Lin. I take it that was a shortened form of her name, a sort of intimate abbreviation?'

'Yes, I imagine so,' Parkin said.

He was looking very unhappy now. His glance had wavered away and he was staring out across the downs.

'What *is* her name?' Tremaine probed. 'You *do* know it?'

'Yes,' Parkin admitted, unwillingly. 'Yes, I do. It's—Elaine.'

There was a sudden silence.

'Oh,' Tremaine said. 'Oh. I see.'

Memories were pressing upon him. A memory of the Chief Constable spending many hours on the scene of the murder and receiving them with a manner that had been both preoccupied and on the alert; a memory of the shadow on his face and the bitterness in his voice when he had spoken of a man being master in his own house.

He recollected Sir Robert Dennell's anxiety to avoid scandal; his eagerness to be informed at once of any development.

And he remembered, too, the hesitancy that had sometimes crept into Parkin's manner when they had first met; the guardedness his intuition had told him had been due to the fact that the inspector had something to conceal.

This was it. This was the thing he had tried to recall. This was what had been on Parkin's mind.

21

EPILOGUE TO MURDER

MORDECAI TREMAINE climbed pantingly up the path towards the seat where Martin Slade was resting. It was an ideal vantage point on the very edge of the cliff where it was possible to sit at ease and gaze out over the panorama of the gorge and the river.

Slade heard the sound of his approach and glanced round.

'Good morning!' he called. 'I see you're indulging in your morning exercise!'

Tremaine covered the remaining few yards and Slade moved one of his sticks to allow him to sit down.

'My goodness,' he observed, 'you certainly have been going at it!'

Tremaine pushed back his pince-nez, breathing hard.

'I was hoping I'd see you. I noticed your car down on the road and your chauffeur told me you might be up this way.'

'You mean you've been looking for me?'

'Yes. I'm in something of a difficulty and I thought maybe you could help me.'

'Naturally I'll do anything I can. What's the trouble?'

'You saw last night's *Courier*?'

Slade raised an eyebrow.

'You mean the news about that fellow Fenn? Yes, I saw it. But surely that isn't your difficulty? It looked to me as though your troubles were over.'

'They aren't exactly over,' Tremaine said. 'Although, of course, a lot of things have been cleared up.'

Slade settled himself more comfortably.

'I must say last night's report was something of a shock. Nobody dreamed what Hardene had been up to—certainly *I* didn't or he wouldn't have been my doctor for so long. Reading between the lines it seemed to me that the police are pretty certain he was responsible for those two murders. I suppose there's no doubt about it? The report was genuine? But it must have been. The *Courier* wouldn't have printed it otherwise.'

'The report was true enough.'

Tremaine leaned back. Jonathan Boyce had kept his word to Rex Linton and had given him the full story. The *Courier* had done it justice and its later editions on the previous day must have caused many Bridgton eyebrows to be raised.

'Well, what's on your mind,' Slade said, glancing at him. 'Come on, let's see if we can sort out what's troubling you.'

'Would you be surprised to hear that Mrs. Colver had been blackmailing Hardene?'

'Mrs. Colver? You mean the housekeeper?' Slade's expression was incredulous. 'You certainly do surprise me. She doesn't look the type.'

'She found out what Hardene had done. He was making regular withdrawals of fifty pounds a month when he died. I don't suppose he paid over the entire fifty but there's no doubt that a large part of it went to her each time.'

'It doesn't sound as though she was pressing him all that hard. Not considering there was murder involved.'

'No, but as you said just now she doesn't seem the black-mailing type. You see, her son's a patient in a sanatorium—incurable. The money helps her to keep things going, and I daresay she's tried all kinds of specialists in the hope of finding one who might be able to do something for him. That sort of thing is expensive.'

'Yes, *I* know all about that,' Slade remarked grimly. 'But if she was blackmailing Hardene it doesn't seem likely that she had anything to do with killing him. She was cutting off her own source of income by putting him out of the way.'

'I don't think she killed Hardene, but at the same time we haven't got the whole story out of her. You see, *she hasn't given up.*'

Slade stared at him for a moment or two, and then shook his head with a smile.

'Sorry. You've lost me.'

'All right,' Tremaine said, and pushed back his pince-nez, 'I'll go on. You don't mind listening to me?'

'I'm enjoying it. Being on the inside of a murder investigation is a new sensation, as I mentioned the other day.'

'As long as I'm not boring you. By talking things over like this, I mean. Doctor Hardene was having an *affaire* with a woman called Elaine. It had been going on for a long time.'

'Yes, I remember your asking me if I knew anything about her. Have you found out anything fresh?'

'Yes, we've found out quite a lot. At first we didn't know any more than her name. She rang up the house on the morning after the murder but she was too quick for the detective who answered the 'phone to put a patrol car on to her. It wasn't until yesterday that we discovered that she's the wife of a—of a prominent person in Bridgton.'

Tremaine deliberately held back the Chief Constable's name. He did not think that at this stage at least it would be a sound policy to reveal that particular item of information.

'I'm seeing daylight,' Slade remarked. 'The husband had found out and was going to start something. Right?'

'More or less. Hardene seems to have known it because he made a note in his diary about trouble that obviously referred to Elaine.'

'And you think the husband actually was doing something about it.'

'Yes. Not long before the murder he was prowling about around Hardene's house. Mrs. Colver saw him, although she didn't know who he was or what he was after.'

Tremaine was sure that his theory was sound. Sir Robert Dennell had known all about his wife and Hardene; that was the reason for the jumpiness of his attitude. And he had kept watch on them. One slip he had made had confirmed that. He had not officially paid a visit to Hardene's house and yet he had mentioned the lane at the rear—a fact he could not possibly have known unless he had been there in person, for its existence had not been discussed at any of their conferences or set down in any report Tremaine had seen.

It was clear now why he *hadn't* gone to the house in his official capacity, although he had spent so much time at the scene of the murder. He had known that the housekeeper had seen him that night in the garden and he had been afraid of being recognized.

Martin Slade was studying him with an ill-concealed air of impatience, clearly waiting for him to continue.

'Do you think it was a case of the eternal triangle, after all? That it was Elaine's husband who killed him and not Fenn?'

'It was certainly a case of the eternal triangle, but it wasn't the husband who murdered Graham Hardene.'

'It wasn't? You mean,' Slade ejaculated, 'that it was the *wife*?'

His tone was eager. Tremaine looked at him thoughtfully. He thought that the time was ripe. He said, quietly:

'What are you going to do about Mrs. Colver?'

Slade's brows drew together in a quick frown.

'I don't understand you.'

'I said just now,' Tremaine went on, still in that quiet, steady voice, 'that she hadn't given up. She knows that we've a good idea what's been going on. But she doesn't believe that we know *all* of it. She thinks that if she can keep her head there's still a chance that she can go on drawing a second income. It's a little—frightening—what a woman will do for someone she loves. Especially what a mother will do for her son.'

'Get to the point, man. What about her?'

'Graham Hardene and two companions were involved in a series of robberies in Canada,' Tremaine said. 'One of them—the man we've known as Fenn—was caught and sent to prison. It looks as though Hardene double-crossed him, and Fenn quite naturally wanted his revenge.'

'That much was in the *Courier* report.'

Tremaine's hand strayed to his pince-nez. He glanced up the path.

'I know,' he said. 'But *this* wasn't in the *Courier*. That it was *you* Doctor Hardene arranged to meet in that empty house near the downs. That it was *you* who killed him.'

For a long interval of time Martin Slade stared at him. And then:

'Would you mind repeating that?' His voice was harshly unnatural. 'I don't think I heard you correctly.'

'It was unexpected when Marton turned up,' Tremaine went on. 'It hadn't occurred to you that Fenn might talk to someone else. You were caught off-balance. That was why you paid Marton to keep him quiet—until you'd had time to plan how best to get rid of him. But you knew more or less when Fenn was likely to arrive, and you had time to get ready for him.'

'I presume,' Slade observed sardonically, 'you mean that *Hardene* had time.'

Tremaine paid no attention to the interruption.

'There were *three* members of the original gang. Hardene, Fenn, and Number Three—*you*. Hardene didn't settle down here in Bridgton alone. The third person seems to have been rather overlooked, but my view is that he was the leader. That's why it was left to Hardene to do the—unpleasant—things. Like killing Marton and that poor devil of a pawnbroker. That's why he kept the appointment in that empty house at your orders. I imagine he thought that you were going to talk over what was to be done about Fenn. The real situation was that you'd made up your mind that Hardene was a menace to you and that it was time to get rid of him.'

Slade made an angry movement.

'You're talking nonsense! I'm not surprised you've been finding difficulties if this is the crazy way your mind's been working! If I'd wanted to meet Hardene for the reason you say, d'you think I'd have needed to go to all that trouble when I could have seen him at his surgery at any time!'

'There were two reasons why the surgery wouldn't have done. In the first place, there was too great a risk that what you had to say to each other might be overheard. And in the second place, you knew that you could never get away with murder under those conditions. By persuading Hardene to meet you in that empty house, after saying that he'd been called out to see a patient, you thought it would look as though he'd made a mistake in the dark and been killed in an accidental scuffle with a tramp. But you made one elementary slip that showed that the murder must have been premeditated.'

Slade's head went up.

'What slip?'

'Your choice of a weapon was made to give the idea that it had been lying close by and your mythical tramp had snatched it up in a rage. But Hardene's body was found *inside the house*.

It was unlikely that there would have been a piece of rock that size in the hall, even though the place was empty. Perhaps you'd planned to drag the body out to the drive and were disturbed by that patrolling policeman. I'm not certain of that any more than I'm certain of your precise motive for killing Hardene. My theory is that you did it because although Fenn knew where to find Hardene he didn't know just where to find *you* or what name you were using. Maybe you thought that with Hardene out of the way you'd be safe. There was even the chance, of course, that Fenn might be connected with the murder and arrested. As a matter of fact, it very nearly *did* happen.'

Slade was clearly making a great effort to keep his voice level.

'You're forgetting something.' His hand went out to one of his sticks. 'This. It would need a healthy and active man to do what you've just accused me of doing.'

Tremaine nodded.

'Yes, I know. But you see, you aren't a cripple at all.'

Martin Slade's grasp tightened upon the stick at his right side but he sat very still.

'It was part of the new character you were playing,' Tremaine went on. 'I began to suspect it that day when I first met you on the downs. You made it clear that you didn't want to stay in my company and you covered the distance to your car at a rate that was a little too fast for a man in your supposed condition. I had a shock when I looked round and saw that you'd gone and that your car was moving off. Incidentally, just after seeing you I met Fenn, and I imagine that the coincidence made me link the two of you together. He was going to meet you, wasn't he? That's why you were waiting on that seat. He did know about you, after all. Tell me, did he go over the cliff accidentally? Or was it *your* doing?'

Slade sat up. He looked carefully all about him and then relaxed with a sigh that was almost one of contentment.

'It was my doing,' he said calmly. 'The fool thought he was going to blackmail me and the chance was too good to miss. No one about and the cliff right behind him. He didn't deserve to get away with such carelessness. It was easy. Just like it was with Hardene. Neither of them suspected what was going to happen to them until it was too late.'

He settled himself against the back of the seat. He seemed quite self-possessed. There was, indeed, an amused smile on his face.

'You've worked it all out, haven't you? Go on, tell me the rest. I find it instructive to have the record played back to me.'

'In your role as a cripple you built up the belief that you couldn't go out unless your hired chauffeur took you when you sent for him, but on the night you killed Hardene your housekeeper and her husband went to the village hall at Seabury and didn't return until late and during their absence you were able to carry out your plan. You were back again by the time they returned from Seabury and of course they had no suspicion that you'd left the house. It's a lonely spot and there wasn't much danger of anyone seeing you.'

'That's why I chose it in the first place,' Slade said. 'I wanted a quiet corner where I wasn't likely to be disturbed and where there wouldn't be too many sympathetic people asking questions about my not being able to walk. With Hardene as my doctor it meant that I could keep in touch with him without anybody realizing there was anything between us.' He nodded in satisfaction. 'It was a perfect set-up. I was a bit removed from Hardene's main practice, of course, but I covered that by saying that he was the only chap who'd ever been able to do anything for me.'

'Naturally, the appointments with the specialists were all non-existent?'

'Oh, naturally. I daren't go near a specialist or I'd have been found out. Hardene used to pretend he'd made the appointments himself and he'd tell that girl of his to note them down as if they were genuine.'

'I can well understand,' Tremaine said, 'how irritated you must have felt when Hardene started to go into politics. He was doing the last thing you wanted by putting himself in the limelight and drawing attention upon himself. When you argued with him about its being dangerous he told you that the more prominent he became the less chance there'd be of being found out; people wouldn't be able to see the wood for the trees.'

'So you know that, do you?' Slade looked at him searchingly, and then nodded. 'Of course. The girl told you. She came back too early—Hardene had got rid of her for a few moments—and heard us talking. I thought I'd managed to carry it off, though.'

'You did. She didn't suspect anything. She isn't a Mrs. Colver. You were the mysterious visitor on the night after the murder, weren't you? It was a big risk to take, but I suppose you thought it might be worth it.'

'I intended to kill her,' Slade said calmly, 'before she got scared and began to talk. I realized after I'd killed Hardene that when she'd had time to think she'd suspect that I'd done it and might go to the police to save herself. She knew that Hardene and I were more than doctor and patient although she didn't know the whole story. She was holding Marton and Wallins over Hardene but she didn't find out why he'd done it.'

'Nevertheless, she was too clever for you that night,' Tremaine observed. 'She was expecting something and stayed awake. When she heard you at the window she gave the alarm—quickly enough to save herself but not so that you'd be caught. She wanted you to get away. She knew that if she was right about you there was a chance of switching her blackmailing tactics on to you. She rang you up the next morning. I don't suppose she dared say much on the 'phone. Did she arrange to meet you somewhere?'

'We met on the downs,' Slade said. 'She wouldn't come any nearer than six feet,' he added, with a dry, reminiscent chuckle. 'Very wise of her. She put it very cleverly. If I paid up and didn't try any funny business she'd keep her mouth shut. Of course, I agreed—at the time. I didn't have any choice.'

He had begun to move restlessly. His eyes were constantly searching the still empty path, flickering over to the gorge that lay beyond the low railing. Tremaine said quickly:

'There isn't much more. When you came to the house on the morning after the murder—you couldn't very well not keep the appointment that had been arranged and in any case you *wanted* to come, so that you could find out what was happening—you saw Fenn. I imagine that *he* saw *you*. It certainly startled you. At first I thought your hesitation was due to the fact that you were crippled, but when Fenn appeared a moment or two later and then it seemed that he had some connection with the murder, I began to wonder. It was only a small point, but all the small points add up to something significant.'

'You surprise me,' Slade said sarcastically. He rose to his feet, no longer a bowed figure but towering menacingly over Tremaine. 'I've listened to you because it amused me but the comedy's over now. Why, you dim-witted old fool, do you think you're going to get away with this? You were in trouble. You thought I might be able to help you. Well, I've talked. I've talked because I knew *you wouldn't be taking it any further*. There are only two of us up here and nobody's ever gone over that cliff and lived to tell the world about it!'

His face was contorted now with passion. Tremaine took off his pince-nez and polished them.

'I suppose,' he said mildly, 'that when you admitted that you and Hardene had often had arguments it was part of the build-up?'

'What else do you think it was? I knew that if I told you we'd been up against each other, and then you found out that I'd told everybody what a good doctor he was, you'd write me off as some harmless crank who'd gone into a panic but hadn't really done anything worth bothering about.'

'And then, when you thought you'd managed that successfully, you scraped up an acquaintance with me so that I could keep you informed about everything that was going on.'

'Of course. I spent a couple of hours running around the district so that I could come across you by *accident*.' There was contempt in the last two words. 'Sage thought I was mad, but it paid dividends.'

'I thought that is what you must have done. You looked for me until you found me—just as *I* looked for *you* this morning.'

Something in Tremaine's voice penetrated Slade's fury. The angry lines of his face settled into a cold mask of awareness.

'What do you mean?'

'I'm not quite such a dim-witted old fool,' Tremaine said, gently. 'Knowing what you'd done—and what you might still do—I didn't come up here without taking precautions. When I cleaned my pince-nez just now it was a signal. Take a look around you.'

Reluctantly, slowly, Martin Slade turned his head. Fifty yards along the path to his left Jonathan Boyce was standing. Slade faced in the other direction, with a sudden, angry hiss. Down the path to the right was Inspector Parkin.

'There are more detectives with them and some right behind me,' Tremaine said. 'I'm afraid it's no good, you know. You're completely surrounded.'

Fear and fury flamed together in the man's face. He was still gripping one of his sticks in his right hand and he swung it high above his head.

'You—'

The stick came down viciously. Tremaine flung himself aside, his heart thumping. The stick missed his head and crashed upon the back of the seat with a violence that must have jarred Slade's arm.

Both Parkin and Boyce were on the move now. Slade glared at them, took a step towards the seat, saw that the way there, too, was barred, and swung around.

The railings were only a few yards away. He leaped towards them, caught the top rail and vaulted over.

Boyce flung himself forward but his outstretched hand missed by several feet.

'Come back, you fool! You'll break your neck!'

Parkin reached the railings. His face was white.

'He'll never make it. The drop's sheer.'

Shakily Tremaine picked himself from the seat where he was still huddled and walked across to Boyce's side. Below him he could hear the desperate man's frantic progress down the bush-studded upper portion of the cliff face.

He leaned over the railings. It was just possible to see the top of Slade's head and his upthrust hands as he searched for fresh holds.

Boyce called again but the man paid no attention. All his energies were being thrust into his fierce effort to climb down the cliff surface to the roadway.

It was hopeless from the start. A dozen yards from the top the bushes thinned out to the bare, relentless rock. They saw Slade's hold slip as a bush gave way at the roots, saw him reach for another and then put all his strength into reaching for the next as that, too, began to fail him.

Only this time there was nothing to grasp.

'Come on!' Boyce said, tight-lipped.

He began to run down the path. Parkin, following him, called out instructions to his subordinates.

Afraid of what he might be going to see and yet unable to hold back, Tremaine went after them.

Oddly, it was not Martin Slade who was chiefly in his mind as he made the journey down the roadway, but Sir Robert Dennell.

He knew now what a bitter burden it was the Chief Constable had been carrying. It had not been fear for himself that had driven him, but a dread that his wife might have committed some rash act. That was why he had called in the Yard so quickly. When he had learned that it had been Graham Hardene who had died there had been nothing else he could do.

He had discovered later that it had not been his wife's hand that had struck Hardene down—no doubt he had been able to check her alibi—but there had been the constant danger that her liaison with the man would be discovered. That was why, Tremaine knew, he had been so irritated at the suggestion that enquiries should be made about Mrs. Masters; he had not been concerned for her but he had not wanted too much additional probing to be done. That was why, also, he had been put out at the mention of the unknown prowler who had been seen at Hardene's house.

Well, there was no reason now why any of it should come out. It could serve in any case no useful purpose. Parkin would be glad of that. Parkin had not been certain, but he had suspected. And his suspicions had caused him more than a little anxiety; loyalty to his chief had been struggling with the duty he owed to Jonathan Boyce.

The ambulance drew up at the side of the road as Tremaine came level with the place where Boyce and Parkin were kneeling among the bushes at the foot of the cliff. He went towards them. Boyce heard him coming and stood up.

'I don't think I'd come any closer,' he said quietly. 'There isn't anything we can do.' He added: 'Perhaps it was as well. It saves a lot of bother this way.'

He looked at Parkin. The inspector knew what was in his mind and he nodded gravely.

'Yes,' he said, 'it saves a lot of bother. I'm—glad.'

Tremaine was glad that all he could see of Martin Slade was a piece of cloth beyond the bushes. He turned away. His legs were feeling weak. He forced himself to think of Margaret Royman.

That was where one's thoughts should be. Not upon wasteful, violent death, but upon beauty and goodness and hope for the future. She would, he felt, be very happy with her reporter.

The ambulance men passed him, carrying a stretcher. He regained the road, where a small crowd was beginning to gather, even in this unfrequented spot, and sat down to wait for Jonathan Boyce.

Well, it was over. There was routine still to be gone through, but the main task was done. The Chief Inspector could collect his bag again and go home.

THE END

FRANCIS DUNCAN

Murder Has a Motive

When Mordecai Tremaine emerges from the little train station, murder is the last thing on his mind. But then again, he has never been able to resist anything in the nature of a mystery – and a mystery is precisely what awaits him in the village of Dalmering.

Rehearsals for the local amateur dramatic production are in full swing – but as Mordecai discovers all too soon, the real tragedy is unfolding offstage. The star of the show has been found dead, and the spotlight is soon on Mordecai, whose reputation in the field of crime-solving precedes him.

With a murderer waiting in the wings, it's up to Mordecai to derail the killer's performance . . . before it's curtains for another victim.

FRANCIS DUNCAN

Murder for Christmas

'Kept guessing to the end, I am left wondering why it has taken so long to discover Francis Duncan . . . With some 20 crime novels to his credit, a relaunch seems long overdue'
Daily Mail

Mordecai Tremaine, former tobacconist and perennial lover of romance novels, has been invited to spend Christmas in the sleepy village of Sherbroome at the country retreat of one Benedict Grame.

Arriving on Christmas Eve, he finds that the revelries are in full flow – but so too are tensions amongst the assortment of guests.

Midnight strikes and the party-goers discover that it's not just presents nestling under the tree . . . there's a dead body too. A dead body that bears a striking resemblance to Father Christmas.

With the snow falling and the suspicions flying, it's up to Mordecai to sniff out the culprit – and prevent someone else from getting murder for Christmas.

'The book nods towards Agatha Christie but retains a crackling atmosphere of dread and horror that will chill the heart however warm your fireside'
Metro

FRANCIS DUNCAN

So Pretty a Problem

Adrian Carthallow, enfant terrible of the art world, is no stranger to controversy. But this time it's not his paintings that have provoked a blaze of publicity – it's the fact that his career has been suddenly terminated by a bullet to the head. Not only that, but his wife has confessed to firing the fatal shot.

Inspector Penross of the town constabulary is, however, less than convinced by Helen Carthallow's story – but has no other explanation for the incident that occurred when the couple were alone in their clifftop house.

Luckily for the Inspector, amateur criminologist Mordecai Tremaine has an uncanny habit of being in the near neighbourhood whenever sudden death makes its appearance. Investigating the killing, Tremaine is quick to realise that however handsome a couple the Carthallows were, and however extravagant a life they led, beneath the surface there's a pretty devil's brew . . .

FRANCIS DUNCAN

Behold a Fair Woman

Mordecai Tremaine's hobby of choice – crime detection – has left him in need of a holiday. A break away from that gruesome business of murder will be just the ticket, and the picturesque island of Moulin d'Or seems to be just the destination.

Amid the sunshine and the sea air, Mordecai falls in with a band of fellow holidaymakers and tries to forget that such a thing as foul play exists. He should have been wiser, of course, because before too long villainy rears its head and a dead body is discovered.

With a killer stalking the sand dunes, it falls to Mordecai to piece together the truth about just who has smuggled murder on to the island idyll . . .

MORE VINTAGE MURDER MYSTERIES

dead good

*For all of you who find
a crime story irresistible.*

Discover the very best crime and thriller books on our
dedicated website – hand-picked by our editorial team
so you have tailored recommendations to help you
choose what to read next.

We'll introduce you to our favourite authors and the
brightest new talent. Read exclusive interviews and
specially commissioned features on everything from the
best classic crime to our top ten TV detectives, join live
webchats and speak to authors directly.

Plus our monthly book competition offers you the
chance to win the latest crime fiction, and there are
DVD box sets and digital devices to be won too.

Sign up for our newsletter at
www.deadgoodbooks.co.uk/signup

Join the conversation on:

penguin.co.uk/vintage